FOUND YET LOST
BY
EDWARD PAYSON ROE

FOUND YET LOST BY EDWARD PAYSON ROE

CHAPTER I
LOVE IN THE WILDERNESS

Hopeless indeed must that region be which May cannot clothe with some degree of beauty and embroider with flowers. On the 5th day of the month the early dawn revealed much that would charm the eyes of all true lovers of nature even in that section of Virginia whose characteristics so grimly correspond with its name—The Wilderness. The low pines and cedars, which abound everywhere, had taken a fresh green; the deciduous trees, the tangled thickets, impenetrable in many places by horse or man, were putting forth a new, tender foliage, tinted with a delicate semblance of autumn hues. Flowers bloomed everywhere, humbly in the grass close to the soil as well as on the flaunting sprays of shrubbery and vines, filling the air with fragrance as the light touched and expanded the petals. Wood-thrushes and other birds sang as melodiously and contentedly as if they had selected some breezy upland forest for their nesting-place instead of a region which has become a synonym for gloom, horror, and death.

Lonely and uninhabited in its normal condition, this forbidding wilderness had become peopled with thousands of men. The Army of the Potomac was penetrating and seeking to pass through it. Vigilant General Lee had observed the movement, and with characteristic boldness and skill ordered his troops from their strong intrenchments on Mine Run toward the Union flank. On this memorable morning the van of his columns wakened from their brief repose but a short distance from the Federal bivouac. Both parties were unconscious of their nearness, for with the exception of a few clearings the dense growth restricted vision to a narrow range. The Union forces were directed in their movements by the compass, as if they were sailors on a fog-enshrouded sea; but they well knew that they were seeking their old antagonist, the Army of Northern Virginia, and that the stubborn tug-of-war might begin at any moment.

When Captain Nichol shook off the lethargy of a brief troubled sleep, he found that the light did not banish his gloomy impressions. Those immediately around him were still slumbering, wrapped in their blankets. Few sounds other than the voices of the awakening birds broke the silence. After a little thought he drew his notebook from his pocket and wrote as follows:

"MY DARLING HELEN—I obey an impulse to write to you this morning. It is scarcely light enough to see as yet; but very soon we shall be on the move again to meet—we known not what, certainly heavy, desperate fighting. I do not know why I am so sad. I have faced the prospect of battles many times before, and have passed through them unharmed, but now I am depressed by an unusual foreboding. Naturally my thoughts turn to you. There was no formal engagement between us when I said those words (so hard to speak) of farewell, nor have I sought to bind you since. Every month has made more clear the uncertainty of life in my calling; and I felt that I had no right to lay upon you any restraint other than that of your own feelings. If the worst happened you would be free as far as I was concerned, and few would know that we had told each other of our love. I wish to tell you of mine once more—not for the last time, I hope, but I don't know. I do love you with my whole heart and soul; and if I am to die in this horrible wilderness, where so many of my comrades died a year ago, my last thoughts will be of you and of the love of God, which your love has made more real to me. I love you too well to wish my death, should it occur, to spoil your young life. I do not ask you to forget me—that would be worse than death, but I ask you to try to be happy and to make others happy as the years pass on. This bloody war will come to an end, will become a memory, and those who perish hope to be remembered; but I do not wish my memory to hang like a cloud over the happy days of peace. I close, my darling, in hope, not fear—hope for you, hope for me, whatever may happen to-day or on coming days of strife. It only remains for me to do my duty. I trust that you will also do yours, which may be even harder. Do not give way to despairing grief if I cannot come back to you in this world. Let your faith in God and hope of a future life inspire and strengthen you in your battles, which may require more courage and unselfishness than mine.

"Yours, either in life or death, ALBERT NICHOL."

He made another copy of this letter, put both in envelopes, and addressed them, then sought two men of his company who came from his native village. They were awake now and boiling their coffee. The officer and the privates had grown up as boys together with little difference of social standing in the democratic town. When off duty, there still existed much of the old familiarity and friendly converse, but when Captain Nichol gave an order, his townsmen immediately became conscious that they were separated from him by the iron wall of military discipline. This characteristic did not alienate his old associates. One of the men hit the truth fairly in saying: "When Cap speaks as Cap, he's as hard and sharp as a bayonet-point; but when a feller is sick and worn out 'tween times you'd think your granny was coddlin' yer."

It was as friend and old neighbor that Nichol approached Sam and Jim Wetherby, two stalwart brothers who had enlisted in his company. "Boys," he said, "I have a favor to ask of you. The Lord only knows how the day will end for any of us. We will take our chances and do our duty, as usual. I hope we may all boil coffee again to-night; but who knows? Here are two letters. If I should fall, and either or both of you come out all right, as I trust you will, please forward them. If I am with you again to-night, return them to me."

"Come, Captain," said Jim, heartily, "the bullet isn't molded that can harm you. You'll lead us into Richmond yet."

"It will not be from lack of goodwill if I don't. I like your spirit; and I believe the army will get there this time whether I'm with it or not. Do as I ask. There is no harm in providing against what may happen. Make your breakfast quickly, for orders may come at any moment;" and he strode away to look after the general readiness of his men.

The two brothers compared the address on the letters and laughed a little grimly. "Cap is a-providing, sure enough," Sam Wetherby remarked. "They are both written to the pretty Helen Kemble that he used to make eyes at in the singing-school. I guess he thinks that you might stop a bullet as well as himself, Jim."

"It's clear he thinks your chances for taking in lead are just as good," replied Jim. "But come, I'm one of them fellows that's never hit till I am hit. One thing at a time, and now it's breakfast."

"Well, hanged if I want to charge under the lead of any other captain!" remarked Sam, meditatively sipping his coffee. "If that girl up yonder knows Cap's worth, she'll cry her eyes out if anything happens to him."

A few moments later the birds fled to the closest cover, startled by the innumerable bugles sounding the note of preparation. Soon the different corps, divisions, and brigades were upon their prescribed lines of march. No movement could be made without revealing the close proximity of the enemy. Rifle-reports from skirmish lines and reconnoitring parties speedily followed. A Confederate force was developed on the turnpike leading southwest from the old Wilderness Tavern; and the fighting began. At about eight o'clock Grant and Meade came up and made their headquarters beneath some pine-trees near the tavern. General Grant could scarcely believe at first that Lee had left his strong intrenchments to give battle in a region little better than a jungle; but he soon had ample and awful proof of the fact. Practically unseen by each other, the two armies grappled like giants in the dark. So thick were the trees and undergrowth that a soldier on a battle line could rarely see a thousand men on either side of him, yet nearly two hundred thousand men matched their deadly strength that day. Hundreds fell, died, and were hidden forever from human eyes.

Thinking to sweep away the rear-guard of Lee's retreating army, Grant ordered a strong advance on the pike in the afternoon. At first it was eminently successful, and if it had been followed up vigorously and steadily, as it undoubtedly would have been if the commander had known what was afterward revealed, it might have resulted in severe disaster to the Confederates. The enemy was pressed back rapidly; and the advancing Union forces were filled with enthusiasm. Before this early success culminated, genuine sorrow saddened every one in Captain Nichol's company. With his face toward the enemy, impetuously leading his men, he suddenly dropped his sword and fell senseless. Sam and Jim Wetherby heard a shell shrieking toward them, and saw it explode directly over their beloved leader. They rushed to his side; blood was pouring over his face, and it also seemed to them that a fragment of the shell had fatally wounded him in the forehead.

"Poor Cap, poor, brave Cap!" ejaculated Sam. "He didn't give us those letters for nothing."

"A bad job, an awfully bad job for us all! curse the eyes that aimed that shell!" growled practical Jim. "Here, take hold. We'll put him in that little dry ditch we just passed, and bury him after the fight, if still on our pins. We can't leave him here to be tramped on."

This they did, then hastily rejoined their company, which had swept on with the battle line. Alas! that battle line and others also were driven back with terrible slaughter before the day closed. Captain Nichol was left in the ditch where he had been placed, and poor Sam Wetherby lay on his back, staring with eyes that saw not at a shattered bird's nest in the bushes above his head. The letter in his pocket mouldered with him.

Jim's begrimed and impassive face disguised an aching heart as he boiled his coffee alone that night. Then, although wearied almost to exhaustion, he gave himself no rest until he had found what promised to be the safest means of forwarding the letter in his pocket.

CHAPTER II
LOVE AT HOME

Long years before the war, happy children were growing in the village of Alton. They studied the history of wars much as they conned their lessons in geography. Scenes of strife belonged to the past, or were enacted among people wholly unlike any who dwelt in their peaceful community. That Americans should ever fight each other was as undreamed of as that the minister should have a pitched battle in the street with his Sunday-school superintendent. They rejoiced mildly when in their progress through the United States history they came to pages descriptive of Indian wars and the Revolutionary struggle, since they found their lessons then more easily remembered than the wordy disputes and little understood decisions of statesmen. The first skating on the pond was an event which far transcended in importance anything related between the green covers of the old history book, while to Albert Nichol the privilege of strapping skates on the feet of little Helen Kemble, and gliding away with her over the smooth ice, was a triumph unknown by any general. He was the son of a plain farmer, and she the daughter of the village banker. Thus, even in childhood, there was thrown around her the glamour of position and reputed wealth—advantages which have their value among the most democratic folk, although slight outward deference may be paid to their possessors. It was the charming little face itself, with its piquant smiles and still more piquant pouts, which won Albert's boyish admiration. The fact that she was the banker's daughter only fired his ambition to be and to do something to make her proud of him.

Hobart Martine, another boy of the village, shared all his schoolmate's admiration for pretty Nellie, as she was usually called. He had been lame from birth, and could not skate. He could only shiver on the bank or stamp around to keep himself warm, while the athletic Al and the graceful little girl passed and repassed, quite forgetting him. There was one thing he could do; and this pleasure he waited for till often numb with cold. He could draw the child on his sled to her home, which adjoined his own.

When it came his turn to do this, and he limped patiently through the snow, tugging at the rope, his heart grew warm as well as his chilled body. She was a rather imperious little belle with the other boys, but was usually gentle with him because he was lame and quiet. When she thanked him kindly and pleasantly at her gate, he was so happy that he could scarcely eat his supper. Then his mother would laugh and say, "You've been with your little sweetheart." He would flush and make no reply.

How little did those children dream of war, even when studying their history lessons! Yet Albert Nichol now lay in the Wilderness jungle. He had done much to make his little playmate proud of him. The sturdy boy developed into a manly man. When he responded to his country's call and raised a company among his old friends and neighbors, Helen Kemble exulted over him tearfully. She gave him the highest tribute within her power and dearest possession—her heart. She made every campaign with him, following him with love's untiring solicitude through the scenes he described, until at last the morning paper turned the morning sunshine into mockery and the songs of the birds into dirges. Captain Nichol's name was on the list of the killed.

With something of the same jealousy, developed and intensified, which he had experienced while watching Albert glide away on the ice with the child adored in a dumb, boyish way, Hobart had seen his old schoolmate depart for the front. Then his rival took the girl from him; now he took her heart. Martine's lameness kept him from being a soldier. He again virtually stood chilled on the bank, with a cold, dreary, hopeless feeling which he believed would benumb his life. He did not know, he was not sure that he had lost Helen beyond hope, until those lurid days when men on both sides were arming and drilling for mutual slaughter. She was always so kind to him, and her tones so gentle when she spoke, that in love's fond blindness he had dared to hope. He eventually learned that she was only sorry for him. He did not, could not, blame her, for he needed but to glance at Nichol's stalwart form, and recall the young soldier's record, in order to know that it would be strange indeed if the girl had chosen otherwise. He would have been more than human if there had not been some bitterness in his heart; but he fought it down honestly, and while pursuing his peaceful avocations engaged in what he believed would be a lifelong battle. He smiled at the girl across the garden fence and called out his cheery "Good-morning." He was her frequent companion by the fireside or on the piazza, according to the season; and he alone of the young men was welcome, for she had little sympathy for those who remained at home without his excuse. He was so bravely her friend, keeping his great love so sternly repressed that she only felt it like a genial warmth in his tones and manner, and believed that he was becoming in truth what he seemed, merely a friend.

On that terrible May morning he was out in the garden and heard her wild, despairing cry as she read the fatal words. He knew that a heavy battle had been begun, and was going down to the gate for his paper, which the newsboy had just left. There was no need of opening it, for the bitter cry he had heard made known to him the one item of intelligence compared with which all else for the time became insignificant. Was it the Devil that inspired a great throb of hope in his heart? At any rate he thought it was, and ground his heel into the gravel as if the serpent's head was beneath it, then limped to Mr. Kemble's door.

The old banker came out to meet him, shaking his gray head and holding the paper in his trembling hand. "Ah!" he groaned, "I've feared it, I've feared it all along, but hoped that it would not be. You've seen Nichol's name—" but he could not finish the sentence.
"No, I have seen nothing; I only heard Helen's cry. That told the whole story."

"Yes. Well, her mother's with her. Poor girl! poor girl! God grant it isn't her death-blow too. She has suffered too much under this long strain of anxiety."

A generous resolve was forming in Martine's mind, and he said earnestly, "We must tide her through this terrible shock. There may be some mistake; he may be only wounded. Do not let her give up hope absolutely. I'll drop everything and go to the battlefield at once. If the worst has in truth happened, I can bring home his remains, and that would be a comfort to her. A newspaper report, made up hastily in the field, is not final. Let this hope break the cruel force of the blow, for it is hard to live without hope."

"Well, Hobart, you ARE a true friend. God bless and reward you! If nothing comes of it for poor Nichol, as I fear nothing will, your journey and effort will give a faint hope to Nellie, and, as you say, break the force of the blow. I'll go and tell her."

Martine went into the parlor, which Helen had decorated with mementoes of her soldier lover. He was alone but a few moments before he heard hasty steps. Helen entered with hot, tearless eyes and an agonized, imploring expression.

"What!" she cried, "is it true that you'll go?"

"Yes, Helen, immediately. I do not think there's reason for despair."

"Oh, God bless you! friend, friend! I never knew what the word meant before. Oh, Hobart, no sister ever lavished love on a brother as I will love you if you bring back my Albert;" and in the impulse of her overwhelming gratitude she buried her face on his shoulder and sobbed aloud. Hope already brought the relief of tears.

He stroked the bowed head gently, saying, "God is my witness, Helen, that I will spare no pains and shrink from no danger in trying to find Captain Nichol. I have known of many instances where the first reports of battles proved incorrect;" and he led her to a chair.

"It is asking so much of you," she faltered.

"You have asked nothing, Helen. I have offered to go, and I AM going. It is a little thing for me to do. You know that my lameness only kept me from joining Captain Nichol's company. Now try to control your natural feelings like a brave girl, while I explain my plans as far as I have formed them."

"Yes, yes! Wait a few moments. Oh, this pain at my heart! I think it would have broken if you hadn't come. I couldn't breathe; I just felt as if sinking under a weight."

"Take courage, Helen. Remember Albert is a soldier."

"IS, IS! Oh, thanks for that little word! You do not believe that he is gone and lost to me?"

"I cannot believe it yet. We will not believe it. Now listen patiently, for you will have your part to do."

"Yes, yes; if I could only do something! That would help me so much.
Oh, if I could only go with you!"
"That would not be best or wise, and might defeat my efforts. I must be free to go where you could not—to visit places unsafe for you. My first step must be to get letters to our State Senator. Your father can write one, and I'll get one or two others. The Senator will give me a letter to the Governor, who in turn will accredit me to the authorities at Washington and the officer in command on the battlefield. You know I shall need passes. Those who go to the extreme front must be able to account for themselves. I will keep in telegraphic communication with you, and you may receive additional tidings which will aid me in my search. Mr. Kemble!" he concluded, calling her father from his perturbed pacing up and down the hall.

"Ah!" said the banker, entering, "this is a hundred-fold better than despairing, useless grief. I've heard the gist of what Hobart has said, and approve it. Now I'll call mother, so that we may all take courage and get a good grip on hope."

They consulted together briefly, and in the prospect of action, Helen was carried through the first dangerous crisis in her experience.

FOUND YET LOST BY EDWARD PAYSON ROE

CHAPTER III
"DISABLED"

Mrs. Martine grieved over her son's unexpected resolve. In her estimation he was engaging in a very dangerous and doubtful expedition. Probably mothers will never outgrow a certain jealousy when they find that another woman has become first in the hearts of their sons. The sense of robbery was especially strong in this case, for Mrs. Martine was a widow, and Hobart an only and idolized child.

The mother speedily saw that it would be useless to remonstrate, and tearfully aided him in his preparations. Before he departed, he won her over as an ally. "These times, mother, are bringing heavy burdens to very many, and we should help each other bear them. You know what Helen is to me, and must be always. That is something which cannot be changed. My love has grown with my growth and become inseparable from my life. I have my times of weakness, but think I can truly say that I love her so well that I would rather make her happy at any cost to myself. If it is within my power, I shall certainly bring Nichol back, alive or dead. Prove your love to me, mother, by cheering, comforting, and sustaining that poor girl. I haven't as much hope of success as I tried to give her, but she needs hope now; she must have it, or there is no assurance against disastrous effects on her health and mind. I couldn't bear that."

"Well, Hobart, if he is dead, she certainly ought to reward you some day."

"We must not think of that. The future is not in our hands. We can only do what is duty now."

Noble, generous purposes give their impress to that index of character, the human face. When Martine came to say good-by to Helen, she saw the quiet, patient cripple in a new light. He no longer secured her strong affection chiefly on the basis of gentle, womanly commiseration. He was proving the possession of those qualities which appeal strongly to the feminine nature; he was showing himself capable of prompt, courageous action, and his plain face, revealing the spirit which animated him, became that of a hero in her eyes. She divined the truth—the love so strong and unselfish that it would sacrifice itself utterly for her. He was seeking to bring back her lover when success in his mission would blot out all hope for him. The effect of his action was most salutary, rousing her from the inertia of grief and despair. "If a mere friend," she murmured, "can be so brave and self-forgetful, I have no excuse for giving away utterly."

She revealed in some degree her new impressions in parting. "Hobart," she said, holding his hand in both of hers, "you have done much to help me. You have not only brought hope, but you have also shown a spirit which would shame me out of a selfish grief. I cannot now forget the claims of others, of my dear father and mother here, and I promise you that I will try to be brave like you, like Albert. I shall not become a weak, helpless burden, I shall not sit still and wring idle hands when others are heroically doing and suffering. Good-by, my friend, my brother. God help us all!"

He felt that she understood him now as never before; and the knowledge inspired a more resolute purpose, if this were possible. That afternoon he was on his way. There came two or three days of terrible suspense for Helen, relieved only by telegrams from Martine as he passed from point to point. The poor girl struggled as a swimmer breasts pitiless waves intervening between him and the shore. She scarcely allowed herself an idle moment; but her effort was feverish and in a measure the result of excitement. The papers were searched for any scrap of intelligence, and the daily mail waited for until the hours and minutes were counted before its arrival.

One morning her father placed Nichol's letter in her hands. They so trembled in the immense hope, the overwhelming emotion which swept over her at sight of the familiar handwriting, that at first she could not open it. When at last she read the prophetic message, she almost blotted out the writing with her tears, moaning, "He's dead, he's dead!" In her morbid, overwrought condition, the foreboding that had been in the mind of the writer was conveyed to hers; and she practically gave up hope for anything better than the discovery and return of his remains. Her father, mother, and intimate friends tried in vain to rally her; but the conviction remained that she had read her lover's farewell words. In spite of the most pathetic and strenuous effort, she could not keep up any longer, and sobbed till she slept in utter exhaustion.

On the following day, old Mr. Wetherby came into the bank. The lines about his mouth were rigid with suppressed feeling. He handed Mr. Kemble a letter, saying in a husky voice, "Jim sent this. He says at the end I was to show it to you." The scrawl gave in brief the details about Captain Nichol already known to the reader, and stated also that Sam Wetherby was missing. "All I know is," wrote the soldier, "that we were driven back, and bullets flew like hail. The brush was so thick I couldn't see five yards either way when I lost sight of Sam."

The colonel of the regiment also wrote to Captain Nichol's father, confirming Private Wetherby's letter. The village had been thrown into a ferment by the tidings of the battle and its disastrous consequences. There was bitter lamentation in many homes. Perhaps the names of Captain Nichol and Helen were oftenest repeated in the little community, for the fact of their mutual hopes was no longer a secret. Even thus early some sagacious people nodded their heads and remarked, "Hobart Martine may have his chance yet." Helen Kemble believed without the shadow of a doubt that all the heart she had for love had perished in the wilderness.

The facts contained in Jim Wetherby's letter were telegraphed to Martine, and he was not long in discovering confirmation of them in the temporary hospitals near the battlefield. He found a man of Captain Nichol's company to whom Jim had related the circumstances. For days the loyal friend searched laboriously the horrible region of strife, often sickened nearly unto death by the scenes he witnessed, for his nature had not been rendered callous by familiarity with the results of war. Then instead of returning home, he employed the influence given by his letters and passes, backed by his own earnest pleading, to obtain permission for a visit to Nichol's regiment. He found it under fire; and long afterward Jim Wetherby was fond of relating how quietly the lame civilian listened to the shells shrieking over and exploding around him. Thus Martine learned all that could be gathered of Nichol's fate, and then, ill and exhausted, he turned his face northward. He felt that it would be a hopeless task to renew his search on the battlefield, much of which had been burned over. He also had the conviction it would be fatal to him to look upon its unspeakable horrors, and breathe again its pestilential air.

He was a sick man when he arrived at home, but was able to relate modestly in outline the history of his efforts, softening and concealing much that he had witnessed. In the delirium of fever which followed, they learned more fully of what he had endured, of how he had forced himself to look upon things which, reproduced in his ravings, almost froze the blood of his watchers.

Helen Kemble felt that her cup of bitterness had been filled anew, yet the distraction of a new grief, in which there was a certain remorseful self-reproach, had the effect of blunting the sharp edge of her first sorrow. In this new cause for dread she was compelled in some degree to forget herself. She saw the intense solicitude of her father and mother, who had been so readily accessory to Martine's expedition; she also saw that his mother's heart was almost breaking under the strain of anxiety. His incoherent words were not needed to reveal that his effort had been prompted by his love. She was one of his watchers, patiently enduring the expressions of regret which the mother in her sharp agony could not repress. Nichol's last letter was now known by heart, its every word felt to be prophetic. She had indeed been called upon to exercise courage and fortitude greater than he could manifest even in the Wilderness battle. Although she often faltered, she did not fail in carrying out his instructions. When at last Martine, a pallid convalescent, could sit in the shade on the piazza, she looked older by years, having, besides, the expression seen in the eyes of some women who have suffered much, and can still suffer much more. In the matter relating to their deepest consciousness, no words had passed between them. She felt as if she were a widow, and hoped he would understand. His full recognition of her position, and acceptance of the fact that she did and must mourn for her lover, his complete self-abnegation, brought her a sense of peace.

The old clock on the landing of the stairway measured off the hours and days with monotonous regularity. Some of the hours and days had been immeasurably longer than the ancient timekeeper had indicated; but in accordance with usual human experiences, they began to grow shorter. Poignant sorrow cannot maintain its severity, or people could not live. Vines, grasses, and flowers covered the graves in Virginia; the little cares, duties, and amenities of life began to screen at times the sorrows that were nevertheless ever present.

"Hobart," Helen said one day in the latter part of June, "do you think you will be strong enough to attend the commemorative services next week? You know they have been waiting for you."

"Yes," he replied quietly; "'and they should not have delayed them so long. It is very sad that so many others have been added since—since—"

"Well, you have not been told, for we have tried to keep every depressing and disquieting influence from you. Dr. Barnes said it was very necessary, because you had seen so much that you should try to forget. Ah, my friend, I can never forget what you suffered for me! Captain Nichol's funeral sermon was preached while you were so ill. I was not present—I could not be. I've been to see his mother often, and she understands me. I could not have controlled my grief, and I have a horror of displaying my most sacred feelings in public. Father and the people also wish you to be present at the general commemorative services, when our Senator will deliver a eulogy on those of our town who have fallen; but I don't think you should go if you feel that it will have a bad effect on you."

"I shall be present, Helen. I suppose my mind has been weak like my body; but the time has come when I must take up life again and accept its conditions as others are doing. You certainly are setting me a good example. I admit that my illness has left a peculiar repugnance to hearing and thinking about the war; it all seemed so very horrible. But if our brave men can face the thing itself, I should be weak indeed if I could not listen to a eulogy of their deeds."

"I am coming to think," resumed Helen, thoughtfully, "that the battle line extends from Maine to the Gulf, and that quiet people like you and me are upon it as truly as the soldiers in the field. I have thought that perhaps the most merciful wounds are often those which kill outright."

"I can easily believe that," he said.

His quiet tone and manner did not deceive her, and she looked at him wistfully as she resumed, "But if they do not kill, the pain must be borne patiently, even though we are in a measure disabled."

"Yes, Helen; and you are disabled in your power to give me what I can never help giving you. I know that. I will not misjudge or presume upon your kindness. We are too good friends to affect any concealments from each other."

"You have expressed my very thought. When you spoke of accepting the conditions of life, I hoped you had in mind what you have said—the conditions of life as they ARE, as we cannot help or change them. We both have got to take up life under new conditions."

"You have; not I, Helen."

Tears rushed to her eyes as she faltered, "I would be transparently false should I affect not to know. What I wish you to feel through the coming months and years is that I cannot—that I am disabled by my wound."

"I understand, Helen. We can go on as we have begun. You have lost, as I have not, for I have never possessed. You will be the greater sufferer; and it will be my dear privilege to cheer and sustain you in such ways as are possible to a simple friend."

She regarded him gratefully, and for the first time since that terrible
May morning the semblance of a smile briefly illumined her face.

CHAPTER IV
MARTINE SEEKS AN ANTIDOTE

It can readily be understood that Martine in his expedition to the South had not limited his efforts solely to his search for Captain Nichol. Wherever it had been within his power he had learned all that he could of other officers and men who had come from his native region; and his letters to their relatives had been in some instances sources of unspeakable comfort. In his visit to the front he had also seen and conversed with his fellow-townsmen, some of whom had since perished or had been wounded. As he grew stronger, Helen wrote out at his dictation all that he could remember concerning these interviews; and these accounts became precious heirlooms in many families.

On the Fourth of July the commemorative oration was delivered by the Senator, who proved himself to be more than senator by his deep, honest feeling and good taste. The "spread eagle" element was conspicuously absent in his solemn, dignified, yet hopeful words. He gave to each their meed of praise. He grew eloquent over the enlisted men who had so bravely done their duty without the incentive of ambition. When he spoke of the honor reflected on the village by the heroism of Captain Nichol, the hearts of the people glowed with gratitude and pride; but thoughts of pity came to all as they remembered the girl, robed in black, who sat with bowed head among them.

"I can best bring my words to a close," said the Senator, "by reading part of a letter written by one of your townsmen, a private in the ranks, yet expressive of feelings inseparable from our common human nature:

"DEAR FATHER—You know I ain't much given to fine feelings or fine words. Poor Sam beat me all holler in such things; but I want you and all the folks in Alton to know that you've got a regular soldier at home. Of course we were all glad to see Bart Martine; and we expected to have a good-natured laugh at his expense when the shells began to fly. Soldiers laugh, as they eat, every chance they get, 'cause they remember it may be the last one. Well, we knew Bart didn't know any more about war than a chicken, and we expected to see him get very nervous and limp off to the rear on the double quick. He didn't scare worth a cent. When a shell screeched over our heads, he just waited till the dinged noise was out of our ears and then went on with his questions about poor Cap and Sam and the others from our town. We were supporting a battery, and most of us lying down. He sat there with us a good hour, telling about the folks at home, and how you were all following us with your thoughts and prayers, and how you all mourned with those who lost friends, and were looking after the children of the killed and wounded.

Fact is, before we knew it we were all on our feet cheering for Alton and the folks at home and the little lame man, who was just as good a soldier as any of us. I tell you he heartened up the boys, what's left of us. I'm sorry to hear he's so sick. If he should die, bury him with a soldier's honors. JAMES WETHERBY."

"These plain, simple, unadorned words," concluded the Senator, "need no comment. Their force and significance cannot be enhanced by anything I can say. I do not know that I could listen quietly to shrieking and exploding shells while I spoke words of courage and good cheer; but I do know that I wish to be among the foremost to honor your modest, unassuming townsman, who could do all this and more."

Martine was visibly distressed by this unexpected feature in the oration and the plaudits which followed. He was too sad, too weak in body and mind, and too fresh from the ghastly battlefield, not to shrink in sensitive pain from personal and public commendation. He evaded his neighbors as far as possible and limped hastily away.

He did not see Helen again till the following morning, for her wound had been opened afresh, and she spent the remainder of the day and evening in the solitude of her room. Martine was troubled at this, and thought she felt as he did.

In the morning she joined him on the piazza. She was pale from her long sad vigil, but renewed strength and a gentle patience were expressed in her thin face.

"It's too bad, Helen," he broke out in unwonted irritation. "I wouldn't have gone if I had known. It was a miserable letting down of all that had gone before—that reference to me."

Now she smiled brightly as she said, "You are the only one present who thought so. Has this been worrying you?"

"Yes, it has. If the speaker had seen what I saw, he would have known better. His words only wounded me."

"He judged you by other men, Hobart. His words would not have wounded very many. I'm glad I heard that letter—that I have learned what I never could from you. I'm very proud of my friend. What silly creatures women are, anyway! They want their friends to be brave, yet dread the consequences of their being so beyond words."

"Well," said Martine, a little grimly, "I'm going to my office to-morrow. I feel the need of a long course of reading in Blackstone."

"You must help keep me busy also," was her reply.

"I've thought about that; yes, a great deal. You need some wholesome, natural interest that is capable of becoming somewhat absorbing. Is it strange that I should recommend one phase of my hobby, flowers? You know that every tree, shrub, and plant on our little place is a sort of a pet with me. You are fond of flowers, but have never given much thought to their care, leaving that to your gardener. Flowers are only half enjoyed by those who do not cultivate them, nurse, or pet them. Then there is such an infinite variety that before you know it your thoughts are pleasantly occupied in experimenting with even one family of plants. It is an interest which will keep you much in the open air and bring you close to Mother Nature."

The result of this talk was that the sad-hearted girl first by resolute effort and then by a growing fondness for the tasks, began to take a personal interest in the daily welfare of her plants. Martine and her father were always on the look-out for something new and rare; and as winter approached, the former had a small conservatory built on the sunny side of the house. They also gave her several caged song-birds, which soon learned to recognize and welcome her. From one of his clients Martine obtained a droll-looking dog that seemed to possess almost human intelligence. In the daily care of living things and dependent creatures that could bloom or be joyous without jarring upon her feelings, as would human mirth or gayety, her mind became wholesomely occupied part of each day; she could smile at objects which did not know, which could not understand.

Still, there was no effort on her part to escape sad memories or the acts and duties which revived them. A noble monument had been erected to Captain Nichol, and one of her chief pleasures was to decorate it with the flowers grown under her own care. Few days passed on which she did not visit one of the families who were or had been represented at the front, while Mrs. Nichol felt that if she had lost a son she had in a measure gained a daughter. As the months passed and winter was wellnigh spent, the wise gossips of the village again began to shake their heads and remark, "Helen Kemble and Bart Martine are very good friends; but I guess that's all it will amount to—all, at any rate, for a long time."

All, for all time, Helen had honestly thought. It might easily have been for all time had another lover sought her, or if Martine himself had become a wooer and so put her on her guard. It was his patient acceptance of what she had said could not be helped, his self-forgetfulness, which caused her to remember his need—a need greatly increased by a sad event. In the breaking up of winter his mother took a heavy cold which ended in pneumonia and death.

The gossips made many plans for him and indulged in many surmises as to what he would do; but he merely engaged the services of an old woman as domestic, and lived on quietly as before. Perhaps he grew a little morbid after this bereavement and clung more closely to his lonely hearth.

This would not be strange. Those who dwell among shadows become ill at ease away from them. Helen was the first to discover this tendency, and to note that he was not rallying as she had hoped he would. He rarely sought their house except by invitation, and then often lapsed into silences which he broke with an evident effort. He never uttered a word of complaint or consciously appealed for sympathy, but was slowly yielding to the steady pressure of sadness which had almost been his heritage. She would have been less than woman if, recalling the past and knowing so well the unsatisfied love in his heart, she had not felt for him daily a larger and deeper commiseration. When the early March winds rattled the casements, or drove the sleety rain against the windows, she saw him in fancy sitting alone brooding, always brooding.

One day she asked abruptly, "Hobart, what are you thinking about so deeply when you are looking at the fire?"

A slow, deep flush came into his face, and he hesitated in his answer. At last he said, "I fear I'm getting into a bad mood, and think I must do something decided. Well, for one thing, the continuance of this war weighs upon my spirit. Men are getting so scarce that I believe they will take me in some capacity. Now that mother is not here, I think I ought to go."

"Oh, Hobart, we would miss you so!" she faltered.

He looked up with a smile. "Yes, Helen, I think you would—not many others, though. You have become so brave and strong that you do not need me any more."

"I am not so brave and strong as I seem. If I were, how did I become so? With the tact and delicacy of a woman, yet with the strength of a man, you broke the crushing force of the first blow, and have helped me ever since."

"You see everything through a very friendly medium. At any rate I could not have been content a moment if I had not done all in my power. You do not need me any longer; you have become a source of strength to others. I cannot help seeing crowded hospital wards; and the thought pursues me that in one of them I might do something to restore a soldier to his place in the field or save him for those at home. I could at least be a hospital nurse, and I believe it would be better for me to be doing some such work."

"I believe it would be better for me also," she answered, her eyes full of tears.

"No, Helen—no, indeed. You have the higher mission of healing the heart-wounds which the war is making in your own vicinity. You should not think of leaving your father and mother in their old age, or of filling their days with anxiety which might shorten their lives."

"It will be very hard for us to let you go. Oh, I did not think I would have to face this also!"

He glanced at her hastily, for there was a sharp distress in her tone, of which she was scarcely conscious herself. Then, as if recollecting himself, he reasoned gently and earnestly: "You were not long in adopting the best antidote for trouble. In comforting others, you have been comforted. The campaign is opening in Virginia; and I think it would be a good and wholesome thing for me to be at work among the wounded. If I can save one life, it will be such a comfort after the war is over."

"Yes," she replied, softly; "the war will be over some day. Albert, in his last letter, said the war would cease, and that happy days of peace were coming. How they can ever be happy days to some I scarcely know; but he seemed to foresee the future when he wrote."

"Helen, I'm going. Perhaps the days of peace will be a little happier if I go."

CHAPTER V
SECOND BLOOM

Martine carried out his purpose almost immediately, seeking the temporary and most exposed hospitals on the extreme left of Grant's army before Petersburg. Indeed, while battles were still in progress he would make his way to the front and become the surgeon's tireless assistant. While thus engaged, even under the enemy's fire, he was able to render services to Jim Wetherby which probably saved the soldier's life. Jim lost his right arm, but found a nurse who did not let him want for anything till the danger point following amputation had passed. Before many weeks he was safe at home, and from him Helen learned more of Martine's quiet heroism than she could ever gather from his letters. In Jim Wetherby's estimation, Cap and Bart Martine were the two heroes of the war.

The latter had found the right antidote. Not a moment was left for morbid brooding. On every side were sharp physical distress, deadly peril to life and limb, pathetic efforts to hold ground against diseases or sloughing wounds. In aiding such endeavor, in giving moral support and physical care, Martine forgot himself. Helen's letters also were an increasing inspiration. He could scarcely take up one of them and say, "Here her words begin to have a warmer tinge of feeling;" but as spring advanced, imperceptibly yet surely, in spite of pauses and apparent retrogressions, just so surely she revealed a certain warmth of sympathy. He was engaged in a work which made it easy for her to idealize him. His unselfish effort to help men live, to keep bitter tears from the eyes of their relatives, appealed most powerfully to all that was unselfish in her nature, and she was beginning to ask, "If I can make this man happier, why should I not do so?" Nichol's letter gained a new meaning in the light of events: "I do not ask you to forget me—that would be worse than death—but I ask you to try to be happy and to make others happy."

"A noble, generous nature prompted those words," she now often mused. "How can I obey their spirit better than in rewarding the man who not only has done so much for me, but also at every cost sought to rescue him?"

In this growing disposition she had no innate repugnance to overcome, nor the shrinking which can neither be defined nor reasoned against. Accustomed to see him almost daily from childhood, conscious for years that he was giving her a love that was virtually homage, she found her heart growing very compassionate and ready to yield the strong, quiet affection which she believed might satisfy him. This had come about through no effort on her part, from no seeking on his, but was the result of circumstances, the outgrowth of her best and most unselfish feelings.

But the effect began to separate itself in character from its causes. All that had gone before might explain why she was learning to love him, and be sufficient reason for this affection, but a woman's love, even that quiet phase developing in Helen's heart, is not like a man's conviction, for which he can give his clear-cut reasons. It is a tenderness for its object—a wish to serve and give all in return for what it receives.

Martine vaguely felt this change in Helen long before he understood it. He saw only a warmer glow of sisterly affection, too high a valuation of his self-denying work, and a more generous attempt to give him all the solace and support within her power.

One day in July, when the war was well over and the field hospitals long since broken up, he wrote from Washington, where he was still pursuing his labors:

"My work is drawing to a close. Although I have not accomplished a tithe of what I wished to do, and have soon so much left undone, I am glad to remember that I have alleviated much pain and, I think, saved some lives. Such success as I have had, dear Helen, has largely been due to you. Your letters have been like manna. You do not know—it would be impossible for you to know—the strength they have given, the inspiration they have afforded. I am naturally very weary and worn physically, and the doctors say I must soon have rest; but your kind words have been life-giving to my soul. I turn to them from day to day as one would seek a cool, unfailing spring. I can now accept life gratefully with the conditions which cannot be changed. How fine is the influence of a woman like you! What deep springs of action it touches! When waiting on the sick and wounded, I try to blend your womanly nature with my coarser fibre. Truly, neither of us has suffered in vain if we learn better to minister to others. I cannot tell you how I long to see the home gardens again; and it now seems that just to watch you in yours will be unalloyed happiness."

Helen smiled over this letter with sweet, deep meanings in her eyes.

One August evening, as the Kemble family sat at tea, he gave them a joyous surprise by appearing at the door and asking in a matter-of-fact voice, "Can you put an extra plate on the table?"

There was no mistaking the gladness of her welcome, for it was as genuine as the bluff heartiness of her father and the gentle solicitude of her mother, who exclaimed, "Oh, Hobart, how thin and pale you are!"

"A few weeks' rest at home will remedy all that," he said. "The heat in Washington was more trying than my work."

"Well, thank the Lord! you ARE at home once more," cried the banker. "I was thinking of drawing on the authorities at Washington for a neighbor who had been loaned much too long."

"Helen," said Martine, with pleased eyes, "how well you look! It is a perfect delight to see color in your cheeks once more. They are gaining, too, their old lovely roundness. I'm going to say what I think right out, for I've been with soldiers so long that I've acquired their bluntness."

"It's that garden work you lured me into," she explained. "I hope you won't think your plants and trees have been neglected."

"Have you been keeping my pets from missing me?"

"I guess they have missed you least of all. Helen has seen to it that they were cared for first," said Mrs. Kemble, emphatically.

"You didn't write about that;" and he looked at the girl gratefully.

"Do you think I could see weeds and neglect just over the fence?" she asked, with a piquant toss of her head.

"Do you think I could believe that you cared for my garden only that your eyes might not be offended?"

"There, I only wished to give you a little surprise. You have treated us to one by walking in with such delightful unexpectedness, and so should understand. I'll show you when you are through supper."

"I'm through now;" and he rose with a promptness most pleasing to her. His gladness in recognizing old and carefully nurtured friends, his keen, appreciative interest in the new candidates for favor that she had planted, rewarded her abundantly.

"Oh," he exclaimed, "what a heavenly exchange from the close, fetid air of hospital wards! Could the first man have been more content in his divinely planted garden?"

She looked at him shyly and thought, "Perhaps when you taste of the fruit of knowledge the old story will have a new and better meaning."

She now regarded him with a new and wistful interest, no longer seeing him through the medium of friendship only. His face, thin and spiritualized, revealed his soul without disguise. It was the countenance of one who had won peace through the divine path of ministry—healing others, himself had been healed. She saw also his unchanged, steadfast love shining like a gem over which flows a crystal current. Its ray was as serene as it was undimmed. It had taken its place as an imperishable quality in his character—a place which it would retain without vicissitude unless some sign from her called it into immediate and strong manifestation. She was in no haste to give this. Time was touching her kindly; the sharp, cruel outlines of the past were softening in the distance, and she was content to remember that the treasure was hers when she was ready for it—a treasure more valued daily.

With exultation she saw him honored by the entire community. Few days passed without new proofs of the hold he had gained on the deepest and best feelings of the people. She who once had pitied now looked up to him as the possessor of that manhood which the most faultless outward semblance can only suggest.

Love is a magician at whose touch the plainest features take on new aspects. Helen's face had never been plain. Even in its anguish it had produced in beholders the profound commiseration which is more readily given when beauty is sorrowful. Now that a new life at heart was expressing itself, Martine, as well as others, could not fail to note the subtle changes. While the dewy freshness of her girlish bloom was absent, the higher and more womanly qualities were now revealing themselves. Her nature had been deepened by her experiences, and the harmony of her life was all the sweeter for its minor chords.

To Martine she became a wonderful mystery, and he almost worshipped the woman whose love he believed buried in an unknown grave, but whose eyes were often so strangely kind. He resumed his old life, but no longer brooded at home, when the autumn winds began to blow. He recognized the old danger and shunned it resolutely. If he could not beguile his thoughts from Helen, it was but a step to her home, and her eyes always shone with a luminous welcome. Unless detained by study of the legal points of some case in hand, he usually found his way over to the Kemble fireside before the evening passed, and his friends encouraged him to come when he felt like it. The old banker found the young man exceedingly companionable, especially in his power to discuss intelligently the new financial conditions into which the country was passing. Helen would smile to herself as she watched the two men absorbed in questions she little understood, and observed her mother nodding drowsily over her knitting. The scene was so peaceful, so cheery, so hopeful against the dark background of the past, that she could not refrain from gratitude. Her heart no longer ached with despairing sorrow, and the anxious, troubled expression had faded out of her parents' faces.

"Yes," she would murmur softly to herself, "Albert was right; the bloody war has ceased, and the happy days of peace are coming. Heaven has blessed him and made his memory doubly blessed, in that he had the heart to wish them to be happy, although he could not live to see them. Unconsciously he took the thorns out of the path which led to his friend and mine. How richly father enjoys Hobart's companionship! He will be scarcely less happy—when he knows—than yonder friend, who is such a very scrupulous friend. Indeed, how either is ever going to know I scarcely see, unless I make a formal statement."

Suddenly Martine turned, and caught sight of her expression.

"All I have for your thoughts! What wouldn't I give to know them!"

Her face became rosier than the firelight warranted as she laughed outright and shook her head.

"No matter," he said; "I am content to hear you laugh like that."

"Yes, yes," added the banker; "Helen's laugh is sweeter to me than any music I ever heard. Thank God! we all can laugh again. I am getting old, and in the course of nature must soon jog on to the better country. When that time comes, the only music I want to hear from earth is good, honest laughter."

"Now, papa, hush that talk right away," cried Helen, with glistening eyes.

"What's the matter?" Mrs. Kemble asked, waking up.

"Nothing, my dear, only it's time for us old people to go to bed."

"Well, I own that it would be more becoming to sleep there than to reflect so unfavorably on your conversation. Of late years talk about money matters always puts me to sleep."

"That wasn't the case, was it, my dear, when we tried to stretch a thousand so it would reach from one January to another?"

"I remember," she replied, smiling and rolling up her knitting, "that we sometimes had to suspend specie payments. Ah, well, we were happy."

When left alone, it was Helen's turn to say, "Now your thoughts are wool-gathering. You don't see the fire when you look at it that way."

"No, I suppose not," replied Martine. "I'll be more frank than you. Your mother's words, 'We were happy,' left an echo in my mind. How experience varies! It is pleasant to think that there are many perfectly normal, happy lives like those of your father and mother."

"That's one thing I like in you, Hobart. You are so perfectly willing that others should be happy."

"Helen, I agree with your father. Your laugh WAS music, the sweetest I ever heard. I'm more than willing that you should be happy. Why should you not be? I have always felt that what he said was true—what he said about the right to laugh after sorrow—but it never seemed so true before. Who could wish to leave blighting sorrow after him? Who could sing in heaven if he knew that he had left tears which could not be dried on earth?"

"You couldn't," she replied with bowed head.

"Nor you, either; nor the brave man who died, to whom I only do justice in believing that he would only be happier could he hear your laugh. Your father's wholesome, hearty nature should teach us to banish every morbid tendency. Let your heart grow as light as it will, my friend. Your natural impulses will not lead you astray. Good-night."

"You feel sure of that?" she asked, giving him a hand that fluttered in his, and looking at him with a soft fire in her eyes.

"Oh, Helen, how distractingly beautiful you are! You are blooming again like your Jack-roses when the second growth pushes them into flower. There; I must go. If I had a stone in my breast instead of a heart—Good-night. I won't be weak again."

CHAPTER VI
MORE THAN REWARD

Helen Kemble's character was simple and direct She was one who lived vividly in the passing hour, and had a greater capacity for deep emotions than for retaining them. The reputation for constancy is sometimes won by those incapable of strong convictions. A scratch upon a rock remains in all its sharpness, while the furrow that has gone deep into the heart of a field is eventually almost hidden by a new flowering growth. The truth was fully exemplified in Helen's case; and a willingness to marry her lifelong lover, prompted at first by a spirit of self-sacrifice, had become, under the influence of daily companionship, more than mere assent. While gratitude and the wish to see the light of a great, unexpected joy come into his eyes remained her chief motives, she had learned that she could attain a happiness herself, not hoped for once, in making him happy.

He was true to his word, after the interview described in the preceding chapter. He did not consciously reveal the unappeased hunger of his heart, but her intuition was never at fault a moment.

One Indian-summer-like morning, about the middle of October, he went over to her home and said, "Helen, what do you say to a long day's outing? The foliage is at its brightest, the air soft as that of June. Why not store up a lot of this sunshine for winter use?"

"Yes, Helen, go," urged her mother. "I can attend to everything."

"A long day, did you stipulate?" said the girl in ready assent; "that means we should take a lunch. I don't believe you ever thought of that."

"We could crack nuts, rob apple-orchards, or if driven to extremity, raid a farmhouse."

"You have heard too much from the soldiers about living off the country. I'd rather raid mamma's cupboard before we start. I'll be ready as soon as you are."

He soon appeared in his low, easy phaeton; and she joined him with the presentiment that there might be even greater gladness in his face by evening than it now expressed. While on the way to the brow of a distant hill which would be their lunching place, they either talked with the freedom of old friends or lapsed into long silences.

At last he asked, "Isn't it a little odd that when with you the sense of companionship is just as strong when you are not talking?"

"It's a comfort you are so easily entertained. Don't you think I'm a rather moderate talker for a woman?"

"Those that talk the most are often least entertaining. I've thought a good deal about it—the unconscious influence of people on one another. I don't mean influence in any moral sense, but in the power to make one comfortable or uncomfortable, and to produce a sense of restfulness and content or to make one ill at ease and nervously desirous of escape."

"And you have actually no nervous desire to escape, no castings around in your mind for an excuse to turn around and drive home?"

"No one could give a surer answer to your question than yourself. I've been thinking of something pleasanter than my enjoyment."

"Well?"

"That your expression has been a very contented one during the last hour. I am coming to believe that you can accept my friendship without effort. You women are all such mysteries! One gets hold of a clew now and then. I have fancied that if you had started out in the spirit of self-sacrifice that I might have a pleasant time, you would be more conscious of your purpose. Even your tact might not have kept me from seeing that you were exerting yourself; but the very genius of the day seems to possess you. Nature is not exerting herself in the least. No breath of air is stirring; all storms are in the past or the future. With a smile on her face, she is just resting in serene content, as you were, I hope. She is softening and obscuring everything distant by an orange haze, so that the sunny present may be all the more real. Days like these will do you good, especially if your face and manner reveal that you can be as truly at rest as Nature."

"Yet what changes may soon pass over the placid scene!"

"Yes, but don't think of them."

"Well, I won't—not now. Yes, you are becoming very penetrating. I am not exerting myself in the least to give you a pleasant time. I am just selfishly and lazily content."

"That fact gives me so much more than content that it makes me happy."

"Hobart, you are the most unselfish man I ever knew."

"Nonsense!"

They had reached their picnic-ground—the edge of a grove whose bright-hued foliage still afforded a grateful shade. The horse was unharnessed and picketed so that he might have a long range for grazing. Then Martine brought the provision basket to the foot of a great oak, and sat down to wait for Helen, who had wandered away in search of wild flowers. At last she came with a handful of late-blooming closed gentians.

"I thought these would make an agreeable feature in your lunch."

"Oh, you are beginning to exert yourself."

"Yes, I have concluded to, a little. So must you, to the extent of making a fire. The rest will be woman's work. I propose to drink your health in a cup of coffee."

"Ah, this is unalloyed," he cried, sipping it later on.

"The coffee?"

"Yes, and everything. We don't foresee the bright days any more than the dark ones. I did not dream of this in Virginia."

"You are easily satisfied. The coffee is smoky, the lunch is cold, winter is coming, and—"

"And I am very happy," he said.

"It would be a pity to disturb your serenity."

"Nothing shall disturb it to-day. Peace is one of the rarest experiences in this world. I mean only to remember that our armies are disbanded and that you are at rest, like Nature."

She had brought a little book of autumn poems, and after lunch read to him for an hour, he listening with the same expression of quiet satisfaction. As the day declined, she shivered slightly in the shade. He immediately arose and put a shawl around her.

"You are always shielding me," she said gently.

"One can do so little of that kind of thing," he replied, "not much more than show intent."

"Now you do yourself injustice." After a moment's hesitancy she added, "I am not quite in your mood to-day, and even Nature, as your ally, cannot make me forget or even wish to forget."

"I do not wish you to forget, but merely cease to remember for a little while. You say Nature is my ally. Listen: already the wind is beginning to sigh in the branches overhead. The sound is low and mournful, as if full of regret for the past and forebodings for the future. There is a change coming. All that I wished or could expect in you was that this serene, quiet day would give you a respite—that complete repose in which the wounded spirit is more rapidly healed and strengthened for the future."

"Have you been strengthened? Have you no fears for the future?"

"No fears, Helen. My life is strong in its negation. The man who is agitated by hopes and fears, who is doomed to disappointments, is the one who has not recognized his limitations, who has not accepted well-defined conditions."

"Hobart, I'm going to put you on your honor now. Remember, and do not answer hastily," and her gaze into his face was searching. Although quiet and perfectly self-controlled, the rich color mounted to her very brow.

"Well, Helen," he asked wonderingly.

"Imagine it possible," she continued with the same earnest gaze, "that you were a woman who has loved as I have loved, and lost as I have. The circumstances are all known, and you have only to recall them. If a man had loved you as you have loved me—"

"But, Helen, can you not believe in a love so strong that it does not ask—"

By a gesture she checked him and repeated, "But if a man had loved you as you have loved me—remember now, on your honor—would you permit him to love with no better reward than the consciousness of being a solace, a help, a sort of buffer between you and the ills of life?"

"But, Helen, I am more than that: I am your friend."

"Indeed you are, the best a woman ever had, or I could not speak as I am doing. Yet what I say is true. From the first it has been your sleepless aim to stand between me and trouble. What have I ever done for you?"

"In giving me your friendship—"

Again she interrupted him, saying, "That virtually means giving you the chance for continued self-sacrifice. Any man or woman in the land would give you friendship on such terms, YOUR terms with me. But you do not answer my question; yet you have answered it over and over again. Were you in my place with your unselfish nature, you could not take so very much without an inevitable longing to return all in your power."

He was deeply agitated. Burying his face in his hands, he said hoarsely, "I must not look at you, or my duty may be too hard. Ah, you are banishing peace and serenity now with a vengeance! I recognize your motive—whither your thoughts are tending. Your conscience, your pity, your exaggerated gratitude are driving you to contemplate a self-sacrifice compared with which mine is as nothing. Yet the possibility of what you suggest is so sweet, so—oh, it is like the reward of heaven for a brief life!" Then he bowed his head lower and added slowly, as if the words were forced from him, "No, Helen, you shall not reward me. I cannot take as pay, or 'return,' as you express it, the reward that you are meditating. I must not remember in after years that my efforts in your behalf piled up such a burdensome sense of obligation that there was but one escape from it."

She came to his side, and removing his hands from his face, retained one of them as she said, gently, "Hobart, I am no longer a shy girl. I have suffered too deeply, I have learned too thoroughly how life may be robbed of happiness, and for a time, almost of hope, not to see the folly of letting the years slip away, unproductive of half what they might yield to you and me. I understand you; you do not understand me, probably because your ideal is too high. You employed an illustration in the narrowest meaning. Is heaven given only as a reward? Is not every true gift an expression of something back of the gift, more than the gift?"

"Helen!"

"Yes, Hobart, in my wish to make you happier I am not bent on unredeemed self-sacrifice. You have been the most skilful of wooers."

"And you are the divinest of mysteries. How have I wooed you?"

"By not wooing at all, by taking a course which compelled my heart to plead your cause, by giving unselfish devotion so unstintedly that like the rain and dew of heaven, it has fostered a new life in my heart, different from the old, yet sweet, real, and precious. I have learned that I can be happier in making you happy. Oh, I shall be no martyr. Am I inconstant because time and your ministry have healed the old wound—because the steady warmth and glow of your love has kindled mine?"

He regarded her with a gaze so rapt, so reverent, so expressive of immeasurable gratitude that her eyes filled with tears. "I think you do understand me," she whispered.

He kissed her hand in homage as he replied, "A joy like this is almost as hard to comprehend at first as an equally great sorrow. My garden teaches me to understand you. A perfect flower-stalk is suddenly and rudely broken. Instead of dying, it eventually sends out a little side-shoot which gives what bloom it can."

"And you will be content with what it can give?"

"I shall be glad with a happiness which almost terrifies me. Only God knows how I have longed for this."

That evening the old banker scarcely ceased rubbing his hands in general felicitation, while practical, housewifely Mrs. Kemble already began to plan what she intended to do toward establishing Helen in the adjoining cottage.

Now that Martine believed his great happiness possible, he was eager for its consummation. At his request the 1st of December was named as the wedding day. "The best that a fireside and evening lamp ever suggested will then come true to me," ha urged. "Since this can be, life is too short that it should not be soon."

Helen readily yielded. Indeed, they were all so absorbed in planning for his happiness as to be oblivious of the rising storm. When at last the girl went to her room, the wind sighed and wailed so mournfully around the house as to produce a feeling of depression and foreboding.

CHAPTER VII
YANKEE BLANK

The wild night storm which followed the most memorable day of his life had no power to depress Martine. In the wavy flames and glowing coals of his open fire he saw heavenly pictures of the future. He drew his mother's low chair to the hearth, and his kindled fancy placed Helen in it. Memory could so reproduce her lovely and familiar features that her presence became almost a reality. In a sense he watched her changing expression and heard her low, mellow tones. The truth that both would express an affection akin to his own grew upon his consciousness like the incoming of a sun-lighted tide. The darkness and storm without became only the background of his pictures, enhancing every prophetic representation. The night passed in ecstatic waking dreams of all that the word "home" suggests when a woman, loved as he loved Helen, was its architect.

The days and weeks which followed were filled with divine enchantment; the prosaic world was transfigured; the intricacies of the law were luminous with the sheen of gold, becoming the quartz veins from which he would mine wealth for Helen; the plants in his little rose-house were cared for with caressing tenderness because they gave buds which would be worn over the heart now throbbing for him. Never did mortal know such unalloyed happiness as blessed Martine, as he became daily more convinced that Helen was not giving herself to him merely from the promptings of compassion.

At times, when she did not know he was listening, he heard her low, sweet laugh; and it had a joyous ring and melody which repeated itself like a haunting refrain of music. He would say smilingly, "It is circumstantial evidence, equivalent to direct proof."

Helen and her mother almost took possession of his house while he was absent at his office, refurnishing and transforming it, yet retaining with reverent memory what was essentially associated with Mrs. Martine. The changing aspects of the house did not banish the old sense of familiarity, but were rather like the apple-tree in the corner of the garden when budding into new foliage and flower. The banker's purse was ever open for all this renovation, but Martine jealously persisted in his resolve to meet every expense himself. Witnessing his gladness and satisfaction, they let him have his way, he meanwhile exulting over Helen's absorbed interest in the adornment of her future home.

The entire village had a friendly concern in the approaching wedding; and the aged gossips never tired of saying, "I told you so," believing that they understood precisely how it had all come about. Even Mrs. Nichol aquiesced with a few deep sighs, assuring herself, "I suppose it's natural. I'd rather it was Bart Martine than anybody else."

A few days before the 1st of December, Martine received a telegram from an aged uncle residing in a distant State. It conveyed a request hard to comply with, yet he did not see how it could be evaded. The despatch was delivered in the evening while he was at the Kembles', and its effect upon the little group was like a bolt out of a clear sky. It ran:

"Your cousin dangerously ill at——Hospital, Washington. Go to him at once, if possible, and telegraph me to come, if necessary."

Hobart explained that this cousin had remained in the army from choice, and that his father, old and feeble, naturally shrank from a journey to which he was scarcely equal. "My hospital experience," he concluded, "leads him to think that I am just the one to go, especially as I can get there much sooner than he. I suppose he is right. Indeed, I do not know of any one else whom he could call upon. It certainly is a very painful duty at this time."

"I can't endure to think of it," Helen exclaimed.

"It's a clear question of conscience, Helen," he replied gently. "Many years have passed since I saw this cousin, yet he, and still more strongly his father, have the claims of kinship. If anything should happen which my presence could avert, you know we should both feel bad. It would be a cloud upon our happiness. If this request had come before you had changed everything for me, you know I would have gone without a moment's hesitation. Very gratitude should make me more ready for duty;" yet he signed deeply.

"But it may delay the wedding, for which the invitations have gone out," protested Mrs. Kemble.

"Possibly it may, if my cousin's life is in danger." Then, brightening up, he added: "Perhaps I shall find that I can leave him in good care for a short time, and then we can go to Washington on our wedding trip. I would like to gain associations with that city different from those I now have."

"Come now," said the banker, hopefully, "if we must face this thing, we must. The probabilities are that it will turn out as Hobart says. At worst it can only be a sad interruption and episode. Hobart will be better satisfied in the end if he does what he now thinks his duty."

"Yours is the right view," assented the young man, firmly. "I shall take the midnight train, and telegraph as soon as I have seen my cousin and the hospital surgeon."

He went home and hastily made his preparations; then, with valise in hand, returned to the Kembles'. The old people bade him Godspeed on his journey, and considerately left him with his affianced.

"Hobart," Helen entreated, as they were parting, "be more than ordinarily prudent. Do not take any risks, even the most trivial, unless you feel you must. Perhaps I'm weak and foolish, but I'm possessed with a strange, nervous dread. This sudden call of duty—for so I suppose I must look upon it—seems so inopportune;" and she hid her tears on his shoulder.

"You are taking it much too seriously, darling," he said, gently drawing her closer to him.

"Yes, my reason tells me that I am. You are only going on a brief journey, facing nothing that can be called danger. Yet I speak as I feel—I cannot help feeling. Give me glad reassurance by returning quickly and safely. Then hereafter I will laugh at forebodings."

"There, you need not wait till I reach Washington. You shall hear from me in the morning, and I will also telegraph when I have opportunity on my journey."

"Please do so, and remember that I could not endure to have my life impoverished again."

Late the following evening, Martine inquired his way to the bedside of his cousin, and was glad indeed to find him convalescent. His own experienced eyes, together with the statement of the sick man and wardmaster, convinced him that the danger point was well passed. In immense relief of mind he said cheerily, "I will watch to-night"; and so it was arranged.

His cousin, soothed and hushed in his desire to talk, soon dropped into quiet slumber, while Martine's thronging thoughts banished the sense of drowsiness. A shaded lamp burned near, making a circle of light and leaving the rest of the ward dim and shadowy. The scene was very familiar, and it was an easy effort for his imagination to place in the adjoining cots the patients with whom, months before, he had fought the winning or losing battle of life. While memory sometimes went back compassionately to those sufferers, his thoughts dwelt chiefly upon the near future, with its certainty of happiness—a happiness doubly appreciated because his renewed experience in the old conditions of his life made the home which awaited him all the sweeter from contrast. He could scarcely believe that he was the same man who in places like this had sought to forget the pain of bereavement and of denial of his dearest wish—he who in the morning would telegraph Helen that the wedding need not even be postponed, or any change made in their plans.

The hours were passing almost unnoted, when a patient beyond the circle of light feebly called for water. Almost mechanically Hobart rose to get it, when a man wearing carpet slippers and an old dressing-gown shuffled noiselessly into view.

"Captain Nichol!" gasped Martine, sinking back, faint and trembling, in his chair.

The man paid no attention, but passed through the circle of light to the patient, gave him a drink, and turned. Martine stared with the paralysis of one looking upon an apparition.

When the figure was opposite to him, he again ejaculated hoarsely,
"Captain Nichol!"
The form in slippers and gray ghostly dressing-gown turned sleepy eyes upon him without the slightest sign of recognition, passed on, and disappeared among the shadows near the wardmaster's room.

A blending of relief and fearful doubt agitated Martine. He knew he had been wide awake and in the possession of every faculty—that his imagination had been playing him no tricks. He was not even thinking of Nichol at the time; yet the impression that he had looked upon and spoken to his old schoolmate, to Helen's dead lover, had been as strong as it was instantaneous. When the man had turned, there had been an unnatural expression, which in a measure dispelled the illusion. After a moment of thought which scorched his brain, he rose and followed the man's steps, and was in time to see him rolling himself in his blanket on the cot nearest the door. From violent agitation, Martine unconsciously shook the figure outlined in the blanket roughly, as he asked, "What's your name?"

"Yankee Blank, doggone yer! Kyant you wake a feller 'thout yankin' 'im out o' baid? What yer want?"

"Great God!" muttered Hobart, tottering back to his seat beside his sleeping cousin, "was there ever such a horrible, mocking suggestion of one man in another? Yankee Blank—what a name! Southern accent and vernacular, yet Nichol's voice! Such similarity combined with such dissimilarity is like a nightmare. Of course it's not Nichol. He was killed nearly two years ago. I'd be more than human if I could wish him back now; but never in my life have I been so shocked and startled. This apparition must account for itself in the morning."

But he could not wait till morning; he could not control himself five minutes. He felt that he must banish that horrible semblance of Nichol from his mind by convincing himself of its absurdity.

He waited a few moments in order to compose his nerves, and then returned. The man had evidently gone to sleep.

"What a fool I am!" Martine again muttered. "Let the poor fellow sleep. The fact that he doesn't know me is proof enough. The idea of wanting any proof! I can investigate his case in the morning, and, no doubt, in broad light that astonishing suggestion of Nichol will disappear."

He was about to turn away when the patient who had called for water groaned slightly. As if his ears were as sensitive to such sounds as those of a mother who hears her child even when it stirs, the man arose. Seeing Martine standing by him, he asked in slight irritation, "What yer want? Why kyant yer say what yer want en have done 'th it? Lemme 'tend ter that feller yander firs'. We uns don't want no mo' stiffs;" and he shuffled with a peculiar, noiseless tread to the patient whose case seemed on his mind. Martine followed, his very hair rising at the well-remembered tones, and the mysterious principle of identity again revealed within the circle of light.

"This is simply horrible!" he groaned inwardly, "and I must have that man account for himself instantly."

"Now I'll 'tend ter yer, but yer mout let a feller sleep when he kin."

"Don't you know me?" faltered Martine, overpowered.

"Naw."

"Please tell me your real name, not your nickname."

"Ain' got no name 'cept Yankee Blank. What's the matter with yer, anyhow?"

"Didn't you ever hear of Captain Nichol?"

"Reckon not. Mout have. I've nussed mo' cap'ins than I kin reckerlect."

"Are you a hospital nurse?"

"Sorter 'spect I am. That's what I does, anyhow. Have you anything agin it? Don't yer come 'ferin' round with me less yer a doctor, astin' no end o' questions. Air you a new doctor?"

"My name is Hobart Martine," the speaker forced himself to say, expecting fearfully a sign of recognition, for the impression that it was Nichol grew upon him every moment, in spite of apparent proof to the contrary.

"Hump! Hob't Ma'tine. Never yeared on yer. Ef yer want ter chin mo' in the mawnin', I'll be yere."

"Wait a moment, Yan—"

"Yankee Blank, I tole yer."

"Well, here's a dollar for the trouble I'm making you," and Martine's face flushed with shame at the act, so divided was his impression about the man.

Yankee Blank took the money readily, grinned, and said, "Now I'll chin till mawnin' ef yer wants hit."

"I won't keep you long. You remind me of—of—well, of Captain Nichol."

"He must 'a' been a cur'ous chap. Folks all say I'm a cur'ous chap."

"Won't you please tell me all that you can remember about yourself?"

"'Tain't much. Short hoss soon curried. Allus ben in hospitals. Had high ole jinks with a wound on my haid. Piece o' shell, they sez, cut me yere," and he pointed to a scar across his forehead. "That's what they tole me. Lor'! I couldn't mek much out o' the gibberish I firs' year, en they sez I talked gibberish too. But I soon got the hang o' the talk in the hospital. Well, ez I wuz sayin', I've allus been in hospitals firs' one, then anuther. I got well, en the sojers call me Yankee Blank en set me waitin' on sick uns en the wounded. That's what I'm a-doin' now."

"You were in Southern hospitals?"

"I reckon. They called the place Richman."

"Why did you come here?"

"Kaze I wuz bro't yere. They said I was 'changed."

"Exchanged, wasn't it?"

"Reckon it was. Anyhow I wuz bro't yere with a lot o' sick fellers. I wuzn't sick. For a long time the doctors kep' a-pesterin' me with questions, but they lemme 'lone now. I 'spected you wuz a new doctor, en at it agin."

"Don't you remember the village of Alton?"

The man shook his head.

"Don't you—" and Martine's voice grew husky—"don't you remember Helen Kemble?"
"A woman?"

"Yes."

"Never yeared on her. I only reckerlect people I've seen in hospitals. Women come foolin' roun' some days, but Lor'! I kin beat any on 'em teekin' keer o' the patients; en wen they dies, I kin lay 'em out. You ast the wardmaster ef I kant lay out a stiff with the best o' 'em."

"That will do. You can go to sleep now."

"All right, Doc. I call everybody doc who asts sech a lot o' questions." He shuffled to his cot and was soon asleep.

FOUND YET LOST BY EDWARD PAYSON ROE

CHAPTER VIII
"HOW CAN I?"

Martine sank into his chair again. Although the conversation had been carried on in low tones, it was the voice of Nichol that he had heard. Closer inspection of the slightly disfigured face proved that, apart from the scar on the forehead, it was the countenance of Nichol. A possible solution of the mystery was beginning to force itself in Hobart's reluctant mind. When Nichol had fallen in the Wilderness, the shock of his injury had rendered him senseless and caused him to appear dead to the hasty scrutiny of Sam and Jim Wetherby. They were terribly excited and had no time for close examination. Nichol might have revived, have been gathered up with the Confederate wounded, and sent to Richmond. There was dire and tremendous confusion at that period, when within the space of two or three days tens of thousands were either killed or disabled. In a Southern hospital Nichol might have recovered physical health while, from injury to the brain, suffering complete eclipse of memory. In this case he would have to begin life anew, like a child, and so would pick up the vernacular and bearing of the enlisted men with whom he would chiefly associate.

Because he remembered nothing and know nothing, he may at first have been tolerated as a "cur'ous chap," then employed as he had explained. He could take the place of a better man where men were greatly needed.

This theory could solve the problem; and Martine's hospital experience prepared his mind to understand what would be a hopeless mystery to many. He was so fearfully excited that he could not remain in the ward. The very proximity to this strange being, who had virtually risen from the dead and appeared to him of all others, was a sort of torture in itself.

What effect would this discovery have on his relations to Helen? He dared not think yet he must think. Already the temptation of his life was forming in his mind. His cousin was sleeping; and with a wild impatience to escape, to get away from all his kind, he stole noiselessly out into the midnight and deserted streets. On, on he went, limping he knew not, cared not where, for his passion and mental agony drove him hither and thither like a leaf before a fitful gale.

"No one knows of this," he groaned. "I can still return and marry Helen. But oh, what a secret to carry!"

Then his heart pleaded. "This is not the lover she lost—only a horrible, mocking semblance. He has lost his own identity; he does not even know himself—would not know her. Ah! I'm not sure of that. I would be dead indeed if her dear features did not kindle my eyes in recognition. It may be that the sight of her face is the one thing essential to restore him. I feel this would be true were it my case. But how can I give her up now? How can?—how can I? Oh, this terrible journey! No wonder Helen had forebodings. She loves me; she is mine. No one else has so good a right. We were to be married only a few hours hence. Then she whom I've loved from childhood would make my home a heaves on earth. And yet—and yet—" Even in the darkness he buried his face in his hands, shuddered, moaned, writhed, and grated his teeth in the torment of the conflict.

Hour after hour he wavered, now on the point of yielding, then stung by conscience into desperate uncertainty. The night was cold, the howling wind would have chilled him at another time, but during his struggle great drops of sweat often poured from his face. Only the eye of God saw that battle, the hardest that was fought and won during the war.

At last, when well out of the city, he lifted his agonized eyes and saw the beautiful hues of morning tingeing the east. Unconsciously, he repeated the sublime, creative words, "Let there be light." It came to him. With the vanishing darkness, he revolted finally against the thought of any shadows existing between him and Helen. She should have all the light that he had, and decide her own course. He had little hope that she would wed him, even if she did not marry Nichol in his present condition—a condition probably only temporary and amenable to skilful treatment.

Wearily he dragged his lame foot back to a hotel in the populous party of the city, and obtained food and wine, for he was terribly exhausted. Next he telegraphed Mr. Kemble:

"Arrived last evening. The wedding will have to be postponed. Will explain later."

"It's the best I can do now," he muttered. "Helen will think it is all due to my cousin's illness." Then he returned to the hospital and found his relative in a state of wonderment at his absence, but refreshed from a good night's rest. Yankee Blank was nowhere to be seen.

"Hobart," exclaimed his cousin, "you look ill—ten years older than you did last night."

"You see me now by daylight," was the quiet reply. "I am not very well."

"It's a perfect shame that I've been the cause of so much trouble, especially when it wasn't necessary."

"Oh, my God!" thought Martine, "there was even no need of this fatal journey." But his face had become grave and inscrutable, and the plea of ill-health reconciled his cousin to the necessity of immediate return. There was no good reason for his remaining, for by a few additional arrangements his relative would do very well and soon be able to take care of himself. Martine felt that he could not jeopardize his hard-won victory by delay, which was as torturing as the time intervening between a desperate surgical operation and the knowledge that it is inevitable.

After seeing that his cousin made a good breakfast, he sought a private interview with the wardmaster. He was able to extract but little information about Yankee Blank more than the man had given himself. "Doctors say he may regain his memory at any time, or it may be a long while, and possibly never," was the conclusion.

"I think I know him," said Martine. "I will bring physician from the city to consult this morning with the surgeon in charge."

"I'm glad to hear it," was the reply. "Something would have to be done soon. He is just staying on here and making himself useful to some extent."

When Martine re-entered the ward, Yankee Blank appeared, grinned, and said affably, "Howdy." Alas! a forlorn, miserable hope that he might have been mistaken was banished from Hobart's mind now that he saw Nichol in the clear light of day. The scar across his forehead and a change of expression, denoting the eclipse of fine, cultivated manhood, could not disguise the unmistakable features. There was nothing to be done but carry out as quickly as possible the purpose which had cost him so dear.

He first telegraphed his uncle to dismiss further anxiety, and that his son would soon be able to visit him. Then the heavy-hearted man sought a physician whom he knew well by reputation.

The consultation was held, and Nichol (as he may be more properly named hereafter) was closely questioned and carefully examined. The result merely confirmed previous impressions. It was explained, as far as explanation can be given of the mysterious functions of the brain, that either the concussion of the exploding shell or the wound from a flying fragment had paralyzed the organ of memory. When such paralysis would cease, if ever, no one could tell. The power to recall everything might return at any moment or it might be delayed indefinitely. A shock, a familiar face, might supply the potency required, or restoration come through the slow, unseen processes of nature. Martine believed that Helen's face and voice would accomplish everything.

He was well known to the medical authorities and had no difficulty in securing belief that he had identified Nichol. He also promised that abundant additional proof should be sent on from Alton, such certainty being necessary to secure the officer's back pay and proper discharge from the service. The surgeon then addressed the man so strangely disabled, "You know I'm in charge of this hospital?"

"I reckon," replied Nichol, anxiously, for the brief experience which he could recall had taught him that the authority of the surgeon-in-chief was autocratic.

"Well, first, you must give up the name of Yankee Blank. Your name hereafter is Captain Nichol."

"All right, Doctor. I'll be a gin'ral ef you sez so."

"Very well; remember your name is Captain Nichol. Next, you must obey this man and go with him. You must do just what he says in all respects. His name is Mr. Hobart Martine."

"Yes, he tole me las' night, Hob't Ma'tine. He took on mighty cur'ous after seein' me."

"Do you understand that you are to mind, to obey him in all respects just as you have obeyed me?"

"I reckon. Will he tek me to anuther hospital?"

"He will take you where you will be well cared for and treated kindly." Having written Nichol's discharge from the hospital, the surgeon turned to other duties.

Martine informed his cousin, as far as it was essential, of the discovery he had made and of the duties which it imposed, then took his leave. Nichol readily accompanied him, and with the exception of a tendency to irritation at little things, exhibited much of the good-natured docility of a child. Martine took him to a hotel, saw that he had a bath, put him in the hands of a barber, and then sent for a clothier. When dressed in clean linen and a dark civilian suit, the appearance of the man was greatly improved. Hobart had set his teeth, and would entertain no thought of compromise with his conscience. He would do by Nichol as he would wish to be done by if their relations were reversed. Helen should receive no greater shock than was inevitable, nor should Nichol lose the advantage of appearing before her in the outward aspect of a gentleman.

Martine then planned his departure so that he would arrive at Alton in the evening—the evening of the day on which he was to have been married. He felt that Mr. Kemble should see Nichol first and hear the strange story; also that the father must break the news to the daughter, for he could not. It was a terrible journey to the poor fellow, for during the long hours of inaction he was compelled to face the probable results of his discovery. The sight of Nichol and his manner was intolerable; and in addition, he was almost as much care as a child. Everything struck him as new and strange, and he was disposed to ask numberless questions. His vernacular, his alternations of amusement and irritation, and the oddity of his ignorance concerning things which should be simple or familiar to a grown man, attracted the attention of his fellow-passengers. It was with difficulty that Martine, by his stern, sad face and a cold, repelling manner, kept curiosity from intruding at every point.

At last, with heart beating thickly, he saw the lights of Alton gleaming in the distance. It was a train not often used by the villagers, and fortunately no one had entered the car who knew him; even the conductor was a stranger. Alighting at the depot, he hastily took a carriage, and with his charge was driven to the private entrance of the hotel. Having given the hackman an extra dollar not to mention his arrival till morning, he took Nichol into the dimly-lighted and deserted parlor and sent for the well-known landlord. Mr. Jackson, a bustling little man, who, between the gossip of the place and his few guests, never seemed to have a moment's quiet, soon entered. "Why, Mr. Martine," he exclaimed, "we wasn't a-lookin' for you yet. News got around somehow that your cousin was dyin' in Washington and that your weddin' was put off too—Why! you look like a ghost, even in this light," and he turned up the lamp.

Martine had told Nichol to stand by a window with his back to the door. He now turned the key, pulled down the curtain, then drew his charge forward where the light fell clear upon his face, and asked, "Jackson, who is that?"

The landlord stared, his jaw fell from sheer astonishment, as he faltered, "Captain Nichol!"

"Yes," said Nichol, with a pleased grin, "that's my new name! Jes' got it, like this new suit o' clo's, bes' I ever had, doggoned ef they ain't. My old name was Yankee Blank."

"Great Scott!" ejaculated Jackson; "is he crazy?"

"Look yere," cried Nichol; "don' yer call me crazy or I'll light on yer so yer won't fergit it."

"There, there!" said Martine, soothingly, "Mr. Jackson doesn't mean any harm. He's only surprised to see you home again."

"Is this home? What's home?"

"It's the town where you were brought up. We'll make you understand about it all before long. Now you shall have some supper. Mr. Jackson is a warm friend of yours, and will see that you have a good one."

"I reckon we'll get on ef he gives me plenty o' fodder. Bring it toreckly, fer I'm hungry. Quit yer starin', kyant yer?" "Don't you know me, Captain Nichol? Why, I—"

"Naw. Never seed ner yeared on yer. Did I ever nuss yer in a hospital?
I kyant reckerlect all on 'em. Get we uns some supper."
"That's the thing to do first, Jackson," added Martine, "Show us upstairs to a private room and wait on us yourself. Please say nothing of this till I give you permission."

They were soon established in a suitable apartment, in which a fire was kindled. Nichol took a rocking-chair and acquiesced in Martine's going out on the pretext of hastening supper.

The landlord received explanations which enabled him to co-operate with Martine. "I could not," said the latter, "take him to his own home without first preparing his family. Neither could I take him to mine for several reasons."

"I can understand some of 'em, Mr. Martine. Why, great Scott! How about your marriage, now that—"

"We won't discuss that subject. The one thing for you to keep in mind is that Nichol lost his memory at the time of his wound. He don't like to be stared at or thought strange. You must humor him much as you would a child. Perhaps the sight of familiar faces and scenes will restore him. Now copy this note in your handwriting and send it to Mr. Kemble. Tell your messenger to be sure to put it into the banker's hands and no other's," and he tore from his note-book a leaf on which was pencilled the following words:

"MR. KEMBLE:

"DEAR SIR—A sick man at the hotel wishes to see you on important business. Don't think it's bad news about Mr. Martine, because it isn't. Please come at once and oblige, HENRY JACKSON."

FOUND YET LOST BY EDWARD PAYSON ROE

CHAPTER IX
SHADOWS OF COMING EVENTS

This first day of winter, her fatal wedding-day, was a sad and strange one to Helen Kemble. The sun was hidden by dark clouds, yet no snow fell on the frozen ground. She had wakened in the morning with a start, oppressed by a disagreeable yet forgotten dream. Hastily dressing, she consoled herself with the hope of a long letter from Martine, explaining everything and assuring her of his welfare; but the early mail brought nothing. As the morning advanced, a telegram from Washington, purposely delayed, merely informed her that her affianced was well and that full information was on its way.

"He has evidently found his cousin very low, and needing constant care," she had sighingly remarked at dinner.

"Yes, Nellie," said the banker, cheerily, "but it is a comfort he is well. No doubt you are right about his cousin, and it has turned out as Hobart feared. In this case it is well he went, for he would always have reproached himself if he had not. The evening mail will probably make all clear."

"It has been so unfortunate!" complained Mrs. Kemble. "If it had only happened a little earlier, or a little later! To have all one's preparations upset and one's plans frustrated is exasperating. Were it not for that journey, Helen would have been married by this time. People come ostensibly to express sympathy, but in reality to ask questions."

"I don't care about people," said Helen, "but the day has been so different from what we expected that it's hard not to yield to a presentiment of trouble. It is so dark and gloomy that we almost need a lamp at midday."

"Well, well," cried hearty Mr. Kemble, "I'm not going to cross any bridges till I come to them. That telegram from Hobart is all we need, to date. I look at things as I do at a bank-bill. If its face is all right, and the bill itself all right, that's enough. You women-folks have such a lot of moods and tenses! Look at this matter sensibly. Hobart was right in going. He's doing his duty, and soon will be back with mind and conscience at rest. It isn't as if he were ill himself."

"Yes, papa, that's just the difference; we women feel, and you men reason. What you say, though, is a good wholesome antidote. I fear I'm a little morbid to-day."

After dinner she and her mother slipped over to the adjoining cottage, which had been made so pretty for her reception. While Mrs. Kemble busied herself here and there, Helen kindled a fire on the hearth of the sitting-room and sat down in the low chair which she knew was designed for her. The belief that she would occupy it daily and be at home, happy herself and, better far, making another, to whom she owed so much, happy beyond even his fondest hope, brought smiles to her face as she watched the flickering blaze.

"Yes," she murmured, "I can make him happier even than he dreams. I know him so well, his tastes, his habits, what he most enjoys, that it will be an easy task to anticipate his wishes and enrich his life. Then he has been such a faithful, devoted friend! He shall learn that his example had not been lost on me."

At this moment the wind rose in such a long mournful, human-like sigh about the house that she started up and almost shuddered. When the evening mail came and brought no letter, she found it hard indeed not to yield to deep depression. In vain her father reasoned with her. "I know all you say sounds true to the ear," she said, "but not to my heart. I can't help it; but I am oppressed with a nervous dread of some impending trouble."

They passed the early hours of the evening as best they could, seeking to divert each other's thoughts. It had been long since the kind old banker was so garrulous, and Helen resolved to reward him by keeping up. Indeed, she shrank from retiring, feeling that through the sleepless night she would be the prey of all sorts of wretched fancies. Never once did her wildest thoughts suggest what had happened, or warn her of the tempest soon to rage in her breast.

Then came the late messenger with the landlord's copied note. She snatched it from the bearer's hand before he could ring the bell, for her straining ears had heard his step even on the gravel walk. Tremblingly she tore open, the envelope in the hall without looking at the address.

"Mr. Jackson said how I was to give it to your father," protested the messenger.

"Well, well," responded Mr. Kemble, perturbed and anxious, "I'm here.
You can go unless there's an answer required.'
"Wasn't told nothin' 'bout one," growled the departing errand-boy.

"Give the note to me, Helen," said her father. "Why do you stare at it so?"

She handed it to him without a word, but looked searchingly in his face, and so did his wife, who had joined him.

"Why, this is rather strange," he said.

"I think it is," added Helen, emphatically.

Mrs. Kemble took the note and after a moment ejaculated: "Well, thank the Lord! it isn't about Hobart."

"No, no," said the banker, almost irritably. "We've all worried about Hobart till in danger of making fools of ourselves. As if people never get sick and send for relatives, or as if letters were never delayed! Why, bless me! haven't we heard to-day that he was well? and hasn't Jackson, who knows more about other people's business than his own, been considerate enough to say that his request has nothing to do with Hobart? It is just as he says, some one is sick and wants to arrange about money matters before banking hours to-morrow. There, it isn't far. I'll soon be back."

"Let me go with you, father," pleaded Helen. "I can stay with Mrs.
Jackson or sit in the parlor till you are through."
"Oh, no, indeed."

"Papa, I AM going with you," said Helen, half-desperately. "I don't believe I am so troubled for nothing. Perhaps it's a merciful warning, and I may be of use to you."

"Oh, let her go, father," said his wife. "She had better be with you than nervously worrying at home. I'll be better satisfied if she is with you."

"Bundle up well, then, and come along, you silly little girl."

Nichol was too agreeably occupied with his supper to miss Hobart, who watched in the darkened parlor for the coming of Mr. Kemble. At last he saw the banker passing through the light streaming from a shop-window, and also recognized Helen at his side. His ruse in sending a note purporting to come from the landlord had evidently failed; and here was a new complication. He was so exhausted in body and mind that he felt he could not meet the girl now without giving way utterly. Hastily returning to the room in which were Nichol and Jackson, he summoned the latter and said, "Unfortunately, Miss Kemble is coming with her father. Keep your counsel; give me a light in another private room; detain the young lady in the parlor, and then, bring Mr. Kemble to me."

"Ah, glad to see you, Mr. Kemble," said the landlord, a moment or two later, with reassuring cheerfulness; "you too, Miss Helen. That's right, take good care of the old gentleman. Yes, we have a sick man here who wants to see you, sir. Miss Helen, take a seat in the parlor by the fire while I turn up the lamp. Guess you won't have to wait long."

"Now, Helen," said her father, smiling at her significantly, "can you trust me out of your sight to go upstairs with Mr. Jackson?"

Much relieved, she smiled in return and sat down to wait.

"Who is this man, Jackson?" Mr. Kemble asked on the stairs.

"Well, sir, he said he would explain everything."

A moment later the banker needed not Martine's warning gesture enjoining silence, for he was speechless with astonishment.

"Mr. Jackson," whispered Martine, "will you please remain in the other room and look after your patient?"

"Hobart," faltered Mr. Kemble, "in the name of all that's strange, what does this mean?"

"It is indeed very strange, sir. You must summon all your nerve and fortitude to help us through. Never before were your strength and good strong common-sense more needed. I've nearly reached the end of my endurance. Please, sir, for Helen's sake, preserve your self-control and the best use of all your faculties, for you must now advise. Mr. Kemble, Captain Nichol is alive."

The banker sank into a chair and groaned. "This would have been glad news to me once; I suppose it should be so now. But how, how can this be?"

"Well, sir, as you say, it should be glad news; it will be to all eventually. I am placed in a very hard position; but I have tried to do my duty, and will."

"Why, Hobart, my boy, you look more worn than you did after your illness. Merciful Heaven! what a complication!"

"A far worse one than you can even imagine. Captain Nichol wouldn't know you. His memory was destroyed at the time of the injury. All before that is gone utterly;" and Martine rapidly narrated what is already known to the reader, concluding, "I'm sorry

Helen came with you, and I think you had better get her home as soon as possible. I could not take him to my home for several reasons, or at least I thought it best not to. It is my belief that the sight of Helen, the tones of her voice, will restore him; and I do not think it best for him to regain his consciousness of the past in a dwelling prepared for Helen's reception as my wife. Perhaps later on, too, you will understand why I cannot see him there. I shall need a home, a refuge with no such associations. Here, on this neutral ground, I thought we could consult, and if necessary send for his parents to-night. I would have telegraphed you, but the case is so complicated, so difficult. Helen must be gradually prepared for the part she must take. Cost me what it may, Nichol must have his chance. His memory may come back instantly and he recall everything to the moment of his injury. What could be more potent to effect this than the sight and voice of Helen? No one here except Jackson is now aware of his condition. If she can restore him, no one else, not even his parents, need know anything about it, except in a general way. It will save a world of disagreeable talk and distress. At any rate, this course seemed the best I could hit upon in my distracted condition."

"Well, Hobart, my poor young friend, you have been tried as by fire," said Mr. Kemble, in a voice broken by sympathy; "God help you and guide us all in this strange snarl! I feel that the first thing to be done is to get Helen home. Such tidings as yours should be broken to her in that refuge only."

"I agree with you most emphatically, Mr. Kemble. In the seclusion of her own home, with none present except yourself and her mother, she should face this thing and nerve herself to act her part, the most important of all. If she cannot awaken Captain Nichol's memory, it is hard to say what will, or when he will be restored."

"Possibly seeing me, so closely associated with her, may have the same effect," faltered the banker.

"I doubt it; but we can try it. Don't expect me to speak while in the hallway. Helen, no doubt, is on the alert, and I cannot meet her to-night. I am just keeping up from sheer force of will. You must try to realize it. This discovery will change everything for me. Helen's old love will revive in all-absorbing power. I've faced this in thought, but cannot in reality NOW—I simply CANNOT. It would do no good. My presence would be an embarrassment to her, and I taxed beyond mortal endurance. You may think me weak, but I cannot help it. As soon as possible I must put you, and if you think best, Captain Nichol's father, in charge of the situation. Jackson can send for his father at once if you wish."

"I do wish it immediately. I can't see my way through this. I would like Dr. Barnes' advice and presence also."

"I think it would be wise, sir. The point I wish to make is that I have done about all that I now can in this affair. My further presence is only another complication. At any rate, I must have a respite—the privilege of going quietly to my own home as soon as possible."

"Oh, Hobart, my heart aches for you; it just ACHES for you. You have indeed been called upon to endure a hundredfold too much in this strange affair. How it will all end God only knows. I understand you sufficiently. Leave the matter to me now. We will have Dr. Barnes and Mr. and Mrs. Nichol here as soon as can be. I suppose I had better see the captain a few moments and then take Helen home."

Martine led the way into the other apartment, where Nichol, rendered good-natured by his supper and a cigar, was conversing sociably with the landlord. Mr. Kemble fairly trembled as he came forward, involuntarily expecting that the man so well known to him must give some sign of recognition.

Nichol paid no heed to him. He had been too long accustomed to see strangers coming and going to give them either thought or attention.

"I say, Hob't Ma'tine," he began, "don' yer cuss me fer eatin' all the supper. I 'lowed ter this Jackson, as yer call 'im, that yer'd get a bite somewhar else, en he 'lowed yer would."

"All right, Nichol; I'm glad you had a good supper."

"I say, Jackson, this Ma'tine's a cur'ous chap—mo cur'ous than I be, I reckon. He's been actin' cur'ous ever since he seed me in the horspital. It's all cur'ous. 'Fore he come, doctors en folks was trying ter fin' out 'bout me, en this Ma'tine 'lows he knows all 'bout me. Ef he wuzn't so orful glum, he'd be a good chap anuff, ef he is cur'ous. Hit's all a-changin' somehow, en yet' tisn't. Awhile ago nobody knowd 'bout me, en they wuz allus a-pesterin' of me with questions. En now Ma'tine en you 'low you know 'bout me, yet you ast questions jes' the same. Like anuff this man yere," pointing with his cigar to Mr. Kemble, who was listening with a deeply-troubled face, "knows 'bout me too, yet wants to ast questions. I don' keer ef I do say it, I had better times with the Johnnies that call me Yankee Blank than I ever had sence. Well, ole duffer [to Mr. Kemble], ast away and git yer load off'n yer mind. I don't like glum faces roun' en folks jes' nachelly bilin' over with questions."

"No, Captain Nichol," said the banker, gravely and sadly, "I've no questions to ask. Good-by for the present."

Nichol nodded a careless dismissal and resumed his reminiscences with Jackson, whose eager curiosity and readiness to laugh were much more to his mind.

Following the noise made by closing the door, Helen's voice rang up from the hall below, "Papa!"

"Yes, I'm coming, dear," he tried to answer cheerily. Then he wrung Martine's hand and whispered, "Send for Dr. Barnes. God knows you should have relief. Tell Jackson also to have a carriage go for Mr. Nichol at once. After the doctor comes you may leave all in our hands. Good-by."
Martine heard the rustle of a lady's dress and retired precipitately.

CHAPTER X
"YOU CANNOT UNDERSTAND"

With an affectation of briskness he was far from feeling, Mr. Kemble came down the stairs and joined his daughter in the hall. He had taken pains to draw his hat well over his eyes, anticipating and dreading her keen scrutiny, but, strange to say, his troubled demeanor passed unnoticed. In the interval of waiting Helen's thoughts had taken a new turn. "Well, papa," she began, as they passed into the street, "I am curious to know about the sick man. You stayed an age, but all the same I'm glad I came with you. Forebodings, presentiments, and all that kind of thing seemed absurd the moment I saw Jackson's keen, mousing little visage. His very voice is like a ray of garish light entering a dusky, haunted room. Things suggesting ghosts and hobgoblins become ridiculously prosaic, and you are ashamed of yourself and your fears."

"Yes, yes," replied Mr. Kemble, yielding to irritation in his deep perplexity, "the more matter-of-fact we are the better we're off. I suppose the best thing to do is just to face what happens and try to be brave."

"Well, papa, what's happened to annoy you to-night? Is this sick man going to make you trouble?"

"Like enough. I hope not. At any rate, he has claims which I must meet."

"Don't you think you can meet them?" was her next anxious query, her mind reverting to some financial obligation.

"We'll see. You and mother'll have to help me out, I guess. I'll tell you both when we get home;" and his sigh was so deep as to be almost a groan.

"Papa," said Helen, earnestly pressing his arm, "don't worry. Mamma and I will stand by you; so will Hobart. He is the last one in the world to desert one in any kind of trouble."

"I know that, no one better; but I fear he'll be in deeper trouble than any of us. The exasperating thing is that there should be any trouble at all. If it had only happened before—well, well, I can't talk here in the street. As you say, you must stand by me, and I'll do the best I can by you and all concerned."

"Oh, papa, there was good cause for my foreboding."

"Well, yes, and no. I don't know. I'm at my wits' end. If you'll be brave and sensible, you can probably do more than any of us."

"Papa, papa, something IS the matter with Hobart," and she drew him hastily into the house, which they had now reached.

Mrs. Kemble met them at the door. Alarmed at her husband's troubled face, she exclaimed anxiously, "Who is this man? What did he want?"

"Come now, mother, give me a chance to get my breath. We'll close the doors, sit down, and talk it all over."

Mrs. Kemble and her daughter exchanged an apprehensive glance and followed with the air of being prepared for the worst.

The banker sat down and wiped the perspiration from his brow, then looked dubiously at the deeply anxious faces turned toward him. "Well," he said, "I'm going to tell you everything as far as I understand it. Now I want to see if you two can't listen calmly and quietly and not give way to useless feeling. There's much to be done, and you especially, Helen, must be in the right condition to do it."

"Oh, papa, why torture me so? Something HAS happened to Hobart. I can't endure this suspense."

"Something has happened to us all," replied her father, gravely. "Hobart has acted like a hero, like a saint; so must you. He is as well and able to go about as you are. I've seen him and talked with him."

"He saw you and not me?" cried the girl, starting up.

"Helen, I entreat, I command you to be composed and listen patiently.
Don't you know him well enough to be sure he had good reasons—"
"I can't imagine a reason," was the passionate reply, as she paced the floor. "What reason could keep me from him? Merciful Heaven! father, have you forgotten that I was to marry him to-day? Well," she added hoarsely, standing before him with hands clinched in her effort at self-restraint, "the reason?"

"Poor fellow! poor fellow! he has not forgotten it," groaned Mr. Kemble. "Well, I might as well out with it. Suppose Captain Nichol was not killed after all?"

Helen sank into a chair as if struck down as Nichol had been himself.

"What!" she whispered; and her face was white indeed.

Mrs. Kemble rushed to her husband, demanding, "Do you mean to tell us that Captain Nichol is alive?"

"Yes; that's just the question we've got to face."

"It brings up another question," replied his wife, sternly. "If he's been alive all this time, why did he not let us know? As far as I can make out, Hobart has found him in Washington—"

"Helen," cried her father to the trembling girl, "for Heaven's sake, be calm!"

"He's alive, ALIVE!" she answered, as if no other thought could exist in her mind. Her eyes were kindling, the color coming into her face, and her bosom throbbed quickly as if her heart would burst its bonds. Suddenly she rushed to her father, exclaiming, "He was the sick man. Oh, why did you not let me see him?"

"Well, well!" ejaculated Mr. Kemble, "Hobart was right, poor fellow! Yes, Helen, Captain Nichol is the sick man, not dangerously ill, however. You are giving ample reason why you should not see him yet; and I tell you plainly you can't see him till you are just as composed as I am."

She burst into a joyous, half-hysterical laugh as she exclaimed, "That's not asking much. I never saw you so moved, papa. Little wonder! The dead is alive again! Oh, papa, papa, you don't understand me at all! Could I hear such tidings composedly—I who have wept so many long nights and days over his death? I must give expression to overwhelming feeling here where it can do no harm, but if I had seen him—when I do see him—ah! he'll receive no harm from me."

"But, Helen, think of Hobart," cried Mrs. Kemble, in sharp distress.

"Mother, mother, I cannot help it. Albert is alive, ALIVE! The old feeling comes back like the breaking up of the fountains of the great deep. You cannot know, cannot understand; Hobart will. I'm sorry, SORRY for him; but he will understand. I thought Albert was dead; I wanted to make Hobart happy. He was so good and kind and deserving that I did love him in a sincere, quiet way, but not with my first love, not as I loved Albert. I thought my love was buried with him; but it has burst the grave as he has. Papa, papa, let me go to him, now, NOW! You say he is sick; it is my place to nurse him back to life. Who has a better right? Why do you not bring him here?"

"Perhaps it will be best, since Helen feels so," said Mr. Kemble, looking at his wife.

"Well, I don't know," she replied with a deep sigh. "We certainly don't wish the public to be looking on any more than we can help. He should be either here or at his own home."

"There's more reason for what you say than you think," Mr. Kemble began.

"There, papa," interrupted Helen, "I'd be more or less than human if I could take! this undreamed-of news quietly, I can see how perplexed and troubled you've been, and how you've kindly tried to prepare me for the tidings. You will find that I have strength of mind to meet all that is required of me. It is all simpler to me than to you, for in a matter of this kind the heart is the guide, indeed, the only guide. Think! If Albert had come back months ago; if Hobart had brought him back wounded and disabled—how would we have acted? Only our belief in his death led to what has happened since, and the fact of life changes everything back to—"

"Now, Helen, stop and listen to me," said her father, firmly. "In one sense the crisis is over, and you've heard the news which I scarcely knew how to break to you. You say you will have strength of mind to meet what is required of you. I trust you may. But it's time you understood the situation as far as I do. Mother's words show she's off the track in her suspicion. Nichol is not to blame in any sense. He is deserving of all sympathy, and yet—oh, dear, it is such a complication!" and the old man groaned as he thought of the personality who best knew himself as Yankee Blank. "The fact is," he resumed to his breathless listeners, "Nichol is not ill at all physically. His mind is affected—"

Mrs. Kemble sank back in her chair, and Helen uttered a cry of dismay.

"Yes, his mind is affected peculiarly. He remembers nothing that happened before he was wounded. You must realize this, Helen; you must prepare yourself for it. His loss of memory is much more sad than if he had lost an arm or a leg. He remembers only what he has picked up since his injury."

"Then, then, he's not insane?" gasped Helen.

"No, no, I should say not," replied her father, dubiously; "yet his words and manner produce much the same effect as if he were—even a stronger effect."

"Oh, this is dreadful!" cried his wife.

"Dreadful indeed, but not hopeless, you know. Keep in mind doctors say that his memory may come back at any time; and Hobart has the belief that the sight and voice of Helen will bring it back."

"God bless Hobart," said Helen, with a deep breath, "and God help him!
His own love inspired that belief. He's right; I know he's right."
"Well, perhaps he is. I don't know. I thought Nichol would recognize me; but there wasn't a sign."

"Oh, papa," cried Helen, smiling through her tears, "there are some things which even your experience and wisdom fail in. Albert will know me. We have talked long enough; now let us act."

"You don't realize it all yet, Helen; you can't. You must remember that Nichol regained consciousness in a Southern hospital. He has learned to talk and act very much like such soldiers as would associate with him."

"The fact that he's alive and that I now may restore him is enough, papa."

"Well, I want Dr. Barnes present when you meet him."

"Certainly; at least within call."

"I must stipulate too," said Mrs. Kemble. "I don't wish the coming scenes to take place in a hotel, and under the eyes of that gossip, Jackson. I don't see why Hobart took him there."

"I do," said Mr. Kemble, standing up for his favorite. "Hobart has already endured more than mortal man ought, yet he has been most delicately considerate. No one but Jackson and Dr. Barnes know about Nichol and his condition. I have also had Nichol's father and mother sent for on my own responsibility, for they should take their share of the matter. Hobart believes that Helen can restore Nichol's memory. This would simplify everything and save many painful impressions. You see, it's such an obscure trouble, and there should be no ill-advised blundering in the matter. The doctors in Washington told Hobart that a slight shock, or the sight of an object that once had the strongest hold upon his thoughts—well, you understand."

"Yes," said Helen, "I DO understand. Hobart is trying to give Albert the very best chance. Albert wrote that his last earthly thoughts would be of me. It is but natural that my presence should kindle those thoughts again. It was like Hobart, who is almost divine in his thoughtfulness of others, to wish to shield Albert from the eyes of even his own father and mother until he could know them, and know us all. He was only taken to the hotel that we all might understand and be prepared to do our part. Papa, bring Albert here and let his father and mother come here also. He should be sacredly shielded in his infirmity, and give a every chance to recover before being seen by others; and please, papa, exact from Jackson a solemn promise not to tattle about Albert."

"Yes, yes; but we have first a duty to perform. Mother, please prepare a little lunch, and put a glass of your old currant wine on the tray. Hobart must not come to a cold, cheerless home. I'll go and have his old servant up and ready to receive him."

"No, mamma, that is still my privilege," said Helen, with a rush, of tears. "Oh, I'm so sorry, SORRY for him! but neither he nor I can help or change what is, what's true."

When the tray was ready, she wrote and sealed these words:

"God bless you, Hobart; God reward you! You have made me feel to-night that earth is too poor, and only heaven rich enough to reward you.

"HELEN."

FOUND YET LOST BY EDWARD PAYSON ROE

CHAPTER XI
MR. KEMBLE'S APPEAL

It often happens that the wife's disposition is an antidote to her husband: and this was fortunately true of Mrs. Jackson. She was neither curious nor gossiping, and with a quick instinct that privacy was desired by Martine, gave at an early hour her orders to close the house for the night. The few loungers, knowing that she was autocratic, slouched off to other resorts. The man and maids of all work were kept out of the way, while she and her husband waited on their unexpected guests. After Mr. Kemble's departure, the errand-boy was roused from his doze behind the stove and seat for Dr. Barnes; then Jackson wrote another note at Martine's dictation:

"MR. WILLIAM NICHOL:

"DEAR SIR—A relative of yours is sick at my house. He came on the evening train. You and your wife had better come at once in the carriage."

Martine retired to the room in which he had seen Mr. Kemble, that he might compose himself before meeting the physician. The sound of Helen's voice, the mere proximity of the girl who at this hour was to have been his wife had not "old chaos" come again for him, were by no means "straws" in their final and crushing weight. Motionless, yet with mind verging on distraction, he sat in the cold, dimly lighted room until aroused by the voice of Dr. Barnes.

"Why, Hobart!" cried his old friend, starting at the bloodshot eyes and pallid face of the young man, "what is the matter? You need me, sure enough, but why on earth are you shivering in this cold room at the hotel?"

Martine again said to Jackson: "Don't leave him," and closed the door. Then, to the physician: "Dr. Barnes, I am ill and worn-out. I know it only too well. You must listen carefully while I in brief tell you why you were sent for; then you and others must take charge and act as you think best. I'm going home. I must have rest and a respite. I must be by myself;" and he rapidly began to sketch his experiences in Washington.

"Hold!" said the sensible old doctor, who indulged in only a few strong exclamations of surprise, which did not interrupt the speaker, "hold! You say you left the ward to think it over, after being convinced that you had discovered Nichol. Did you think it over quietly?"

"Quietly!" repeated Martine, with intense bitterness. "Would a man, not a mummy, think over such a thing quietly? Judge me as you please, but I was tempted as I believe never man was before. I fought the Devil till morning."

"I thought as much," said the doctor, grasping Martine's hand, then slipping a finger on his pulse. "You fought on foot too, didn't you?"

"Yes, I walked the streets as if demented."

"Of course. That in part accounts for your exhaustion. Have you slept much since?"

"Oh, Doctor, let me get through and go home!"

"No, Hobart, you can't get through with me till I am with you. My dear fellow, do you think that I don't understand and sympathize with you? There's no reason why you should virtually risk your life for Captain Nichol again. Take this dose of quinine at once, and then proceed. I can catch on rapidly. First answer, how much have you slept since?"

"The idea of sleep! You can remedy this, Doctor, after my part in this affair is over. I must finish now. Helen may return, and I cannot meet her, nor am I equal to seeing Mr. and Mrs. Nichol. My head feels queer, but I'll get through somehow, if the strain is not kept up too long;" and he finished in outline his story. In conclusion he said, "You will understand that you are now to have charge of Nichol. He is prepared by his experience to obey you, for he has always been in hospitals, where the surgeon's will is law. Except with physicians, he has a sort of rough waywardness, learned from the soldiers."

"Yes, I understand sufficiently now to manage. You put him in my charge, then go home, and I'll visit you as soon as I can."

"One word more, Doctor. As far as you think best, enjoin reticence on Jackson. If the sight of Helen restores Nichol, as I believe it will, little need ever be said about his present condition. Jackson would not dare to disobey a physician's injunction."

"Don't you dare disobey them, either. I'll manage him too. Come."

Nichol had slept a good deal during the latter part of his journey, and now was inclined to wakefulness—a tendency much increased by his habit of waiting on hospital patients at night. In the eager and curious Jackson he had a companion to his mind, who stimulated in him a certain child-like vanity.

"Hello, Ma'tine," he said, "ye're gittin' tired o' me, I reckon, ye're off so much. I don't keer. This yere Jackson's a lively cuss, en I 'low we'll chin till mawnin'."

"Yes, Nichol, Mr. Jackson is a good friend of yours; and here is another man who is more than a friend. You remember what the surgeon at the hospital said to you?"

"I reckon," replied Nichol, anxiously. "Hain't I minded yer tetotally?"

"Yes, you have done very well indeed—remarkably well, since you knew I was not a doctor. Now this man is a doctor—the doctor I was to bring you to. You won't have to mind me any more, but you must mind this man, Dr. Barnes, in all respects, just as you did the doctors in the hospitals. As long as you obey him carefully he will be very good to you."

"Oh, I'll mind, Doctor," said Nichol, rising and assuming the respectful attitude of a hospital nurse. "We uns wuz soon larned that't wuzn't healthy to go agin the doctor. When I wuz Yankee Blank, 'fo' I got ter be cap'n, I forgot ter give a Johnny a doze o' med'cine, en I'm doggoned ef the doctor didn't mek me tek it myse'f. Gee wiz! sech a time ez I had! Hain't give the doctors no trouble sence."

"All right, Captain Nichol," said Dr. Barnes, quietly, "I understand my duties, and I see that you understand yours. As you say, doctors must be obeyed, and I already see that you won't make me or yourself any trouble. Good-night, Hobart, I'm in charge now."

"Good-night, Doctor. Mr. Jackson, I'm sure you will carry out Dr. Barnes' wishes implicitly."
"Yer'd better, Jackson," said Nichol, giving him a wink. "A doctor kin give yer high ole jinks ef ye're not keerful."

Martine now obeyed the instinct often so powerful in the human breast as well as in dumb animals, and sought the covert, the refuge of his home, caring little whether he was to live or die. When he saw the lighted windows of Mr. Kemble's residence, he moaned as if in physical pain. A sudden and immeasurable longing to see, to speak with Helen once before she was again irrevocably committed to Nichol, possessed him. He even went to her gate to carry out his impulse, then curbed himself and returned resolutely to his dwelling. As soon as his step was on the porch, the door opened and Mr. Kemble gave him the warm grasp of friendship. Without a word, the two men entered the sitting-room, sat down by the ruddy fire, and looked at each other, Martine with intense, questioning anxiety in his haggard face. The banker nodded gravely as he said, "Yes, she knows."

"It's as I said it would be?" Martine added huskily, after a moment or two.

"Well, my friend, she said you would understand her better than any one else. She wrote you this note."

Martine's hands so trembled that he could scarcely break the seal. He sat looking at the tear-blurred words some little time, and grew evidently calmer, then faltered, "Yes, it's well to remember God at such a time. He has laid heavy burdens upon me. He is responsible for them, not I. If I break, He also will be responsible."

"Hobart," said Mr. Kemble, earnestly, "you must not break under this, for our sake as well as your own. I have the presentiment that we shall all need you yet, my poor girl perhaps most of all. She doesn't, she can't realize it. Now, the dead is alive again. Old girlish impulses and feelings are asserting themselves. As is natural, she is deeply excited; but this tidal wave of feeling will pass, and then she will have to face both the past and future. I know her well enough to be sure she could never be happy if this thing wrecked you. And then, Hobart," and the old man sank his voice to a whisper, "suppose—suppose Nichol continues the same."

"He cannot," cried Martine, almost desperately. "Oh, Mr. Kemble, don't suggest any hope for me. My heart tells me there is none, that there should not be any. No, she loved him as I have loved her from childhood. She is right. I do understand her so well that I know what the future will be."

"Well," said Mr. Kemble, firmly, as he rose, "she shall never marry him as he is, with my consent. I don't feel your confidence about Helen's power to restore him. I tell you, Hobart, I'm in sore straits. Helen is the apple of my eye. She is the treasure of our old age. God knows I remember what you have done for her and for us in the past; and I feel that we shall need you in the future. You've become like a son to mother and me, and you must stand by us still. Our need will keep you up and rally you better than all Dr. Barnes' medicine. I know you well enough to know that. But take the medicine all the same; and above all things, don't give way to anything like recklessness and despair. As you say, God has imposed the burden. Let him give you the strength to bear it, and other people's burdens too, as you have in the past. I must go now. Don't fail me."

Wise old Mr. Kemble had indeed proved the better physician. His misgivings, fears, and needs, combined with his honest affection, had checked the cold, bitter flood of despair which had been overwhelming Martine. The morbid impression that he would be only another complication, and of necessity an embarrassment to Helen and her family, was in a measure removed. Mere words of general condolence would not have helped him; an appeal like that to the exhausted soldier, and the thought that the battle for him was not yet over, stirred the deep springs of his nature and slowly kindled the purpose to rally and be ready. He rose, ate a little of the food, drank the wine, then looked around the beautiful apartment prepared for her who was to have been his wife, "I have grown weak and reckless," he said. "I ought to have known her well enough—I do know her so well—as to be sure that I would cloud her happiness if this thing destroyed me."

CHAPTER XII
"YOU MUST REMEMBER"

Mr. And Mrs. Nichol wonderingly yet promptly complied with the request for their presence, meantime casting about in their minds as to the identity of the relative who had summoned them so unexpected. Mr. Kemble arrived at the hotel at about the same moment as they did, and Jackson was instructed to keep the carriage in waiting. "It was I who sent for you and your wife," said the banker. "Mr. Martine, if possible, would have given you cause for a great joy only; but I fear it must be tempered with an anxiety which I trust will not be long continued;" and he led the way into the parlor.

"Is it—can it be about Albert?" asked Mrs. Nichols trembling, and sinking into a chair.

"Yes, Mrs. Nichol. Try to keep your fortitude, for perhaps his welfare depends upon it."

"Oh, God be praised! The hope of this never wholly left me, because they didn't find his body."

Dr. Barnes came down at once, and with Mr. Kemble tried to soothe the strong emotions of the parents, while at the same time enlightening them as to their son's discovery and condition.

"Well," said Mr. Nichol, in strong emphasis; "Hobart Martine is one of a million."

"I think he ought to have brought Albert right to me first," Mrs. Nichol added, shaking her head and wiping her eyes. "After all, a mother's claim—"

"My dear Mrs. Nichol," interrupted Dr. Barnes, "there was no thought of undervaluing your claim on the part of our friend Hobart. He has taken what he believed, and what physicians led him to believe, was the best course to restore your son. Besides, Mr. Martine is a very sick man. Even now he needs my attention more than Captain Nichol. You must realize that he was to have married Miss Kemble to-day; yet he brings back your son, sends for Mr. Kemble in order that his daughter, as soon as she can realize the strange truth, may exert her power. He himself has not seen the girl who was to have been his bride."

"Wife, wife," said Mr. Nichol, brokingly, "no mortal man could do more for us than Hobart Martine, God bless him!"

"Mrs. Nichol," began Mr. Kemble, "my wife and Helen both unite in the request that you and your husband bring your son at once to our house; perhaps you would rather meet him in the privacy—"

"Oh, no, no!" she cried, "I cannot wait. Please do not think I am insensible to all this well-meant kindness; but a mother's heart cannot wait. He'll know ME—me who bore him and carried him on my breast."

"Mrs. Nichol, you shall see him at once," said the doctor. "I hope it will be as you say; but I'm compelled to tell you that you may be disappointed. There's no certainty that this trouble will pass away at once under any one's influence. You and your husband come with me. Mr. Kemble, I will send Jackson down, and so secure the privacy which you would kindly provide. I will be present, for I may be needed."

He led the way, the mother following with the impetuosity and abandon of maternal love, and the father with stronger and stranger emotions than he had ever known, but restrained in a manner natural to a quiet, reticent man. They were about to greet one on whom they had once centred their chief hopes and affection, yet long mourned as dead. It is hard to imagine the wild tumult of their feelings. Not merely by words, but chiefly by impulse, immediate action, could they reveal how profoundly they were moved.

With kindly intention, as he opened the door of the apartment, the doctor began, "Mr. Jackson, please leave us a few—"

Mrs. Nichol saw her son and rushed upon him, crying, "Albert, Albert!" It was enough at that moment that she recognized him; and the thought that he would not recognize her was banished. With an intuition of heart beyond all reasoning, she felt that he who had drawn his life from her must know her and respond to nature's first strong tie.

In surprise, Nichol had risen, then was embarrassed to find an elderly woman sobbing on his breast and addressing him in broken, endearing words by a name utterly unfamiliar. He looked wonderingly at his father, who stood near, trembling and regarding him through tear-dimmed eyes with an affectionate interest, impressive even to his limited perceptions.

"Doctor," he began over his mother's head, "what in thunder does all this here mean? Me 'n' Jackson was chinnin' comf't'bly, when sud'n you uns let loose on me two crazy old parties I never seed ner yeared on. Never had folks go on so 'bout me befo'. Beats even that Hob't Ma'tine," and he showed signs of rising irritation.

"Albert, Albert!" almost shrieked Mrs. Nichol, "don't you know me—ME, your own mother?"

"Naw."

At the half-indignant, incredulous tone, yet more than all at the strange accent and form of this negative, the poor woman was almost beside herself. "Merciful God!" she cried, "this cannot be;" and she sank into a chair, sobbing almost hysterically.

For reasons of his own, Dr. Barnes did not interfere. Nature in powerful manifestations was actuating the parents; and he decided, now that things had gone so far, to let the entire energy of uncurbed emotion, combined with all the mysterious affinity of the closest kinship, exert its influence on the clogged brain of his patient.

For a few moments Mrs. Nichol was too greatly overcome to comprehend anything clearly; her husband, on the other hand, was simply wrought up to his highest capacity for action. His old instinct of authority returned, and he seized his son's hand and began, "Now, see here, Albert, you were wounded in your head—"

"Yes, right yere," interrupted Nichol, pointing to his scar. "I knows all 'bout that, but I don't like these goin's on, ez ef I wuz a nachel-bawn fool, en had ter bleve all folks sez. I've been taken in too often. When I wuz with the Johnnies they'd say ter me, 'Yankee Blank, see that ar critter? That's a elephant.' When I'd call it a elephant, they'd larf an' larf till I flattened out one feller's nose. I dunno nothin' 'bout elephants; but the critter they pinted at wuz a cow. Then one day they set me ter scrubbin' a nigger to mek 'im white, en all sech doin's, till the head-doctor stopped the hull blamed nonsense. S'pose I be a cur'ous chap. I ain't a nachel-bawn ijit. When folks begin ter go on, en do en say things I kyant see through, then I stands off en sez, 'Lemme 'lone.' The hospital doctors wouldn't 'low any foolin' with me 't all."

"I'm not allowing any fooling with you," said Dr. Barnes, firmly. "I wish you to listen to that man and woman, and believe all they say. The hospital doctors would give you the same orders."

"All right, then," assented Nichol, with a sort of grimace of resignation. "Fire away, old man, an' git through with yer yarn so Jackson kin come back. I wish this woman wouldn't take on so. Hit makes me orful oncomf't'ble, doggoned ef hit don't."

The rapid and peculiar utterance, the seemingly unfeeling words of his son, stung the father into an ecstasy of grief akin to anger. A man stood before him, as clearly recognized as his own image in a mirror. The captain was not out of his mind in any familiar sense of the word; he remembered distinctly what had happened for months past. He must recall, he must be MADE to recollect the vital truths of his life on which not only his happiness but that of others depended. Although totally ignorant of what the wisest can explain but vaguely, Mr. Nichol was bent on restoring his son by the sheer force of will, making him remember by telling him what he should and must recall. This he tried to do with strong, eager insistence. "Why, Albert," he urged, "I'm your father; and that's your mother."

Nichol shook his head and looked at the doctor, who added gravely,
"That's all true."
"Yes," resumed Mr. Nichol, with an energy and earnestness of utterance which compelled attention. "Now listen to reason. As I was saying, you were wounded in the head, and you have forgotten what happened before you were hurt. But you must remember, you must, indeed, or you will break your mother's heart and mine, too."

"But I tell yer, I kyant reckerlect a thing befo' I kinder waked up in the hospital, en the Johnnies call me Yankee Blank. I jes' wish folks would lemme alone on that pint. Hit allus bothers me en makes me mad. How kin I reckerlect when I kyant?" and he began to show signs of strong vexation.

Dr. Barnes was about to interfere when Mrs. Nichol, who had grown calmer, rose, took her son's hand, and said brokenly: "Albert, look me in the face, your mother's face, and try, TRY with all your heart and soul and mind. Don't you remember ME?"

It was evident that her son did try. His brow wrinkled in the perplexed effort, and he looked at her fixedly for a moment or more; but no magnetic current from his mother's hand, no suggestion of the dear features which had bent over him in childhood and turned toward him in love and pride through subsequent years found anything in his arrested consciousness answering to her appeal.

The effort and its failure only irritated him, and he broke out: "Now look yere, I be as I be. What's the use of all these goin's on? Doctor, if you sez these folks are my father and mother, so be it. I'm learning somethin' new all the time. This ain't no mo' quar, I s'pose, than some other things. I've got to mind a doctor, for I've learned that much ef I hain't nuthin' else, but I want you uns to know that I won't stan' no mo' foolin'. Doctors don't fool me, en they've got the po'r ter mek a feller do ez they sez, but other folks is got ter be keerful how they uses me."

Mrs. Nichol again sank into her chair and wept bitterly; her husband at last remained silent in a sort of inward, impotent rage of grief. There was their son, alive and in physical health, yet between him and them was a viewless barrier which they could not break through.

The strange complications, the sad thwartings of hope which must result unless he was restored, began to loom already in the future.

Dr. Barnes now came forward and said: "Captain Nichol, you are as you are at this moment, but you must know that you are not what you were once. We are trying to restore you to your old self. You'd be a great deal better off if we succeed. You must help us all you can. You must be patient, and try all the time to recollect. You know I am not deceiving you, but seeking to help you. You don't like this. That doesn't matter. Didn't you see doctors do many things in hospitals which the patients didn't like?"

"I reckon," replied Nichol, growing reasonable at once when brought on familiar ground.

"Well, you are my patient. I may have to do some disagreeable things, but they won't hurt you. It won't be like taking off an arm or a leg. You have seen that done, I suppose?"

"You bet!" was the eager, proud reply. "I used to hold the fellows when they squirmed."

"Now hold yourself. Be patient and good-natured. While we are about it, I want to make every appeal possible to your lost memory, and I order you to keep on trying to remember till I say: 'Through for the present.' If we succeed, you'll thank me all the days of your life. Anyhow, you must do as I say."

"Oh, I know that."

"Well, then, your name is Captain Nichol. This is Mr. Nichol, your father; this lady is your mother. Call them father and mother when you speak to them. Always speak kindly and pleasantly. They'll take you to a pleasant home when I'm through with you, and you must mind them. They'll be good to you everyway."

Nichol grinned acquiescence and said: "All right, Doctor."

"Now you show your good sense. We'll have you sound and happy yet." The doctor thought a moment and then asked: "Mr. Nichol, I suppose that after our visit to Mr. Kemble, you and your wife would prefer to take your son home with you?"

"Certainly," was the prompt response.

"I would advise you to do so. After our next effort, however it results, we all will need rest and time for thought. Captain, remain here a few moments with your father and mother. Listen good-naturedly and answer pleasantly to whatever they may say to you. I will be back soon."

FOUND YET LOST BY EDWARD PAYSON ROE

CHAPTER XIII
"I'M HELEN"

Dr. Barnes descended the stairs to the parlor where Mr. Kemble impatiently awaited him. "Well?" said the banker, anxiously.

"I will explain while on the way to your house. The carriage is still ready, I suppose?" to Jackson.

"Yes," was the eager reply; "how did he take the meeting of his parents?"

"In the main as I feared. He does not know them yet. Mr. Jackson, you and I are somewhat alike in one of our duties. I never talk about my patients. If I did, I ought to be drummed out of the town instead of ever being called upon again. Of course you feel that you should not talk about your guests. You can understand why the parties concerned in this matter would not wish to have it discussed in the village."

"Certainly, Doctor, certainly," replied Jackson, reddening, for he knew something of his reputation for gossip. "This is no ordinary case."

"No, it is not. Captain Nichol and his friends would never forgive any one who did not do right by them now. In about fifteen minutes or so I will return. Have the carriage wait for me at Mr. Kemble's till again wanted. You may go back to the captain and do your best to keep him wide-awake."

Jackson accompanied them to the conveyance and said to the man on the box: "Obey all Dr. Barnes's orders."

As soon as the two men were seated, the physician began: "Our first test has failed utterly;" and he briefly narrated what had occurred, concluding, "I fear your daughter will have no better success. Still, it is perhaps wise to do all we can, on the theory that these sudden shocks may start up the machinery of memory. Nichol is excited; such powers as he possesses are stimulated to their highest activity, and he is evidently making a strong effort to recall the past, I therefore now deem it best to increase the pressure on his brain to the utmost. If the obstruction does not give way, I see no other course than to employ the skill of experts and trust to the healing processes of time."

"I am awfully perplexed, Doctor," was the reply. "You must be firm with me on one point, and you know your opinion will have great weight. Under no sentimental sense of duty, or even of affection, must Helen marry Nichol unless he is fully restored and given time to prove there is no likelihood of any return of this infirmity."

"I agree with you emphatically. There is no reason for such self-sacrifice on your daughter's part. Nichol would not appreciate it. He is not an invalid; on the contrary, a strong, muscular man, abundantly able to take care of himself under the management of his family."

"He has my profound sympathy," continued Mr. Kemble, "but giving that unstintedly is a very different thing from giving him my only child."

"Certainly. Perhaps we need not say very much to Miss Helen on this point at present. Unless he becomes his old self she will feel that she has lost him more truly than if he were actually dead. The only deeply perplexing feature in the case is its uncertainty. He may be all right before morning, and he may never recall a thing that happened before the explosion of that shell."

The carriage stopped, and Mr. Kemble hastily led the way to his dwelling. Helen met them at the door. "Oh, how long you have been!" she protested; "I've just been tortured by suspense."

Dr. Barnes took her by the hand and led her to the parlor. "Miss Helen," he said gravely, "if you are not careful you will be another patient on my hands. Sad as is Captain Nichol's case, he at least obeys me implicitly; so must you. Your face is flushed, your pulse feverish, and—"

"Doctor," cried the girl, "you can't touch the disease till you remove the cause. Why is he kept so long from me?"

"Helen, child, you MUST believe that the doctor—that we all—are doing our best for you and Nichol," said Mr. Kemble, anxiously. "His father and mother came to the hotel. It was but natural that they should wish to see him at once. How would we feel?"

"Come, Helen, dear, you must try to be more calm," urged the mother, gently, with her arm around her daughter's neck. "Doctor, can't you give her something to quiet her nerves?"

"Miss Helen, like the captain, is going to do just as I say, aren't you? You can do more for yourself than I can do for you. Remember, you must act intelligently and cooperate with me. His father, and especially his mother, exhibited the utmost degree of emotion and made the strongest appeals without effect. Now we must try different tactics. All must be quiet and nothing occur to confuse or irritate him."

"Ah, how little you all understand me! The moment you give me a chance to act I can be as calm as you are. It's this waiting, this torturing suspense that I cannot endure. Hobart would not have permitted it. He knows, he understands. Every effort will fail till Albert sees me. It will be a cause for lasting gratitude to us both that I should be the one to restore him. Now let me manage. My heart will guide me better than your science."

"What will you do?" inquired her father, in deep solicitude.

"See, here's his picture," she replied, taking it from a table near—"the one he gave me just before he marched away. Let him look at that and recall himself. Then I will enter. Oh, I've planned it all! My self-control will be perfect. Would I deserve the name of woman if I were weak or hysterical? No, I would do my best to rescue any man from such a misfortune, much more Albert, who has such sacred claims."

"That's a good idea of yours about the photograph. Well, I guess I must let Nature have her own way again, only in this instance I advise quiet methods."

"Trust me, Doctor, and you won't regret it."

"Nerve yourself then to do your best, but prepare to be disappointed for the present. I do not and cannot share in your confidence."

"Of course you cannot," she said, with a smile which illuminated her face into rare beauty. "Only love and faith could create my confidence."

"Miss Helen," was the grave response, "would love and faith restore
Captain Nichol's right arm if he had lost it?"
"Oh, but that's different," she faltered.

"I don't know whether it is or not. We are experimenting. There may be a physical cause obstructing memory which neither you nor any one can now remove. Kindness only leads me to temper your hope."

"Doctor," she said half-desperately, "it is not hope; it is belief. I could not feel as I do if I were to be disappointed."

"Ah, Miss Helen, disappointment is a very common experience. I must stop a moment and see one who has learned this truth pretty thoroughly. Then I will bring Nichol and his parents at once."

Tears filled her eyes. "Yes, I know," she sighed; "my heart just bleeds for him, but I cannot help it. Were I not sure that Hobart understands me better than any one else, I should be almost distracted. This very thought of him nerves me. Think what he did for Albert from a hard sense of duty. Can I fail? Good-by, and please, PLEASE hasten."

Martine rose to greet the physician with a clear eye and a resolute face. "Why, why!" cried Dr. Barnes, cheerily, "you look a hundred per cent better. That quinine—"

"There, Doctor, I don't undervalue your drugs; but Mr. Kemble has been to see me and appealed to me for help—to still be on hand if needed. Come, I've had my hour for weakness. I am on the up-grade now. Tell me how far the affair has progressed."

"Haven't time, Hobart. Since Mr. Kemble's treatment is so efficacious, I'll continue it. You will be needed, you will indeed, no matter how it all turns out. I won't abandon my drugs, either. Here, take this."

Martine took the medicine as administered. "Now when you feel drowsy, go to sleep," added the doctor.

"Tell me one thing—has she seen him yet?"

"No; his father and mother have, and he does not know them. It's going to be a question of time, I fear."

"Helen will restore him."

"So she believes, or tries to. I mercifully shook her faith a little. Well, she feels for you, old fellow. The belief that you understand her better than any one has great sustaining power."

"Say I won't fail her; but I entreat that you soon let me know the result of the meeting."

"I'll come in," assented the doctor, as he hastily departed. Then he added sotto voce, "If you hear anything more under twelve or fifteen hours, I'm off my reckoning."

Re-entering the carriage, he was driven rapidly to the hotel. Jackson had played his part, and had easily induced Nichol to recount his hospital experience in the presence of his parents, who listened in mingled wonder, grief, and impotent protest.

"Captain, put on your overcoat and hat and come with me," said the doctor, briskly. "Your father and mother will go with us."

"Good-by, Jackson," said Nichol, cordially. "Ye're a lively cuss, en I hopes we'll have a chaince to chin agin."

With a blending of hope and of fear, his parents followed him. The terrible truth of his sensibility to all that he should recognize and remember became only the more appalling as they comprehended it. While it lost none of its strangeness, they were compelled to face and to accept it as they could not do at first.

"Now, Captain," said the doctor, after they were seated in the carriage, "listen carefully to me. It is necessary that you recall what happened before you were wounded. I tell you that you must do it if you can, and you know doctors must be obeyed."

"Look yere, Doctor, ain't I a-tryin'? but I tell yer hit's like tryin' ter lift myself out o' my own boots."

"Mind, now, I don't say you must remember, only try your best. You can do that?"

"I reckon."

"Well, you are going to the house of an old friend who knew you well before you were hurt. You must pay close heed to all she says just as you would to me. You must not say any rude, bad words, such as soldiers often use, but listen to every word she says. Perhaps you'll know her as soon as you see her. Now I've prepared you. I won't be far off."

"Don't leave me, Doctor. I jes' feels nachelly muxed up en mad when folks pester me 'bout what I kyant do."

"You must not get angry now, I can tell you. That would never do at all. I FORBID it."

"There, there now, Doctor, I won't, doggone me ef I will," Nichol protested anxiously.

Mr. Kemble met them at the door, and the captain recognized him instantly.

"Why, yere's that sensible ole feller what didn't want to ast no questions," he exclaimed.

"You are right, Captain Nichol, I have no questions to ask."

"Well, ef folks wuz all like you I'd have a comf't'ble time"

"Come with me, Captain," said the physician, leading the way into the parlor. Mr. Kemble silently ushered Mr. and Mrs. Nichol into the sitting-room on the opposite side of the hall and placed them in the care of his wife. He then went into the back parlor in which was Helen, now quiet as women so often are in emergencies. Through a slight opening between the sliding-door she looked, with tightly clasped hands and parted lips, at her lover. At first she was conscious of little else except the overwhelming truth that before her was one she had believed dead. Then again surged up with blinding force the old feeling which had possessed her when she saw him last—when he had impressed his farewell kiss upon her lips. Remembering the time for her to act was almost at hand, she became calm—more from the womanly instinct to help him than from the effort of her will.

Dr. Barnes said to Nichol, "Look around. Don't you think you have seen this room before? Take your time and try to remember."

The captain did as he was bidden, but soon shook his head. "Hit's right purty, but I don't reckerlect."

"Well, sit down here, then, and look at that picture. Who is it?"

"Why, hit's me—me dressed up as cap'n," ejaculated Nichol, delightedly.

"Yes, that was the way you looked and dressed before you were wounded."

"How yer talk! This beats anythin' I ever yeared from the Johnnies."

"Now, Captain Nichol, you see we are not deceiving you. We called you captain. There's your likeness, taken before you were hurt and lost your memory, and you can see for yourself that you were a captain. You must think how much there is for you to try to remember. Before you went to the war, long before you got hurt, you gave this likeness of yourself to a young lady that you thought a great deal of. Can't you recall something about it?"

Nichol wrinkled his scarred forehead, scratched his head, and hitched uneasily in his chair, evidently making a vain effort to penetrate the gloom back of that vague awakening in the Southern hospital. At last he broke out in his usual irritation, "Naw, I kyant, doggon—"

"Hush! you must not use that word here. Don't be discouraged. You are trying; that's all I ask," and the doctor laid a soothing hand on his shoulder. "Now, Captain, I'll just step in the next room. You think quietly as you can about the young lady to whom you gave that picture of yourself."

Nichol was immensely pleased with his photograph, and looked at it in all its lights. While thus gratifying a sort of childish vanity, Helen entered noiselessly, her blue eyes, doubly luminous from the pallor of her face, shining like sapphires. So intent was her gaze that one might think it would "kindle a soul under the ribs of death."

At last Nichol became conscious of her presence and started, exclaiming, "Why, there she is herself."

"OH, Albert, you DO know me," cried the girl, rushing toward him with outstretched hand.

He took it unhesitatingly, saying with a pleased wonder, "Well, I reckon I'm comin' round. Yer the young lady I give this picture to?"

"I'm Helen," she breathed, with an indescribable accent of tenderness and gladness.

"Why, cert'ny. The doctor tole me 'bout you."

"But you remember me yourself?" she pleaded. "You remember what you said to me when you gave me this picture?" and she looked into his eyes with an expression which kindled even his dull senses.

"Oh, shucks!" he said slowly, "I wish I could. I'd like ter 'blige yer, fer ye're right purty, en I am a-tryin' ter mind the doctor."

Such a sigh escaped her that one might think her heart and hope were going with it. The supreme moment of meeting had come and gone, and he did not know her; she saw and felt in her inmost soul that he did not. The brief and illusive gleam into the past was projected only from the present, resulting from what he had been told, not from what he recalled.

She withdrew her hand, turned away, and for a moment or two her form shook with sobs she could not wholly stifle. He looked on perplexed and troubled, then broke out, "I jes' feels ez ef I'd split my blamed ole haid open—"

She checked him by a gesture. "Wait," she cried, "sit down." She took a chair near him and hastily wiped her eyes. "Perhaps I can help you remember me. You will listen closely, will you not?"

"I be dog—oh, I forgot," and he looked toward the back parlor apprehensively. "Yes, mees, I'll do anythin' yer sez."

"Well, once you were a little boy only so high, and I was a little girl only so high. We both lived in this village and we went to school together. We studied out of the same books together. At three o'clock in the afternoon school was out, and then we put our books in our desks and the teacher let us go and play. There was a pond of water, and it often froze over with smooth black ice. You and I used to go together to that pond; and you would fasten my skates on my feet—"

"Hanged ef I wouldn't do it agin," he cried, greatly pleased. "Yer beats 'em all. Stid o' astin' questions, yer tells me all 'bout what happened. Why, I kin reckerlect it all ef I'm tole often anuff."

With a sinking heart she faltered on, "Then you grew older and went away to school, and I went away to school. We had vacations; we rode on horseback together. Well, you grew to be as tall as you are now; and then came a war and you wore a captain's uniform, like—like that you see in your likeness, and—and—" she stopped. Her rising color became a vivid flush; she slowly rose as the thought burned its way into her consciousness that she was virtually speaking to a stranger. Her words were bringing no gleams of intelligence into his face; they were throwing no better, no stronger light upon the past than if she were telling the story to a great boy. Yet he was not a boy. A man's face was merely disfigured (to her eyes) by a grin of pleasure instead of a pleased smile; and a man's eyes were regarding her with an unwinking stare of admiration. She was not facing her old playmate, her old friend and lover, but a being whose only consciousness reached back but months, through scenes, associations coarse and vulgar like himself. She felt this with an intuition that was overwhelming. She could not utter another syllable, much less speak of the sacred love of the past. "O God!" she moaned in her heart, "the man has become a living grave in which his old self is buried. Oh, this is terrible, terrible!"

As the truth grew upon her she sprang away, wringing her hands and looking upon him with an indescribable expression of pity and dread. "Oh," she now moaned aloud, "if he had only come back to me mutilated in body, helpless! but this change—"

She fled from the room, and Nichol stared after her in perplexed consternation.

CHAPTER XIV
"FORWARD! COMPANY A"

When Mrs. Kemble was left alone with Captain Nichol's parents in the sitting-room, she told them of Helen's plan of employing the photograph in trying to recall their son to himself. It struck them as an unusually effective method. Mrs. Kemble saw that their anxiety was so intense that it was torture for them to remain in suspense away from the scene of action. It may be added that her own feelings also led her to go with them into the back parlor, where all that was said by Nichol and her daughter could be heard. Her solicitude for Helen was not less than theirs for their son; and she felt the girl might need both motherly care and counsel. She was opposed even more strenuously than her husband to any committal on the daughter's part to her old lover unless he should become beyond all doubt his former self. At best, it would be a heavy cross to give up Martine, who had won her entire affection. Helen's heart presented a problem too deep for solution. What would—what could—Captain Nichol be to her child in his present condition, should it continue?

It was but natural, therefore, that she and her husband should listen to Helen's effort to awaken memories of the past with profound anxiety. How far would she go? If Nichol were able to respond with no more appreciative intelligence than he had thus far manifested, would a sentiment of pity and obligation carry her to the point of accepting him as he was, of devoting herself to one who, in spite of all their commiseration and endeavors to tolerate, might become a sort of horror in their household! It was with immense relief that they heard her falter in her story, for they quickly divined that there was nothing in him which responded to her effort. When they heard her rise and moan, "If he had only come back to me mutilated in body, helpless! but this change—" they believed that she was meeting the disappointment as they could wish.

Mr. and Mrs. Nichol heard the words also, and while in a measure compelled to recognize their force, they conveyed a meaning hard to accept. The appeal upon which so much hope had been built had failed. In bitterness of soul, the conviction grew stronger that their once brave, keen-minded son would never be much better than an idiot.

Then Helen appeared among them as pale, trembling, and overwhelmed as if she had seen a spectre. In strong reaction from her effort and blighted hope she was almost in a fainting condition. Her mother's arms received her and supported her to a lounge; Mrs. Nichol gave way to bitter weeping; Mr. Kemble wrung the father's hand in sympathy, and then at his wife's request went for restoratives. Dr. Barnes closed the sliding-doors and prudently reassured Nichol: "You have done your best, Captain, and that is all I asked of you. Remain here quietly and look at your picture for a little while, and then you shall have a good long rest."

"I did try, Doctor," protested Nichol, anxiously. "Gee wiz! I reckon a feller orter try ter please sech a purty gyurl. She tole me lots. Look yere, Doctor, why kyan't I be tole over en over till I reckerlect it all?"

"Well, we'll see, Captain. It's late now, and we must all have a rest.
Stay here till I come for you."
Nichol was so pleased with his photograph that he was well content in its contemplation. The physician now gave his attention to Helen, who was soon so far restored as to comprehend her utter failure. Her distress was great indeed, and for a few moments diverted the thoughts of even Mr. and Mrs. Nichol from their own sad share in the disappointment.

"Oh, oh!" sobbed Helen, "this is the bitterest sorrow the war has brought us yet."

"Well, now, friends," said Dr. Barnes, "it's time I had my say and gave my orders. You must remember that I have not shared very fully in your confidence that the captain could be restored by the appeals you have made; neither do I share in this abandonment to grief now. As the captain says, he is yet simply unable to respond. We must patiently wait and see what time and medical skill can do for him. There is no reason whatever for giving up hope. Mrs. Kemble, I would advise you to take Miss Helen to her room, and you, Mr. Nichol, to take your wife and son home. I will call in the morning, and then we can advise further."

His counsel was followed, the captain readily obeying when told to go with his parents. Then the physician stepped over to Martine's cottage and found, as he supposed, that the opiate and exhausted nature had brought merciful oblivion.

It was long before Helen slept, nor would she take anything to induce sleep. She soon became quiet, kissed her mother, and said she wished to be alone. Then she tried to look at the problem in all its aspects, and earnestly asked for divine guidance. The decision reached in the gray dawn brought repose of mind and body.

It was late in the afternoon when Martine awoke with a dull pain in his head and heart. As the consciousness of all that had happened returned, he remembered that there was good reason for both. His faithful old domestic soon prepared a dainty meal, which aided in giving tone to his exhausted system. Then he sat down by his fire to brace himself for the tidings he expected to hear. Helen's chair was empty. It would always be hers, but hope was gone that she would smile from it upon him during the long winter evenings. Already the room was darkening toward the early December twilight, and he felt that his life was darkening in like manner. He was no longer eager to hear what had occurred. The mental and physical sluggishness which possessed him was better than sharp pain; he would learn all soon enough—the recognition, the beginning of a new life which inevitably would drift further and further from him. His best hope was to get through the time, to endure patiently and shape his life so as to permit as little of its shadow as possible to fall upon hers. But as he looked around the apartment and saw on every side the preparations for one who had been his, yet could be no longer, his fortitude gave way, and he buried his face in his hands.

So deep was his painful revery that he did not hear the entrance of Dr. Barnes and Mr. Kemble. The latter laid a hand upon his shoulder and said kindly, "Hobart, my friend, it is just as I told you it would be. Helen needs you and wishes to see you."
Martine started up, exclaiming, "He must have remembered her."

Mr. Kemble shook his head. "No, Hobart," said the doctor, "she was as much of a stranger to him as you were. There were, of course, grounds for your expectation and hers also, but we prosaic physiologists have some reason for our doubtings as well as you for your beliefs. It's going to be a question of time with Nichol. How are you yourself? Ah, I see," he added, with his finger on his patient's pulse. "With you it's going to be a question of tonics."

"Yes, I admit that," Martine replied, "but perhaps of tonics other than those you have in mind. You said, sir [to Mr. Kemble], that Helen wished to see me?"

"Yes, when you feel well enough."

"I trust you will make yourselves at home," said Martine, hastily preparing to go out.

"But don't you wish to hear more about Nichol?" asked the doctor, laughing.

"Not at present. Good-by."

Yet he was perplexed how to meet the girl who should now have been his wife; and he trembled with strange embarrassment as he entered the familiar room in which he had parted from her almost on the eve of their wedding. She was neither perplexed nor embarrassed, for she had the calmness of a fixed purpose. She went swiftly to him, took his hand, led him to a chair, then sat down beside him. He looked at her wonderingly and listened sadly as she asked, "Hobart, will you be patient with me again?"

"Yes," he replied after a moment, yet he sighed deeply in foreboding.

Tears came into her eyes, yet her voice did not falter as she continued: "I said last night that you would understand me better than any one else; so I believe you will now. You will sustain and strengthen me in what I believe to be duty."

"Yes, Helen, up to the point of such endurance as I have. One can't go beyond that."

"No, Hobart, but you will not fail me, nor let me fail. I cannot marry Captain Nichol as he now is"—there was an irrepressible flash of joy in his dark eyes—"nor can I," she added slowly and sadly, "marry you." He was about to speak, but she checked him and resumed. "Listen patiently to me first. I have thought and thought long hours, and I think I am right. You, better than I, know Captain Nichol's condition—its sad contrast to his former noble self. The man we once knew is veiled, hidden, lost—how can we express it? But he exists, and at any time may find and reveal himself. No one, not even I, can revolt at what he is now as he will revolt at it all when his true consciousness returns. He has met with an immeasurable misfortune. He is infinitely worse off than if helpless—worse off than if he were dead, if this condition is to last; but it may not last. What would he think of me if I should desert him now and leave him nothing to remember but a condition of which he could only think with loathing? I will hide nothing from you, Hobart, my brave, true friend—you who have taught me what patience means. If you had brought him back utterly helpless, yet his old self in mind, I could have loved him and married him, and you would have sustained me in that course. Now I don't know. My future, in this respect, is hidden like his. The shock I received last night, the revulsion of feeling which followed, leaves only one thing clear. I must try to do what is right by him; it will not be easy. I hope you will understand. While I have the deepest pity that a woman can feel, I shrink from him NOW, for the contrast between his former self and his present is so terrible. Oh, it is such a horrible mystery! All Dr. Barnes's explanations do not make it one bit less mysterious and dreadful. Albert took the risk of this; he has suffered this for his country. I must suffer for him; I must not desert him in his sad extremity. I must not permit him to awake some day and learn from others what he now is, and that I, the woman he loved, of all others, left him to his degradation. The consequences might be more fatal than the injury which so changed him. Such action on my part might destroy him morally. Now his old self is buried as truly as if he had died. I could never look him in the face again if I left him to take his chances in life with no help from me, still less if I did that which he could scarcely forgive. He could not understand all that has happened since we thought him dead. He would only remember that I deserted him in his present pitiable plight. Do you understand me, Hobart?"

"I must, Helen."

"I know how hard it is for you. Can you think I forget this for a moment? Yet I send for you to help, to sustain me in a purpose which changes our future so greatly. Do you not remember what you said once about accepting the conditions of life as they are? We must do this again, and make the best of them."

"But if—suppose his memory does not come back. Is there to be no hope?"

"Hobart, you must put that thought from you as far as you can. Do you not see whither it might lead? You would not wish Captain Nichol to remain as he is?"

"Oh," he cried desperately, "I'm put in a position that would tax any saint in the calendar."

"Yes, you are. The future is not in our hands. I can only appeal to you to help me do what I think is right NOW."

He thought a few moments, took his resolve, then gave her his hand silently. She understood him without a word.

The news of the officer's return and of his strange condition was soon generally known in the village; but his parents, aided by the physician, quickly repressed those inclined to call from mere curiosity. At first Jim Wetherby scouted the idea that his old captain would not know him, but later had to admit the fact with a wonder which no explanations satisfied. Nichol immediately took a fancy to the one-armed veteran, who was glad to talk by the hour about soldiers and hospitals.

Before any matured plan for treatment could be adopted Nichol became ill, and soon passed into the delirium of fever. "The trouble is now clear enough," Dr. Barnes explained. "The captain has lived in hospitals and breathed a tainted atmosphere so long that his system is poisoned. This radical change of air has developed the disease."

Indeed, the typhoid symptoms progressed so rapidly as to show that the robust look of health had been in appearance only. The injured, weakened brain was the organ which suffered most, and in spite of the physician's best efforts his patient speedily entered into a condition of stupor, relieved only by low, unintelligible mutterings. Jim Wetherby became a tireless watcher, and greatly relieved the grief-stricken parents. Helen earnestly entreated that she might act the part of nurse also, but the doctor firmly forbade her useless exposure to contagion. She drove daily to the house, yet Mrs.

Nichol's sad face and words could scarcely dissipate the girl's impression that the whole strange episode was a dream.

At last it was feared that the end was near. One night Dr. Barnes, Mr. and Mrs. Nichol, and Jim Wetherby were watching in the hope of a gleam of intelligence. He was very low, scarcely more than breathing, and they dreaded lest there might be no sign before the glimmer of life faded out utterly.

Suddenly the captain seemed to awake, his glassy eyes kindled, and a noble yet stern expression dignified his visage. In a thick voice he said, "For—" Then, as if all the remaining forces of life asserted themselves, he rose in his bed and exclaimed loudly, "Forward! Company A. Guide right. Ah!" He fell back, now dead in very truth.

"Oh!" cried Jim Wetherby, excitedly, "them was the last words I heard from him just before the shell burst, and he looks now just as he did then."

"Yes," said Dr. Barnes, sadly and gravely, "memory came back to him at the point where he lost it. He has died as we thought at first—a brave soldier leading a charge."

The stern, grand impress of battle remained upon the officer's countenance. Friends and neighbors looked upon his ennobled visage with awe, and preserved in honored remembrance the real man that temporarily had been obscured. Helen's eyes, when taking her farewell look, were not so blinded with tears but that she recognized his restored manhood. Death's touch had been more potent than love's appeal.

In the Wilderness, upon a day fatal to him and so many thousands, Captain Nichol had prophesied of the happy days of peace. They came, and he was not forgotten.

One evening Dr. Barnes was sitting with Martine and Helen at their fireside. They had been talking about Nichol, and Helen remarked thoughtfully, "It was so very strange that he should have regained his memory in the way and at the time he did."

"No," replied the physician, "that part of his experience does not strike me as so very strange. In typhoid cases a lucid interval is apt to precede death. His brain, like his body, was depleted, shrunken slightly by disease. This impoverishment probably removed the cerebral obstruction, and the organ of memory renewed its action at the point where it had been arrested. My theory explains his last ejaculation, 'Ah!' It was his involuntary exclamation as he again heard the shell burst. The reproduction in his mind of this explosion killed him instantly after all. He was too enfeebled to bear the shock. If he had passed from delirium into quiet sleep—ah, well! he is dead, and that is all we can know with certainty."

"Well," said Martine, with a deep breath, "I am glad he had every chance that it was possible for us to give him."

"Yes, Hobart," added his wife, gently, "you did your whole duty, and I do not forget what it cost you."

QUEEN OF SPADES

"Mother," remarked Farmer Banning, discontentedly, "Susie is making a long visit."

"She is coming home next week," said his cheery wife. She had drawn her low chair close to the air-tight stove, for a late March snowstorm was raging without.

"It seems to me that I miss her more and more."

"Well, I'm not jealous."

"Oh, come, wife, you needn't be. The idea! But I'd be jealous if our little girl was sorter weaned away from us by this visit in town."

"Now, see here, father, you beat all the men I ever heard of in scolding about farmers borrowing, and here you are borrowing trouble."

"Well, I hope I won't have to pay soon. But I've been thinking that the old farmhouse may look small and appear lonely after her gay winter. When she is away, it's too big for me, and a suspicion lonely for us both. I've seen that you've missed her more than I have."

"I guess you're right. Well, she's coming home, as I said, and we must make home seem home to her. The child's growing up. Why, she'll be eighteen week after next. You must give her something nice on her birthday."

"I will," said the farmer, his rugged, weather-beaten face softening with memories. "Is our little girl as old as that? Why, only the other day I was carrying her on my shoulder to the barn and tossing her into the haymow. Sure enough, the 10th of April will be her birthday. Well, she shall choose her own present."

On the afternoon of the 5th of April he went down the long bill to the station, and was almost like a lover in his eagerness to see his child. He had come long before the train's schedule time, but was rewarded at last. When Susie appeared, she gave him a kiss before every one, and a glad greeting which might have satisfied the most exacting of lovers. He watched her furtively as they rode at a smart trot up the hill. Farmer Banning kept no old nags for his driving, but strong, well-fed, spirited horses that sometimes drew a light vehicle almost by the reins. "Yes," he thought, "she has grown a little citified. She's paler, and has a certain air or style that don't seem just natural to the hill. Well, thank the Lord! she doesn't seem sorry to go up the hill once more."

"There's the old place, Susie, waiting for you," he said. "It doesn't look so very bleak, does it, after all the fine city houses you've seen?"

"Yes, father, it does. It never appeared so bleak before."

He looked at his home, and in the late gray afternoon, saw it in a measure with her eyes—the long brown, bare slopes, a few gaunt old trees about the house, and the top boughs of the apple-orchard behind a sheltering hill in the rear of the dwelling.

"Father," resumed the girl, "we ought to call our place the Bleak House. I never so realized before how bare and desolate it looks, standing there right in the teeth of the north wind."

His countenance fell, but he had no time for comment. A moment later Susie was in her mother's arms. The farmer lifted the trunk to the horse-block and drove to the barn. "I guess it will be the old story," he muttered. "Home has become 'Bleak House.' I suppose it did look bleak to her eyes, especially at this season. Well, well, some day Susie will go to the city to stay, and then it will be Bleak House sure enough."

"Oh, father," cried his daughter when, after doing his evening work, he entered with the shadow of his thoughts still upon his face—"oh, father, mother says I can choose my birthday present!"

"Yes, Sue; I've passed my word."

"And so I have your bond. My present will make you open your eyes."

"And pocket-book too, I suppose. I'll trust you, however, not to break me. What is it to be?"

"I'll tell you the day before, and not till then."

After supper they drew around the stove. Mrs. Banning got out her knitting, as usual, and prepared for city gossip. The farmer rubbed his hands over the general aspect of comfort, and especially over the regained presence of his child's bright face. "Well, Sue," he remarked, "you'll own that this room IN the house doesn't look very bleak?"

"No, father, I'll own nothing of the kind. Your face and mother's are not bleak, but the room is."

"Well," said the farmer, rather disconsolately, "I fear the old place has been spoiled for you. I was saying to mother before you came home—"

"There now, father, no matter about what you were saying. Let Susie tell us why the room is bleak."

The girl laughed softly, got up, and taking a billet of wood from the box, put it into the air-tight. "The stove has swallowed it just as old Trip did his supper. Shame! you greedy dog," she added, caressing a great Newfoundland that would not leave her a moment. "Why can't you learn to eat your meals like a gentleman?" Then to her father, "Suppose we could sit here and see the flames curling all over and around that stick. Even a camp in the woods is jolly when lighted up by a flickering blaze."

"Oh—h!" said the farmer; "you think an open fire would take away the bleakness?"

"Certainly. The room would be changed instantly, and mother's face would look young and rosy again. The blue-black of this sheet-iron stove makes the room look blue-black."

"Open fires don't give near as much heat," said her father, meditatively. "They take an awful lot of wood; and wood is getting scarce in these parts."

"I should say so! Why don't you farmers get together, appoint a committee to cut down every tree remaining, then make it a State-prison offence ever to set out another? Why, father, you cut nearly all the trees from your lot a few years ago and sold the wood. Now that the trees are growing again, you are talking of clearing up the land for pasture. Just think of the comfort we could get out of that wood-lot! What crop would pay better? All the upholsterers in the world cannot furnish a room as an open hardwood fire does; and all the produce of the farm could not buy anything else half so nice."

"Say, mother," said her father, after a moment, "I guess I'll get down that old Franklin from the garret to-morrow and see if it can't furnish this room."

The next morning he called rather testily to the hired man, who was starting up the lane with an axe, "Hiram, I've got other work for you. Don't cut a stick in that wood-lot unless I tell you."

The evening of the 9th of April was cool but clear, and the farmer said, genially, "Well, Sue, prospects good for fine weather on your birthday. Glad of it; for I suppose you will want me to go to town with you for your present, whatever it is to be."

"You'll own up a girl can keep a secret now, won't you?"

"He'll have to own more'n that," added his wife; "he must own that an ole woman hasn't lost any sleep from curiosity."

"How much will be left me to own to-morrow night?" said the farmer, dubiously. "I suppose Sue wants a watch studded with diamonds, or a new house, or something else that she darsn't speak of till the last minute, even to her mother."

"Nothing of the kind. I want only all your time tomorrow, and all
Hiram's time, after you have fed the stock."
"All our time!

"Yes, the entire day, in which you both are to do just what I wish. You are not going gallivanting to the city, but will have to work hard."

"Well, I'm beat! I don't know what you want any more than I did at first."

"Yes, you do—your time and Hiram's."

"Give it up. It's hardly the season for a picnic. We might go fishing—"

"We must go to bed, so as to be up early, all hands."

"Oh, hold on, Sue; I do like this wood-fire. If it wouldn't make you vain, I'd tell you how—"

"Pretty, father. Say it out."

"Oh, you know it, do you? Well, how pretty you look in the firelight. Even mother, there, looks ten years younger. Keep your low seat, child, and let me look at you. So you're eighteen? My! my! how the years roll around! It WILL be Bleak House for mother and me, in spite of the wood-fire, when you leave us."

"It won't be Bleak House much longer," she replied with a significant little nod.

The next morning at an early hour the farmer said, "All ready, Sue. Our time is yours till night; so queen it over us." And black Hiram grinned acquiescence, thinking he was to have an easy time.

"Queen it, did you say?" cried Sue, in great spirits. "Well, then, I shall be queen of spades. Get 'em, and come with me. Bring a pickaxe, too." She led the way to a point not far from the dwelling, and resumed: "A hole here, father, a hole there, Hiram, big enough for a small hemlock, and holes all along the northeast side of the house. Then lots more holes, all over the lawn, for oaks, maples, dogwood, and all sorts to pretty trees, especially evergreens.'

"Oh, ho!" cried the farmer; "now I see the hole where the woodchuck went in."

"But you don't see the hole where he's coming out. When that is dug, even the road will be lined with trees. Foolish old father! you thought I'd be carried away with city gewgaws, fine furniture, dresses, and all that sort of thing. You thought I'd be pining for what you couldn't afford, what wouldn't do you a particle of good, nor me either, in the long run. I'm going to make you set out trees enough to double the value of your place and take all the bleakness and bareness from this hillside. To-day is only the beginning. I did get some new notions in the city which made me discontented with my home, but they were not the notions you were worrying about. In the suburbs I saw that the most costly houses were made doubly attractive by trees and shrubbery, and I knew that trees would grow for us as well as for millionaires—My conscience! if there isn't—" and the girl frowned and bit her lips.

"Is that one of the city beaux you were telling us about?" asked her father, sotto voce.

"Yes; but I don't want any beaux around to-day. I didn't think he'd be so persistent." Then, conscious that she was not dressed for company, but for work upon which she had set her heart, she advanced and gave Mr. Minturn a rather cool greeting.

But the persistent beau was equal to the occasion. He had endured Sue's absence as long as he could, then had resolved on a long day's siege, with a grand storming-onset late in the afternoon.

"Please, Miss Banning," he began, "don't look askance at me for coming at this unearthly hour. I claim the sacred rites of hospitality. I'm an invalid. The doctor said I needed country air, or would have prescribed it if given a chance. You said I might come to see you some day, and by playing Paul Pry I found out, you remember, that this was your birthday, and—"

"And this is my father, Mr. Minturn."

Mr. Minturn shook the farmer's hand with a cordiality calculated to awaken suspicions of his designs in a pump, had its handle been thus grasped. "Mr. Banning will forgive me for appearing with the lark," he continued volubly, determining to break the ice. "One can't get the full benefit of a day in the country if he starts in the afternoon."

The farmer was polite, but nothing more. If there was one thing beyond all others with which he could dispense, it was a beau for Sue.

Sue gave her father a significant, disappointed glance, which meant, "I won't get my present to day"; but he turned and said to Hiram, "Dig the hole right there, two feet across, eighteen inches deep." Then he started for the house. While not ready for suitors, his impulse to bestow hospitality was prompt.

The alert Mr. Minturn had observed the girl's glance, and knew that the farmer had gone to prepare his wife for a guest. He determined not to remain unless assured of a welcome. "Come, Miss Banning," he said, "we are at least friends, and should be frank. How much misunderstanding and trouble would often be saved if people would just speak their thought! This is your birthday—YOUR DAY. It should not be marred by any one. It would distress me keenly if I were the one to spoil it. Why not believe me literally and have your way absolutely about this day? I could come another time. Now show that a country girl, at least, can speak her mind."

With an embarrassed little laugh she answered, "I'm half inclined to take you at your word; but it would look so inhospitable."

"Bah for looks! The truth, please. By the way, though, you never looked better than in that trim blue walking-suit."

"Old outgrown working-suit, you mean. How sincere you are!"

"Indeed I am. Well, I'm de trop; that much is plain. You will let me come another day, won't you?"

"Yes, and I'll be frank too and tell you about THIS day. Father's a busy man, and his spring work is beginning, but as my birthday-present he has given me all his time and all Hiram's yonder. Well, I learned in the city how trees improved a home; and I had planned to spend this long day in setting out trees—planned it ever since my return. So you see—"

"Of course I see and approve," cried Minturn. "I know now why I had such a wild impulse to come out here to-day. Why, certainly. Just fancy me a city tramp looking for work, and not praying I won't find it, either. I'll work for my board. I know how to set out trees. I can prove it, for I planted those thrifty fellows growing about our house in town. Think how much more you'll accomplish, with another man to help—one that you can order around to your heart's content."

"The idea of my putting you to work!"

"A capital idea! and if a man doesn't work when a woman puts him at it he isn't worth the powder—I won't waste time even in original remarks. I'll promise you there will be double the number of trees out by night. Let me take your father's spade and show you how I can dig. Is this the place? If I don't catch up with Hiram, you may send the tramp back to the city." And before she could remonstrate, his coat was off and he at work.

Laughing, yet half in doubt, she watched him. The way he made the earth fly was surprising. "Oh, come," she said after a few moments, "you have shown your goodwill. A steam-engine could not keep it up at that rate."

"Perhaps not; but I can. Before you engage me, I wish you to know that
I am equal to old Adam, and can dig."
"Engage you!" she thought with a little flutter of dismay. "I could manage him with the help of town conventionalities; but how will it be here? I suppose I can keep father and Hiram within earshot, and if he is so bent on—well, call it a lark, since he has referred to that previous bird, perhaps I might as well have a lark too, seeing it's my birthday." Then she spoke. "Mr. Minturn!"

"I'm busy."

"But really—"

"And truly tell me, am I catching up with Hiram?"

"You'll get down so deep that you'll drop through if you're not careful."

"There's nothing like having a man who is steady working for you. Now, most fellows would stop and giggle at such little amusing remarks."

"You are soiling your trousers."

"Yes, you're right. They ARE mine. There; isn't that a regulation hole?

'Two feet across and eighteen deep.'"
"Yah! yah!" cackled Hiram; "eighteen foot deep! Dat ud be a well."

"Of course it would, and truth would lie at its bottom. Can I stay,
Miss Banning?"
"Did you ever see the like?" cried the farmer, who had appeared, unnoticed.

"Look here, father," said the now merry girl, "perhaps I was mistaken.
This—"
"Tramp—" interjected Minturn.

"Says he's looking for work and knows how to set out trees."

"And will work all day for a dinner," the tramp promptly added.

"If he can dig holes at that rate, Sue," said her father, catching their spirit, "he's worth a dinner. But you're boss to-day; I'm only one of the hands."

"I'm only another," said Minturn, touching his hat.

"Boss, am I? I'll soon find out. Mr. Minturn, come with me and don a pair of overalls. You shan't put me to shame, wearing that spick-and-span suit, neither shall you spoil it. Oh, you're in for it now! You might have escaped, and come another day, when I could have received you in state and driven you out behind father's frisky bays. When you return to town with blistered hands and aching bones, you will at least know better another time."

"I don't know any better this time, and just yearn for those overalls."

"To the house, then, and see mother before you become a wreck."

Farmer Banning looked after him and shook his head. Hiram spoke his employer's thought, "Dar ar gem'lin act like he gwine ter set hisself out on dis farm."

Sue had often said, "I can never be remarkable for anything; but I won't be commonplace." So she did not leave her guest in the parlor while she rushed off for a whispered conference with her mother. The well-bred simplicity of her manner, which often stopped just short of brusqueness, was never more apparent than now. "Mother!" she called from the parlor door.

The old lady gave a few final directions to her maid-of-all-work, and then appeared.

"Mother, this is Mr. Minturn, one of my city friends, of whom I have spoken to you. He is bent on helping me set out trees."

"Yes, Mrs. Banning, so bent that your daughter found that she would have to employ her dog to get me off the place."

Now, it had so happened that in discussing with her mother the young men whom she had met, Sue had said little about Mr. Minturn; but that little was significant to the experienced matron. Words had slipped out now and then which suggested that the girl did more thinking than talking concerning him; and she always referred to him in some light which she chose to regard as ridiculous, but which had not seemed in the least absurd to the attentive listener. When her husband, therefore, said that Mr. Minturn had appeared on the scene, she felt that an era of portentous events had begun. The trees to be set out would change the old place greatly, but a primeval forest shading the door would be as nothing compared with the vicissitude which a favored "beau" might produce. But mothers are more unselfish than fathers, and are their daughters' natural allies unless the suitor is objectionable. Mrs. Banning was inclined to be hospitable on general principles, meantime eager on her own account to see something of this man, about whom she had presentiments. So she said affably, "My daughter can keep her eye on the work which she is so interested in, and yet give you most of her time.—Susan, I will entertain Mr. Minturn while you change your dress."

She glanced at her guest dubiously, receiving for the moment the impression that the course indicated by her mother was the correct one. The resolute admirer knew well what a fiasco the day would be should the conventionalities prevail, and so said promptly: "Mrs. Banning, I appreciate your kind intentions, and I hope some day you may have the chance to carry them out. To-day, as your husband understands, I am a tramp from the city looking for work. I have found it, and have been engaged.—Miss Banning, I shall hold you inflexibly to our agreement—a pair of overalls and dinner."

Sue said a few words of explanation. Her mother laughed, but urged, "Do go and change your dress."

"I protest!" cried Mr. Minturn. "The walking-suit and overalls go together."

"Walking-suit, indeed!" repeated Sue, disdainfully. "But I shall not change it. I will not soften one feature of the scrape you have persisted in getting yourself into."

"Please don't."

"Mr. Minturn," said the matron, with smiling positiveness, "Susie is boss only out of doors; I am, in the house. There is a fresh-made cup of coffee and some eggs on toast in the dining-room. Having taken such an early start, you ought to have a lunch before being put to work."

"Yes," added Sue, "and the out-door boss says you can't go to work until at least the coffee is sipped."

"She's shrewd, isn't she, Mrs. Banning? She knows she will get twice as much work out of me on the strength of that coffee. Please get the overalls. I will not sip, but swallow the coffee, unless it's scalding, so that no time may be lost. Miss Banning must see all she had set her heart upon accomplished to-day, and a great deal more."

The matron departed on her quest, and as she pulled out the overalls, nodded her head significantly. "Things will be serious sure enough if he accomplishes all he has set his heart on," she muttered. "Well, he doesn't seem afraid to give us a chance to see him. He certainly will look ridiculous in these overalls, but not much more so than Sue in that old dress. I do wish she would change it."

The girl had considered this point, but with characteristic decision had thought: "No; he shall see us all on the plainest side of our life. He always seemed a good deal of an exquisite in town, and he lives in a handsome house. If to-day's experience at the old farm disgusts him, so be it. My dress is clean and tidy, if it is outgrown and darned; and mother is always neat, no matter what she wears. I'm going through the day just as I planned; and if he's too fine for us, now is the time to find it out. He may have come just for a lark, and will laugh with his folks to-night over the guy of a girl I appear; but I won't yield even to the putting of a ribbon in my hair."

Mrs. Banning never permitted the serving of cold slops for coffee, and Mr. Minturn had to sip the generous and fragrant beverage slowly. Meanwhile, his thoughts were busy. "Bah! for the old saying, 'Take the goods the gods send,'" he mused. "Go after your goods and take your pick. I knew my head was level in coming out. All is just as genuine as I supposed it would be—simple, honest, homely. The girl isn't homely, though, but she's just as genuine as all the rest, in that old dress which fits her like a glove. No shams and disguises on this field-day of my life. And her mother! A glance at her comfortable amplitude banished my one fear. There's not a sharp angle about her. I was satisfied about Miss Sue, but the term 'mother-in-law' suggests vague terrors to any man until reassured.—Ah, Miss Banning," he said, "this coffee would warm the heart of an anchorite. No wonder you are inspired to fine things after drinking such nectar."

"Yes, mother is famous for her coffee. I know that's fine, and you can praise it; but I'll not permit any ironical remarks concerning myself."

"I wouldn't, if I were you, especially when you are mistress of the situation. Still, I can't help having my opinion of you. Why in the world didn't you choose as your present something stylish from the city?"

"Something, I suppose you mean, in harmony with my very stylish surroundings and present appearance."

"I didn't mean anything of the kind, and fancy you know it. Ah! here are the overalls. Now deeds, not words. I'll leave my coat, watch, cuffs, and all impedimenta with you, Mrs. Banning. Am I not a spectacle to men and gods?" he added, drawing up the garment, which ceased to be nether in that it reached almost to his shoulders.

"Indeed you are," cried Sue, holding her side from laughing. Mrs. Banning also vainly tried to repress her hilarity over the absurd guy into which the nattily-dressed city man had transformed himself.

"Come," he cried, "no frivolity! You shall at least say I kept my word about the trees to-day." And they started at once for the scene of action, Minturn obtaining on the way a shovel from the tool-room.

"To think she's eighteen years old and got a beau!" muttered the farmer, as he and Hiram started two new holes. They were dug and others begun, yet the young people had not returned. "That's the way with young men nowadays—'big cry, little wool.' I thought I was going to have Sue around with me all day. Might as well get used to it, I suppose. Eighteen! Her mother's wasn't much older when—yes, hang it, there's always a WHEN with these likely girls. I'd just like to start in again on that day when I tossed her into the haymow."

"What are you talking to yourself about, father?"

"Oh! I thought I had seen the last of you to-day."

"Perhaps you will wish you had before night."

"Well, now, Sue! the idea of letting Mr. Minturn rig himself out like that! There's no use of scaring the crows so long before corn-planting." And the farmer's guffaw was quickly joined by Hiram's broad "Yah! yah!"

She frowned a little as she said, "He doesn't look any worse than I do."

"Come, Mr. Banning, Solomon in all his glory could not so take your daughter's eye to-day as a goodly number of trees standing where she wants them. I suggest that you loosen the soil with the pickaxe, then I can throw it out rapidly. Try it."

The farmer did so, not only for Minturn, but for Hiram also. The lightest part of the work thus fell to him. "We'll change about," he said, "when you get tired."

But Minturn did not get weary apparently, and under this new division of the toil the number of holes grew apace.

"Sakes alive, Mr. Minturn!" ejaculated Mr. Banning, "one would think you had been brought up on a farm."

"Or at ditch-digging," added the young man. "No; my profession is to get people into hot water and then make them pay roundly to get out. I'm a lawyer. Times have changed in cities. It's there you'll find young men with muscle, if anywhere. Put your hand here, sir, and you'll know whether Miss Banning made a bad bargain in hiring me for the day."

"Why!" exclaimed the astonished farmer, "you have the muscle of a blacksmith."

"Yes, sir; I could learn that trade in about a month."

"You don't grow muscle like that in a law-office?"

"No, indeed; nothing but bills grow there. A good fashion, if not abused, has come in vogue, and young men develop their bodies as well as brains. I belong to an athletic club in town, and could take to pugilism should everything else fail."

"Is there any prospect of your coming to that?" Sue asked mischievously.

"If we were out walking, and two or three rough fellows gave you impudence—" He nodded significantly.

"What could you do against two or three? They'd close on you."

"A fellow taught to use his hands doesn't let men close on him."

"Yah, yah! reckon not," chuckled Hiram. One of the farm household had evidently been won.

"It seems to me," remarked smiling Sue, "that I saw several young men in town who appeared scarcely equal to carrying their canes."

"Dudes?"

"That's what they are called, I believe."

"They are not men. They are neither fish, flesh, nor fowl, but the beginning of the great downward curve of evolution. Men came up from monkeys, it's said, you know, but science is in despair over the final down-comes of dudes. They may evolute into grasshoppers."

The farmer was shaken with mirth, and Sue could not help seeing that he was having a good time. She, however, felt that no tranquilly exciting day was before her, as she had anticipated. What wouldn't that muscular fellow attempt before night? He possessed a sort of vim and cheerful audacity which made her tremble, "He is too confident," she thought, "and needs a lesson. All this digging is like that of soldiers who soon mean to drop their shovels. I don't propose to be carried by storm just when he gets ready. He can have his lark, and that's all to-day. I want a good deal of time to think before I surrender to him or any one else."

During the remainder of the forenoon these musings prevented the slightest trace of sentimentality from appearing in her face or words. She had to admit mentally that Minturn gave her no occasion for defensive tactics. He attended as strictly to business as did Hiram, and she was allowed to come and go at will. At first she merely ventured to the house, to "help mother," as she said. Then, with growing confidence, she went here and there to select sites for trees; but Minturn dug on no longer "like a steam-engine," yet in an easy, steady, effective way that was a continual surprise to the farmer.

"Well, Sue," said her father at last, "you and mother ought to have an extra dinner; for Mr. Minturn certainly has earned one."

"I promised him only a dinner," she replied; "nothing was said about its being extra."

"Quantity is all I'm thinking of," said Minturn. "I have the sauce which will make it a feast."

"Beckon it's gwine on twelve," said Hiram, cocking his eye at the sun.
"Hadn't I better feed de critters?"
"Ah, old man! own up, now; you've got a backache," said Minturn.

"Dere is kin' ob a crik comin'—"

"Drop work, all hands," cried Sue. "Mr. Minturn has a 'crik' also, but he's too proud to own it. How you'll groan for this to-morrow, sir!"

"If you take that view of the case, I may be under the necessity of giving proof positive to the contrary by coming out to-morrow."

"You're not half through yet. The hardest part is to come."

"Oh, I know that," he replied; and he gave her such a humorously appealing glance that she turned quickly toward the house to hide a conscious flush.

The farmer showed him to the spare-room, in which he found his belongings. Left to make his toilet, he muttered, "Ah, better and better! This is not the regulation refrigerator into which guests are put at farmhouses. All needed for solid comfort is here, even to a slight fire in the air-tight. Now, isn't that rosy old lady a jewel of a mother-in-law? She knows that a warm man shouldn't get chilled just as well as if she had studied athletics. Miss Sue, however, is a little chilly. She's on the fence yet. Jupiter! I AM tired. Oh, well, I don't believe I'll have seven years of this kind of thing. You were right, though, old man, if your Rachel was like mine. What's that rustle in the other room? She's dressing for dinner. So must I; and I'm ready for it. If she has romantic ideas about love and lost appetites, I'm a goner."

When he descended to the parlor, his old stylish self again, Sue was there, robed in a gown which he had admired before, revealing the fact to her by approving glances. But now he said, "You don't look half so well as you did before."

"I can't say that of you," she replied.

"A man's looks are of no consequence."

"Few men think so."

"Oh, they try to please such critical eyes as I now am meeting."

"And throw dust in them too sometimes."

"Yes; gold dust, often. I haven't much of that."

"It would be a pity to throw it away if you had."

"No matter how much was thrown, I don't think it would blind you, Miss Banning."
The dining-room door across the hall opened, and the host and hostess appeared. "Why, father and mother, how fine you look!"

"It would be strange indeed if we did not honor this day," said Mrs. Banning. "I hope you have not so tired yourself, sir, that you cannot enjoy your dinner. I could scarcely believe my eyes as I watched you from the window."

"I am afraid I shall astonish you still more at the table. I am simply ravenous."

"This is your chance," cried Sue. "You are now to be paid in the coin you asked for."

Sue did remark to herself by the time they reached dessert and coffee, "I need have no scruples in refusing a man with such an appetite; he won't pine. He is a lawyer, sure enough. He is just winning father and mother hand over hand."

Indeed, the bosom of good Mrs. Banning must have been environed with steel not to have had throbs of goodwill toward one who showed such hearty appreciation of her capital dinner. But Sue became only the more resolved that she was not going to yield so readily to this muscular suitor who was digging and eating his way straight into the hearts of her ancestors, and she proposed to be unusually elusive and alert during the afternoon. She was a little surprised when he resumed his old tactics.

After drinking a second cup of coffee, he rose, and said, "As an honest man, I have still a great deal to do after such a dinner."

"Well, it has just done me good to see you," said Mrs. Banning, smiling genially over her old-fashioned coffee-pot. "I feel highly complimented."

"I doubt whether I shall be equal to another such compliment before the next birthday. I hope, Miss Susie, you have observed my efforts to do honor to the occasion?"

"Oh," cried the girl, "I naturally supposed you were trying to get even in your bargain."

"I hope to be about sundown. I'll get into those overalls at once, and
I trust you will put on your walking-suit."

"Yes, it will be a walking-suit for a short time. We must walk to the wood-lot for the trees, unless you prefer to ride.—Father, please tell Hiram to get the two-horse wagon ready."

When the old people were left alone, the farmer said, "Well, mother, Sue HAS got a suitor, and if he don't suit her—" And then his wit gave out.

"There, father, I never thought you'd come to that. It's well she has, for you will soon have to be taken care of."

"He's got the muscle to do it. He shall have my law-business, anyway."

"Thank the Lord, it isn't much; but that's not saying he shall have Sue."
"Why, what have you against him?"

"Nothing so far. I was only finding out if you had anything against him."

"Lawyers, indeed! What would become of the men if women turned lawyers. Do you think Sue—"
"Hush!"

They all laughed till the tears came when Minturn again appeared dressed for work; but he nonchalantly lighted a cigar and was entirely at his ease.

Sue was armed with thick gloves and a pair of pruning-nippers. Minturn threw a spade and pickaxe on his shoulder, and Mr. Banning, whom Sue had warned threateningly "never to be far away," tramped at their side as they went up the lane. Apparently there was no need of such precaution, for the young man seemed wholly bent on getting up the trees, most of which she had selected and marked during recent rambles. She helped now vigorously, pulling on the young saplings as they loosened the roots, then trimming them into shape. More than once, however, she detected glances, and his thoughts were more flattering than she imagined. "What vigor she has in that supple, rounded form! Her very touch ought to put life into these trees; I know it would into me. How young she looks in that comical old dress which barely reaches her ankles! Yes, Hal Minturn; and remember, that trim little ankle can put a firm foot down for or against you—so no blundering."

He began to be doubtful whether he would make his grand attack that day, and finally decided against it, unless a very favorable opportunity occurred, until her plan of birthday-work had been carried out and he had fulfilled the obligation into which he had entered in the morning. He labored on manfully, seconding all her wishes, and taking much pains to get the young trees up with an abundance of fibrous roots. At last his assiduity induced her to relent a little, and she smiled sympathetically as she remarked, "I hope you are enjoying yourself. Well, never mind; some other day you will fare better."

"Why should I not enjoy myself?" he asked in well-feigned surprise. "What condition of a good time is absent? Even an April day has forgotten to be moody, and we are having unclouded, genial sunshine. The air is delicious with springtime fragrance. Were ever hemlocks so aromatic as these young fellows? They come out of the ground so readily that one would think them aware of their proud destiny. Of course I'm enjoying myself. Even the robins and sparrows know it, and are singing as if possessed."

"Hadn't you better give up your law-office and turn farmer?"

"This isn't farming. This is embroidery-work."

"Well, if all these trees grow they will embroider the old place, won't they?"

"They'll grow, every mother's son of 'em."

"What makes you so confident?"

"I'm not confident. That's where you are mistaken." And he gave her such a direct, keen look that she suddenly found something to do elsewhere.

"I declare!" she exclaimed mentally, "he seems to read my very thoughts."

At last the wagon was loaded with trees enough to occupy the holes which had been dug, and they started for the vicinity of the farmhouse again. Mr. Banning had no match-making proclivities where Sue was concerned, as may be well understood, and had never been far off. Minturn, however, had appeared so single-minded in his work, so innocent of all designs upon his daughter, that the old man began to think that this day's performance was only a tentative and preliminary skirmish, and that if there were danger it lurked in the unknown future. He was therefore inclined to be less vigilant, reasoning philosophically, "I suppose it's got to come some time or other. It looks as if Sue might go a good deal further than this young man and fare worse. But then she's only eighteen, and he knows it. I guess he's got sense enough not to plant his corn till the sun's higher. He can see with half an eye that my little girl isn't ready to drop, like an over-ripe apple." Thus mixing metaphors and many thoughts, he hurried ahead to open the gate for Hiram.

"I'm in for it now," thought Sue, and she instinctively assumed an indifferent expression and talked volubly of trees.

"Yes, Miss Banning," he said formally, "by the time your hair is tinged with gray the results of this day's labor will be seen far and wide. No passenger in the cars, no traveller in the valley, but will turn his eyes admiringly in this direction."

"I wasn't thinking of travellers," she answered, "but of making an attractive home in which I can grow old contentedly. Some day when you have become a gray-haired and very dignified judge you may come out and dine with us again. You can then smoke your cigar under a tree which you helped to plant."

"Certainly, Miss Banning. With such a prospect, how could you doubt that I was enjoying myself? What suggested the judge? My present appearance?"

The incongruity of the idea with his absurd aspect and a certain degree of nervousness set her off again, and she startled the robins by a laugh as loud and clear as their wild notes.

"I don't care," she cried. "I've had a jolly birthday, and am accomplishing all on which I had set my heart."

"Yes, and a great deal more, Miss Banning," he replied with a formal bow. "In all your scheming you hadn't set your heart on my coming out and—does modesty permit me to say it?—helping a little."

"Now, you HAVE helped wonderfully, and you must not think I don't appreciate it."

"Ah, how richly I am rewarded!"

She looked at him with a laughing and perplexed little frown, but only said, "No irony, sir."

By this time they had joined her father and begun to set out the row of hemlocks. To her surprise, Sue had found herself a little disappointed that he had not availed himself of his one opportunity to be at least "a bit friendly" as she phrased it. It was mortifying to a girl to be expecting "something awkward to meet" and nothing of the kind take place. "After all," she thought, "perhaps he came out just for a lark, or, worse still, is amusing himself at my expense; or he may have come on an exploring expedition and plain old father and mother, and the plain little farmhouse, have satisfied him. Well, the dinner wasn't very plain, but he may have been laughing in his sleeve at our lack of style in serving it. Then this old dress! I probably appear to him a perfect guy." And she began to hate it, and devoted it to the rag-bag the moment she could get it off.

This line of thought, once begun, seemed so rational that she wondered it had not occurred to her before. "The idea of my being so ridiculously on the defensive!" she thought. "No, it wasn't ridiculous either, as far as my action went, for he can never say I ACTED as if I wanted him to speak. My conceit in expecting him to speak the moment he got a chance WAS absurd. He has begun to be very polite and formal. That's always the way with men when they want to back out of anything. He came out to look us over, and me in particular; he made himself into a scarecrow just because I looked like one, and now will go home and laugh it all over with his city friends. Oh, why did he come and spoil my day? Even he said it WAS my day, and he has done a mean thing in spoiling it. Well, he may not carry as much self-complacency back to town as he thinks he will. Such a cold-blooded spirit, too!—to come upon us unawares in order to spy out everything, for fear he might get taken in! You were very attentive and flattering in the city, sir, but now you are disenchanted. Well, so am I."

Under the influence of this train of thought she grew more and more silent. The sun was sinking westward in undimmed splendor, but her face was clouded. The air was sweet, balmy, well adapted to sentiment and the setting out of trees, but she was growing frosty.

"Hiram," she said shortly, "you've got that oak crooked; let me hold it." And thereafter she held the trees for the old colored man as he filled in the earth around them.

Minturn appeared as oblivious as he was keenly observant. At first the change in Sue puzzled and discouraged him; then, as his acute mind sought her motives, a rosy light began to dawn upon him. "I may be wrong," he thought, "but I'll take my chances in acting as if I were right before I go home."

At last Hiram said: "Reckon I'll have to feed de critters again;" and he slouched off.

Sue nipped at the young trees further and further away from the young man who must "play spy before being lover." The spy helped Mr. Banning set out the last tree. Meantime, the complacent farmer had mused: "The little girl's safe for another while, anyhow. Never saw her more offish; but things looked squally about dinner-time. Then, she's only eighteen; time enough years hence." At last he said affably, "I'll go in and hasten supper, for you've earned it if ever a man did, Mr. Minturn. Then I'll drive you down to the evening train." And he hurried away.

Sue's back was toward them, and she did not hear Minturn's step until he was close beside her. "All through," he said; "every tree out. I congratulate you; for rarely in this vale of tears are plans and hopes crowned with better success."

"Oh, yes," she hastened to reply; "I am more than satisfied. I hope that you are too."

"I have no reason to complain," he said. "You have stood by your morning's bargain, as I have tried to."

"It was your own fault, Mr. Minturn, that it was so one-sided. But I've no doubt you enjoy spicing your city life with a little lark in the country."

"It WAS a one-sided bargain, and I have had the best of it."

"Perhaps you have," she admitted. "I think supper will be ready by the time we are ready for it." And she turned toward the house. Then she added, "You must be weary and anxious to get away."

"You were right; my bones DO ache. And look at my hands. I know you'll say they need washing; but count the blisters."

"I also said, Mr. Minturn, that you would know better next time. So you see I was right then and am right now."

"Are you perfectly sure?"

"I see no reason to think otherwise." In turning, she had faced a young sugar-maple which he had aided her in planting early in the afternoon. Now she snipped at it nervously with her pruning-shears, for he would not budge, and she felt it scarcely polite to leave him.

"Well," he resumed, after an instant, "it has a good look, hasn't it, for a man to fulfil an obligation literally?"

"Certainly, Mr. Minturn," and there was a tremor in her tone; "but you have done a hundred-fold more than I expected, and never were under any obligations."

"Then I am free to begin again?"

"You are as free now as you have been all day to do what you please."
And her shears were closing on the main stem of the maple. He caught

and stayed her hand. "I don't care!" she cried almost passionately. "Come, let us go in and end this foolish talk."

"But I do care," he replied, taking the shears from her, yet retaining her hand in his strong grasp. "I helped you plant this tree, and whenever you see it, whenever you care for it, when, in time, you sit under its shade or wonder at its autumn hues, I wish you to remember that I told you of my love beside it. Dear little girl, do you think I am such a blind fool that I could spend this long day with you at your home and not feel sorry that I must ever go away? If I could, my very touch should turn the sap of this maple into vinegar. To-day I've only tried to show how I can work for you. I am eager to begin again, and for life."

At first Sue had tried to withdraw her hand, but its tenseness relaxed. As he spoke, she turned her averted face slowly toward him, and the rays of the setting sun flashed a deeper crimson into her cheeks. Her honest eyes looked into his and were satisfied. Then she suddenly gathered the young tree against her heart and kissed the stem she had so nearly severed. "This maple is witness to what you've said," she faltered. "Ah! but it will be a sugar-maple in truth; and if petting will make it live—there, now! behave! The idea! right out on this bare lawn! You must wait till the screening evergreens grow before—Oh, you audacious—I haven't promised anything."

"I promise everything. I'm engaged, and only taking my retaining-fees."

"Mother," cried Farmer Banning at the dining-room window, "just look yonder!"

"And do you mean to say, John Banning, that you didn't expect it?"

"Why, Sue was growing more and more offish."

"Of course! Don't you remember?"

"Oh, this unlucky birthday! As if trees could take Sue's place!"

"Yah!" chuckled Hiram from the barn door, "I knowed dat ar gem'lin was a-diggin' a hole fer hisself on dis farm."

"Mr. Minturn—" Sue began as they came toward the house arm in arm.

"Hal—" he interrupted.

"Well, then, Mr. Hal, you must promise me one thing in dead earnest. I'm the only chick father and mother have. You must be very considerate of them, and let me give them as much of my time as I can. This is all that I stipulate; but this I do."

"Sue," he said in mock solemnity, "the prospects are that you'll be a widow."

"Why do you make such an absurd remark?"

"Because you have struck amidships the commandment with the promise, and your days will be long in the land. You'll outlive everybody."

"This will be no joke for father and mother."

So it would appear. They sat in the parlor as if waiting for the world to come to an end— as indeed it had, one phase of it, to them. Their little girl, in a sense, was theirs no longer.

"Father, mother," said Sue, demurely, "I must break some news to you."

"It's broken already," began Mrs. Banning, putting her handkerchief to her eyes.

Sue's glance renewed her reproaches for the scene on the lawn; but Minturn went promptly forward, and throwing his arm around the matron's plump shoulders, gave his first filial kiss.

"Come, mother," he said, "Sue has thought of you both; and I've given her a big promise that I won't take any more of her away than I can help. And you, sir," wringing the farmer's hand, "will often see a city tramp here who will be glad to work for his dinner. These overalls are my witness."

Then they became conscious of his absurd figure, and the scene ended in laughter that was near akin to tears.

The maple lived, you may rest assured; and Sue's children said there never was such sugar as the sap of that tree yielded.

All the hemlocks, oaks, and dogwood thrived as if conscious that theirs had been no ordinary transplanting; while Minturn's half-jesting prophecy concerning the travellers in the valley was amply fulfilled.

AN UNEXPECTED RESULT

"Jack, she played with me deliberately, heartlessly. I can never forgive her."

"In that case, Will, I congratulate you. Such a girl isn't worth a second thought, and you've made a happy escape."

"No congratulations, if you please. You can talk coolly, because in regard to such matters you are cool, and, I may add, a trifle cold. Ambition is your mistress, and a musty law-book has more attractions for you than any woman living. I'm not so tempered. I am subject to the general law of nature, and a woman's love and sympathy are essential to success in my life and work."

"That's all right; but there are as good fish—"

"Oh, have done with your trite nonsense," interrupted Will Munson, impatiently. "I'd consult you on a point of law in preference to most of the gray-beards, but I was a fool to speak of this affair. And yet as my most intimate friend—"

"Come, Will, I'm not unfeeling;" and John Ackland rose and put his hand on his friend's shoulder. "I admit that the subject is remote from my line of thought and wholly beyond my experience. If the affair is so serious I shall take it to heart."

"Serious! Is it a slight thing to be crippled for life?"

"Oh, come, now," said Ackland, giving his friend a hearty and encouraging thump, "you are sound in mind and limb; what matters a scratch on the heart to a man not twenty-five?"

"Very well; I'll say no more about it. When I need a lawyer I'll come to you. Good-by; I sail for Brazil in the morning."

"Will, sit down and look me in the eyes," said Ackland, decisively.
"Will, forgive me. You are in trouble. A man's eyes usually tell me
more than all his words, and I don't like the expression of yours.
There is yellow fever in Brazil."
"I know it," was the careless reply.

"What excuse have you for going?"

"Business complications have arisen there, and I promptly volunteered to go. My employers were kind enough to hesitate and warn me, and to say that they could send a man less valuable to them, but I soon overcame their objections."

"That is your excuse for going. The reason I see in your eyes. You are reckless, Will."

"I have reason to be."

"I can't agree with you, but I feel for you all the same. Tell me all about it, for this is sad news to me. I had hoped to join you on the beach in a few days, and to spend August with you and my cousin. I confess I am beginning to feel exceedingly vindictive toward this pretty little monster, and if any harm comes to you I shall be savage enough to scalp her."

"The harm has come already, Jack. I'm hit hard. She showed me a mirage of happiness that has made my present world a desert. I am reckless; I'm desperate. You may think it is weak and unmanly, but you don't know anything about it. Time or the fever may cure me, but now I am bankrupt in all that gives value to life. A woman with an art so consummate that it seemed artless, deliberately evoked the best there was in me, then threw it away as indifferently as a cast-off glove."

"Tell me how it came about."

"How can I tell you? How can I in cold blood recall glances, words, intonations, the pressure of a hand that seemed alive with reciprocal feeling? In addition to her beauty she had the irresistible charm of fascination. I was wary at first, but she angled for me with a skill that would have disarmed any man who did not believe in the inherent falseness of woman. The children in the house idolized her, and I have great faith in a child's intuitions."

"Oh, that was only a part of her guile," said Ackland, frowningly.

"Probably; at any rate she has taken all the color and zest out of my life. I wish some one could pay her back in her own coin. I don't suppose she has a heart; but I wish her vanity might be wounded in a way that would teach her a lesson never to be forgotten."

"It certainly would be a well-deserved retribution," said Ackland, musingly.

"Jack, you are the one, of all the world, to administer the punishment. I don't believe a woman's smiles ever quickened your pulse one beat."

"You are right, Will, it is my cold-bloodedness—to put your thought in plain English—that will prove your best ally."

"I only hope that I am not leading you into danger. You will need an Indian's stoicism."

"Bah! I may fail ignominiously, and find her vanity invulnerable, but I pledge you my word that I will avenge you if it be within the compass of my skill. My cousin, Mrs. Alston, may prove a useful ally. I think you wrote me that the name of this siren was Eva Van Tyne?"

"Yes; I only wish she had the rudiments of a heart, so that she might feel in a faint, far-off way a little of the pain she has inflicted on me. Don't let her make you falter or grow remorseful, Jack. Remember that you have given a pledge to one who may be dead before you can fulfil it."

Ackland said farewell to his friend with the fear that he might never see him again, and a few days later found himself at a New England seaside resort, with a relentless purpose lurking in his dark eyes. Mrs. Alston did unconsciously prove a useful ally, for her wealth and elegance gave her unusual prestige in the house, and in joining her party Ackland achieved immediately all the social recognition he desired.

While strolling with this lady on the piazza he observed the object of his quest, and was at once compelled to make more allowance than he had done hitherto for his friend's discomfiture. Two or three children were leaning over the young girl's chair, and she was amusing them by some clever caricatures. She was not so interested, however, but that she soon noted the new-comer, and bestowed upon him from time to time curious and furtive glances. That these were not returned seemed to occasion her some surprise, for she was not accustomed to be so utterly ignored, even by a stranger. A little later Ackland saw her consulting the hotel register.

"I have at least awakened her curiosity," he thought.

"I've been waiting for you to ask me who that pretty girl is," said Mrs. Alton, laughing; "you do indeed exceed all men in indifference to women."

"I know all about that girl," was the grim reply. "She has played the very deuce with my friend Munson."

"Yes," replied Mrs. Alston, indignantly, "it was the most shameful piece of coquetry I ever saw. She is a puzzle to me. To the children and the old people in the house she is consideration and kindness itself; but she appears to regard men of your years as legitimate game and is perfectly remorseless. So beware! She is dangerous, invulnerable as you imagine yourself to be. She will practice her wiles upon you if you give her half a chance, and her art has much more than her pretty face to enforce it. She is unusually clever."

Ackland's slight shrug was so contemptuous that his cousin was nettled, and she thought, "I wish the girl could disturb his complacent equanimity just a little. It vexes one to see a man so indifferent; it's a slight to woman;" and she determined to give Miss Van Tyne the vantage-ground of an introduction at the first opportunity.

And this occurred before the evening was over. To her surprise Ackland entered into an extended conversation with the enemy. "Well," she thought, "if he begins in this style there will soon be another victim. Miss Van Tyne can talk to as bright a man as he is and hold her own. Meanwhile she will assail him in a hundred covert ways. Out of regard for his friend he should have shown some disapproval of her; but there he sits quietly talking in the publicity of the parlor."

"Mrs. Alston," said a friend at her elbow, "you ought to forewarn your cousin and tell him of Mr. Munson's fate."

"He knows all about Mr. Munson," was her reply. "Indeed, the latter is his most intimate friend. I suppose my cousin is indulging in a little natural curiosity concerning this destroyer of masculine peace, and if ever a man could do so in safety he can."

"Why so?"

"Well, I never knew so unsusceptible a man. With the exception of a few of his relatives, he has never cared for ladies' society."

Mrs. Alston was far astray in supposing that curiosity was Ackland's motive in his rather prolonged conversation with Miss Van Tyne. It was simply part of his tactics, for he proposed to waste no time in skirmishing or in guarded and gradual approaches. He would cross weapons at once, and secure his object by a sharp and aggressive campaign. His object was to obtain immediately some idea of the calibre of the girl's mind, and in this respect he was agreeably surprised, for while giving little evidence of thorough education, she was unusually intelligent and exceedingly quick in her perceptions. He soon learned also that she was gifted with more than woman's customary intuition, that she was watching his face closely for meanings that he might not choose to express in words or else to conceal by his language. While he feared that his task would be far more difficult than he expected, and that he would have to be extremely guarded in order not to reveal his design, he was glad to learn that the foe was worthy of his steel. Meanwhile her ability and self-reliance banished all compunction. He had no scruples in humbling the pride of a woman who was at once so proud, so heartless, and so clever. Nor would the effort be wearisome, for she had proved herself both amusing and interesting. He might enjoy it quite as much as an intricate law case.

Even prejudiced Ackland, as he saw her occasionally on the following day, was compelled to admit that she was more than pretty. Her features were neither regular nor faultless. Her mouth was too large to be perfect, and her nose was not Grecian; but her eyes were peculiarly fine and illumined her face, whose chief charm lay in its power of expression. If she chose, almost all her thoughts and feelings could find their reflex there. The trouble was that she could as readily mask her thought and express what she did not feel. Her eyes were of the darkest blue and her hair seemed light in contrast. It was evident that she had studied grace so thoroughly that her manner and carriage appeared unstudied and natural. She never seemed self-conscious, and yet no one had ever seen her in an ungainly posture or had known her to make an awkward gesture. This grace, however, like a finished style in writing, was tinged so strongly with her own individuality that it appeared original as compared with the fashionable monotony which characterized the manners of so many of her age. She could not have been much more than twenty; and yet, as Mrs. Alston took pains to inform her cousin, she had long been in society, adding, "Its homage is her breath of life, and from all I hear your friend Munson has had many predecessors. Be on your guard."

"Your solicitude in my behalf is quite touching," he replied. "Who is this fair buccaneer that has made so many wrecks and exacts so heavy a revenue from society? Who has the care of her and what are her antecedents?"

"She is an orphan, and possessed, I am told, of considerable property in her own name. A forceless, nerveless maiden aunt is about the only antecedent we see much of. Her guardian has been here once or twice, but practically she is independent."

Miss Van Tyne's efforts to learn something concerning Ackland were apparently quite as casual and indifferent and yet were made with utmost skill. She knew that Mrs. Alston's friend was something of a gossip; and she led her to speak of the subject of her thoughts with an indirect finesse that would have amused the young man exceedingly could he have been an unobserved witness. When she learned that he was Mr. Munson's intimate friend and that he was aware of her treatment of the latter, she was somewhat disconcerted. One so forewarned might not become an easy prey. But the additional fact that he was almost a woman-hater put her upon her mettle at once, and she felt that here was a chance for a conquest such as she had never made before. She now believed that she had discovered the key to his indifference. He was ready enough to amuse himself with her as a clever woman, but knew her too well to bestow upon her even a friendly thought.

"If I can bring him to my feet it will be a triumph indeed," she murmured exultantly; "and at my feet he shall be if he gives me half a chance." Seemingly he gave her every chance that she could desire, and while he scarcely made any effort to seek her society, she noted with secret satisfaction that he often appeared as if accidentally near her, and that he ever made it the easiest and most natural thing in the world for her to join him. His conversation was often as gay and unconventional as she could wish; but she seldom failed to detect in it an uncomfortable element of satire and irony. He always left her dissatisfied with herself and with a depressing consciousness that she had made no impression upon him.

His conquest grew into an absorbing desire; and she unobtrusively brought to bear upon him every art and fascination that she possessed. Her toilets were as exquisite as they were simple. The children were made to idolize her more than ever; but Ackland was candid enough to admit that this was not all guile on her part, for she was evidently in sympathy with the little people, who can rarely be imposed upon by any amount of false interest. Indeed, he saw no reason to doubt that she abounded in good-nature toward all except the natural objects of her ruling passion; but the very skill and deliberateness with which she sought to gratify this passion greatly increased his vindictive feeling. He saw how naturally and completely his friend had been deceived and how exquisite must have been the hopes and anticipations so falsely raised. Therefore he smiled more grimly at the close of each succeeding day, and was more than ever bent upon the accomplishment of his purpose.

At length Miss Van Tyne changed her tactics and grew quite oblivious to Ackland's presence in the house; but she found him apparently too indifferent to observe the fact. She then permitted one of her several admirers to become devoted; Ackland did not offer the protest of even a glance. He stood, as it were, just where she had left him, ready for an occasional chat, stroll, or excursion, if the affair came about naturally and without much effort on his part. She found that she could neither induce him to seek her nor annoy him by an indifference which she meant should be more marked than his own.

Some little time after there came a windy day when the surf was so heavy that there were but few bathers. Ackland was a good swimmer, and took his plunge as usual. He was leaving the water when Miss Van Tyne ran down the beach and was about to dart through the breakers in her wonted fearless style.

"Be careful," he said to her; "the undertow is strong, and the man who has charge of the bathing is ill and not here. The tide is changing—in fact, running out already, I believe."

But she would not even look at him, much less answer. As there were other gentlemen present, he started for his bath-house, but had proceeded but a little way up the beach before a cry brought him to the water's edge instantly.

"Something is wrong with Miss Van Tyne," cried half a dozen voices.
"She ventured out recklessly, and it seems as if she couldn't get back."
At that moment her form rose on the crest of a wave, and above the thunder of the surf came her faint cry, "Help!"

The other bathers stood irresolute, for she was dangerously far out, and the tide had evidently turned. Ackland, on the contrary, dashed through the breakers and then, in his efforts for speed, dived through the waves nearest to the shore. When he reached the place where he expected to find her he saw nothing for a moment or two but great crested billows that every moment were increasing in height under the rising wind. For a moment he feared that she had perished, and the thought that the beautiful creature had met her death so suddenly and awfully made him almost sick and faint. An instant later, however, a wave threw her up from the trough of the sea into full vision somewhat on his right, and a few strong strokes brought him to her side.

"Oh, save me!" she gasped.

"Don't cling to me," he said sternly. "Do as I bid you. Strike out for the shore if you are able; if not, lie on your back and float."

She did the latter, for now that aid had reached her she apparently recovered from her panic and was perfectly tractable. He placed his left hand under her and struck out quietly, aware that the least excitement causing exhaustion on his part might cost both of them their lives.

As they approached the shore a rope was thrown to them, and Ackland, who felt his strength giving way, seized it—desperately. He passed his arm around his companion with a grasp that almost made her breathless, and they were dragged half suffocated through the water until strong hands on either side rushed them through the breakers.

Miss Van Tyne for a moment or two stood dazed and panting, then disengaged herself from the rather warm support of the devoted admirer whom she had tried to play against Ackland, and tried to walk, but after a few uncertain steps fell senseless on the sand, thus for the moment drawing to herself the attention of the increasing throng. Ackland, glad to escape notice, was staggering off to his bath-house when several ladies, more mindful of his part in the affair than the men had been, overtook him with a fire of questions and plaudits.

"Please leave me alone," he said almost savagely, without looking around.

"What a bear he is! Any one else would have been a little complacent over such an exploit," they chorused, as they followed the unconscious girl, who was now being carried to the hotel.

Ackland locked the door of his little apartment and sank panting on the bench. "Maledictions on her!" he muttered. "At one time there was a better chance of her being fatal to me than to Munson with his yellow-fever tragedy in prospect. Her recklessness to-day was perfectly insane. If she tries it again she may drown for all that I care, or at least ought to care." His anger appeared to act like a tonic, and he was soon ready to return to the house. A dozen sprang forward to congratulate him, but they found such impatience and annoyance at all reference to the affair that with many surmises the topic was dropped.

"You are a queer fellow," remarked his privileged cousin, as he took her out to dinner. "Why don't you let people speak naturally about the matter, or rather, why don't you pose as the hero of the occasion?"

"Because the whole affair was most unnatural, and I am deeply incensed. In a case of necessity I am ready to risk my life, although it has unusual attractions for me; but I'm no melodramatic hero looking for adventures. What necessity was there in this case? It is the old story of Munson over again in another guise. The act was that of an inconsiderate, heartless woman who follows her impulses and inclinations, no matter what may be the consequences." After a moment he added less indignantly, "I must give her credit for one thing, angry as I am—she behaved well in the water, otherwise she would have drowned me."

"She is not a fool. Most women would have drowned you."

"She is indeed not a fool; therefore she's the more to blame. If she is ever so reckless again, may I be asleep in my room. Of course one can't stand by and see a woman drown, no matter who or what she is."

"Jack, what made her so reckless?" Mrs. Alston asked, with a sudden intelligence lighting up her face.

"Hang it all! How should I know? What made her torture Munson? She follows her impulses, and they are not always conducive to any one's well-being, not even her own."

"Mark my words, she has never shown this kind of recklessness before."

"Oh, yes, she has. She was running her horse to death the other hot morning and nearly trampled on a child;" and he told of an unexpected encounter while he was taking a rather extended ramble.

"Well," exclaimed Mrs. Alston, smiling significantly, "I think I understand her symptoms better than you do. If you are as cold-blooded as you seem, I may have to interfere."

"Oh, bah!" he answered impatiently. "Pardon me, but I should despise myself forever should I become sentimental, knowing what I do."

"Jack, had you no compunctions when fearing that such a beautiful girl might perish? We are going to have an awful night. Hear the wind whistle and moan, and the sky is already black with clouds. The roar of the surface grows louder every hour. Think of that lovely form being out in those black angry waves, darted at and preyed upon by horrible slimy monsters. Oh, it fairly makes my flesh creep!"

"And mine too," he said with a strong gesture of disgust; "especially when I remember that I should have kept her company, for of course I could not return without her. I confess that when at first I could not find her I was fairly sick at the thought of her fate. But remember how uncalled for it all was—quite as much so as that poor Will Munson is on his way to die with the yellow fever, like enough."

"Jack," said his cousin, affectionately, laying her hand on his arm, "blessings on your courage to-day! If what might have happened so easily had occurred, I could never have looked upon the sea again without a shudder. I should have been tormented by a horrible memory all my life. It was brave and noble—"

"Oh, hush!" he said angrily. "I won't hear another word about it even from you. I'm not brave and noble. I went because I was compelled to go; I hated to go. I hate the girl, and have more reason now than ever. If we had both drowned, no doubt there would have been less trouble in the world. There would have been one lawyer the less, and a coquette extinguished. Now we shall both prey on society in our different ways indefinitely."

"Jack, you are in an awful mood to-day."

"I am; never was in a worse."

"Having so narrowly escaped death, you ought to be subdued and grateful."

"On the contrary, I'm inclined to profanity. Excuse me; don't wish any dessert. I'll try a walk and a cigar. You will now be glad to be rid of me on any terms."

"Stay, Jack. See, Miss Van Tyne has so far recovered as to come down.
She looked unutterable things at you as she entered."
"Of course she did. Very few of her thoughts concerning me or other young men would sound well if uttered. Tell your friends to let this topic alone, or I shall be rude to them," and without a glance toward the girl he had rescued he left the dining-room.

"Well, well," murmured Mrs. Alston, "I never saw Jack in such a mood before. It is quite as unaccountable as Miss Tyne's recklessness. I wonder what is the matter with HIM."

Ackland was speedily driven back from his walk by the rain, which fact he did not regret, for he found himself exhausted and depressed. Seeking a retired piazza in order to be alone, he sat down with his hat drawn over his eyes and smoked furiously. Before very long, however, he was startled out of a painful revery by a timid voice saying:

"Mr. Ackland, won't you permit me to thank you?"

He rose. Miss Van Tyne stood before him with outstretched hand. He did not notice it, but bowing coldly, said:

"Please consider that you have thanked me and let the subject drop."

"Do not be so harsh with me," she pleaded. "I cannot help it if you are. Mr. Ackland, you saved my life."

"Possibly."

"And possibly you think that it is scarcely worth saving."

"Possibly your own conscience suggested that thought to you."

"You are heartless," she burst out indignantly. He began to laugh.
"That's a droll charge for you to make," he said.
She looked at him steadfastly for a moment, and then murmured: "You are thinking of your friend, Mr. Munson."

"That would be quite natural. How many more can you think of?"

"You are indeed unrelenting," she faltered, tears coming into her eyes; "but I cannot forget that but for you I should now be out there"—and she indicated the sea by a gesture, then covered her face with her hands, and shuddered.

"Do not feel under obligations. I should have been compelled to do as much for any human being. You seem to forget that I stood an even chance of being out there with you, and that there was no more need of the risk than there was that my best friend's life should be blight—"

"You—you out there?" she cried, springing toward him and pointing to the sea.

"Certainly. You cannot suppose that having once found you, I could come ashore without you. As it was, my strength was rapidly giving way, and were it not for the rope—"

"Oh, forgive me," she cried passionately, seizing his hand in spite of him. "It never entered my mind that you could drown. I somehow felt that nothing could harm you. I was reckless—I didn't know what I was doing—I don't understand myself any more. Please—please forgive me, or I shall not sleep to-night."

"Certainly," he said lightly, "if you will not refer to our little episode again."

"Please don't speak in that way," she sighed, turning away.

"I have complied with your request."

"I suppose I must be content," she resumed sadly. Then turning her head slowly toward him she added hesitatingly: "Will you forgive me for—for treating your friend—"

"No," he replied, with such stern emphasis that she shrank from him and trembled.

"You are indeed heartless," she faltered, as she turned to leave him.

"Miss Van Tyne," he said indignantly, "twice you have charged me with being heartless. Your voice and manner indicate that I would be unnatural and unworthy of respect were I what you charge. In the name of all that's rational what does this word 'heartless' mean to you? Where was your heart when you sent my friend away so wretched and humbled that he is virtually seeking the death from which you are so glad to escape?"

"I did not love him," she protested faintly.

He laughed bitterly, and continued, "Love! That's a word which I believe has no meaning for you at all, but it had for him. You are a remarkably clever woman, Miss Van Tyne. You have brains in abundance. See, I do you justice. What is more, you are beautiful and can be so fascinating that a man who believed in you might easily worship you. You made him believe in you. You tried to beguile me into a condition that with my nature would be ruin indeed. You never had the baby plea of a silly, shallow woman. I took pains to find that out the first evening we met. In your art of beguiling an honest, trusting man you were as perfect as you were remorseless, and you understood exactly what you were doing."

For a time she seemed overwhelmed by his lava-like torrent of words, and stood with bowed head and shrinking, trembling form; but when he ceased she turned to him and said bitterly and emphatically:

"I did NOT understand what I was doing, nor would my brain have taught me were I all intellect like yourself. I half wish you had left me to drown," and with a slight, despairing gesture she turned away and did not look back.

Ackland's face lighted up with a sudden flash of intelligence and deep feeling. He started to recall her, hesitated, and watched her earnestly until she disappeared; then looking out on the scowling ocean, he took off his hat and exclaimed in a deep, low tone:

"By all that's divine, can this be? Is it possible that through the suffering of her own awakening heart she is learning to know the pain she has given to others? Should this be true, the affair is taking an entirely new aspect, and Munson will be avenged as neither of us ever dreamed would be possible."

He resumed his old position and thought long and deeply, then rejoined his cousin, who was somewhat surprised to find that his bitter mood had given place to his former composure.

"How is this, Jack?" she asked. "As the storm grows wilder without, you become more serene."

"Only trying to make amends for my former bearishness," he said carelessly, but with a little rising color.

"I don't understand you at all," she continued discontentedly. "I saw you sulking in that out-of-the-way corner, and I saw Miss Van Tyne approach you hesitatingly and timidly, with the purpose, no doubt, of thanking you. Of course I did not stay to watch, but a little later I met Miss Van Tyne, and she looked white and rigid. She has not left her room since."

"You take a great interest in Miss Van Tyne. It is well you are not in my place."

"I half wish I was and had your chances. You are more pitiless than the waves from which you saved her."

"I can't help being just what I am," he said coldly. "Good-night." And he too disappeared for the rest of the evening.

The rain continued to fall in blinding torrents, and the building fairly trembled under the violence of the wind. The guests drew together in the lighted rooms, and sought by varied amusements to pass the time until the fierceness of the storm abated, few caring to retire while the uproar of the elements was so great.

At last as the storm passed away, and the late-rising moon threw a sickly gleam on the tumultuous waters, Eva looked from her window with sleepless eyes, thinking sadly and bitterly of the past and future. Suddenly a dark figure appeared on the beach in the track of the moonlight. She snatched an opera-glass, but could not recognize the solitary form. The thought would come, however, that it was Ackland; and if it were, what were his thoughts and what place had she in them? Why was he watching so near the spot that might have been their burial-place?

"At least he shall not think that I can stolidly sleep after what has occurred," she thought, and she turned up her light, opened her window, and sat down by it again. Whoever the unseasonable rambler might be, he appeared to recognize the gleam from her window, for he walked hastily down the beach and disappeared. After a time she darkened her room again and waited in vain for his return. "If it were he, he shuns even the slightest recognition," she thought despairingly; and the early dawn was not far distant when she fell into an unquiet sleep.

For the next few days Miss Van Tyne was a puzzle to all except Mrs. Alston. She was quite unlike the girl she had formerly been, and she made no effort to disguise the fact. In the place of her old exuberance of life and spirits, there was lassitude and great depression. The rich color ebbed steadily from her face, and dark lines under her eyes betokened sleepless nights. She saw the many curious glances in her direction, but apparently did not care what was thought or surmised. Were it not that her manner to Ackland was so misleading, the tendency to couple their names together would have been far more general. She neither sought nor shunned his society; in fact, she treated him as she did the other gentlemen of her acquaintance. She took him at his word. He had said he would forgive her on condition that she would not speak of what he was pleased to term that "little episode," and she never referred to it.

Her aunt was as much at fault as the others, and one day querulously complained to Mrs. Alston that she was growing anxious about Eva. "At first I thought she was disappointed over the indifference of that icy cousin of yours; but she does not appear to care a straw for him. When I mention his name she speaks of him in a natural, grateful way, then her thoughts appear to wander off to some matter that is troubling her. I can't find out whether she is ill or whether she has heard some bad news of which she will not speak. She never gave me or any one that I know of much of her confidence."

Mrs. Alston listened but made no comments. She was sure she was right in regard to Miss Van Tyne's trouble, but her cousin mystified her. Ackland had become perfectly inscrutable. As far as she could judge by any word or act of his he had simply lost his interest in Miss Van Tyne, and that was all that could be said; and yet a fine instinct tormented Mrs. Alston with the doubt that this was not true, and that the young girl was the subject of a sedulously concealed scrutiny. Was he watching for his friend or for his own sake, or was he, in a spirit of retaliation, enjoying the suffering of one who had made others suffer? His reserve was so great that she could not pierce it, and his caution baffled even her vigilance. But she waited patiently, assured that the little drama must soon pass into a more significant phase.

And she was right. Miss Van Tyne could not maintain the line of action she had resolved upon. She had thought, "I won't try to appear happy when I am not. I won't adopt the conventional mask of gayety when the heart is wounded. How often I have seen through it and smiled at the transparent farce—farce it seemed then, but I now fear it was often tragedy. At any rate there was neither dignity nor deception in it. I have done with being false, and so shall simply act myself and be a true woman. Though my heart break a thousand times, not even by a glance shall I show that it is breaking for him. If he or others surmise the truth, they may; let them. It is a part of my penance; and I will show the higher, stronger pride of one who makes no vain, useless pretence to happy indifference, but who can maintain a self-control so perfect that even Mrs. Alston shall not see one unmaidenly advance or overture."

She succeeded for a time, as we have seen, but she overrated her will and underrated her heart, that with deepening intensity craved the love denied her. With increasing frequency she said to herself, "I must go away. My only course is to hide my weakness and never see him again. He is inflexible, yet his very obduracy increases my love a hundred-fold."

At last after a lonely walk on the beach she concluded, "My guardian must take me home on Monday next. He comes to-night to spend Sunday with us, and I will make preparations to go at once."

Although her resolution did not fail her, she walked forward more and more slowly, her dejection and weariness becoming almost overpowering. As she was turning a sharp angle of rocks that jutted well down to the water she came face to face with Ackland and Mrs. Alston. She was off her guard; and her thoughts of him had been so absorbing that she felt he must be conscious of them. She flushed painfully and hurried by with slight recognition and downcast face, but she had scarcely passed them when, acting under a sudden impulse, she stopped and said in a low tone:

"Mr. Ackland—"

He turned expectantly toward her. For a moment she found it difficult to speak, then ignoring the presence of Mrs. Alston, resolutely began:

"Mr. Ackland, I must refer once more to a topic which you have in a sense forbidden. I feel partially absolved, however, for I do not think you have forgiven me anything. At any rate I must ask your pardon once more for having so needlessly and foolishly imperilled your life. I say these words now because I may not have another opportunity; we leave on Monday." With this she raised her eyes to his with an appeal for a little kindness which Mrs. Alston was confident could not be resisted. Indeed, she was sure that she saw a slight nervous tremor in Ackland's hands, as if he found it hard to control himself. Then he appeared to grow rigid. Lifting his hat, he said gravely and unresponsively:

"Miss Van Tyne, you now surely have made ample amends. Please forget the whole affair."

She turned from him at once, but not so quickly but that both he and his cousin saw the bitter tears that would come. A moment later she was hidden by the angle of the rock. As long as she was visible Ackland watched her without moving, then he slowly turned to his cousin, his face as inscrutable as ever. She walked at his side for a few moments in ill-concealed impatience, then stopped and said decisively:

"I'll go no further with you to-day. I am losing all respect for you."

Without speaking, he turned to accompany her back to the house. His reticence and coldness appeared to annoy her beyond endurance, for she soon stopped and sat down on a ledge of the rocks that jutted down the beach where they had met Miss Van Tyne.

"John, you are the most unnatural man I ever saw in my life," she began angrily.

"What reason have you for so flattering an opinion," he asked coolly.

"You have been giving reason for it every day since you came here," she resumed hotly. "I always heard it said that you had no heart; but I defended you and declared that your course toward your mother even when a boy showed that you had, and that you would prove it some day. But I now believe that you are unnaturally cold, heartless, and unfeeling. I had no objection to your wounding Miss Van Tyne's vanity and encouraged you when that alone bid fair to suffer. But when she proved she had a heart and that you had awakened it, she deserved at least kindness and consideration on your part. If you could not return her affection, you should have gone away at once; but I believe that you have stayed for the sole and cruel purpose of gloating over her suffering."

"She has not suffered more than my friend, or than I would if—"

"You indeed! The idea of your suffering from any such cause! I half believe you came here with the deliberate purpose of avenging your friend, and that you are keeping for his inspection a diary in which the poor girl's humiliation to-day will form the hateful climax."

They did not dream that the one most interested was near. Miss Van Tyne had felt too faint and sorely wounded to go further without rest. Believing that the rocks would hide her from those whose eyes she would most wish to shun, she had thrown herself down beyond the angle and was shedding the bitterest tears that she had ever known. Suddenly she heard Mrs. Alston's words but a short distance away, and was so overcome by their import that she hesitated what to do. She would not meet them again for the world, but felt so weak that she doubted whether she could drag herself away without being discovered, especially as the beach trended off to the left so sharply a little further on that they might discover her. While she was looking vainly for some way of escape she heard Ackland's words and Mrs. Alston's surmise in reply that he had come with the purpose of revenge. She was so stung by their apparent truth that she resolved to clamber up through an opening of the rocks if the thing were possible. Panting and exhausted she gained the summit, and then hastened to an adjacent grove, as some wounded, timid creature would run to the nearest cover. Ackland had heard sounds and had stepped around the point of the rocks just in time to see her disappearing above the bank. Returning to Mrs. Alston, he said impatiently:

"In view of your opinions my society can have no attractions for you.

Shall I accompany you to the hotel?"

"No," was the angry reply. "I'm in no mood to speak to you again to-day."

He merely bowed and turned as if to pursue his walk. The moment she was hidden, however, he also climbed the rocks in time to see Miss Van Tyne entering the grove. With swift and silent tread he followed her, but could not at once discover her hiding-place. At last passionate sobs made it evident that she was concealed behind a great oak a little on his left. Approaching cautiously, he heard her moan:

"Oh, this is worse than death! He makes me feel as if even God had no mercy for me. But I will expiate my wrong; I will, at the bitterest sacrifice which a woman can make."

She sprang up to meet Ackland standing with folded arms before her. She started violently and leaned against the tree for support. But the weakness was momentary, for she wiped the tears from her eyes, and then turned to him so quietly that only her extreme pallor proved that she realized the import of her words.

"Mr. Ackland," she asked, "have you Mr. Munson's address?"

It was his turn now to start, but he merely answered: "Yes."

"Do—do you think he still cares for me?"

"Undoubtedly."

"Since then you are so near a friend, will you write to him that I will try"—she turned away and would not look at him as, after a moment's hesitation, she concluded her sentence—"I will try to make him as happy as I can."

"Do you regret your course?" he asked with a slight tremor in his voice.

"I regret that I misled—that I wronged him beyond all words. I am willing to make all the amends in my power."

"Do you love him?"

She now turned wholly away and shook her head.

"And yet you would marry him?"

"Yes, if he wished it, knowing all the truth."

"Can you believe he would wish it?" he asked indignantly. "Can you believe that any man—"

"Then avenge him to your cruel soul's content," she exclaimed passionately. "Tell him that I have no heart to give to him or to any one. Through no effort or fault of mine I overheard Mrs. Alston's words and yours. I know your design against me. Assuage your friend's grief by assuring him of your entire success, of which you are already so well aware. Tell him how you triumphed over an untaught, thoughtless girl who was impelled merely by the love of power and excitement, as you are governed by ambition and a remorseless will. I did not know—I did not understand how cruel I was, although now that I do know I shall never forgive myself. But if you had the heart of a man you might have seen that you were subjecting me to torture. I did not ask or expect that you should care for me; but I had a right to hope for a little kindness, a little manly and delicate consideration, a little healing sympathy for the almost mortal wound that you have made. But I now see that you have stood by and watched like a grand inquisitor. Tell your friend that you have transformed the thoughtless girl into a suffering woman. I cannot go to Brazil. I cannot face dangers that might bring rest. I must keep my place in society—keep it too under a hundred observant and curious eyes. You have seen it all of late in this house; I was too wretched to care. It was a part of my punishment, and I accepted it. I would not be false again even in trying to conceal a secret which it is like death to a woman to reveal. I only craved one word of kindness from you. Had I received it, I would have gone away in silence and suffered in silence. But your course and what I have heard have made me reckless and despairing. You do not leave me even the poor consolation of self-sacrifice. You are my stony-hearted fate. I wish you had left me to drown. Tell your friend that I am more wretched than he ever can be, because I am a woman. Will he be satisfied?"

"He ought to be," was the low, husky reply.

"Are you proud of your triumph?"

"No, I am heartily ashamed of it; but I have kept a pledge that will probably cost me far more than it has you."

"A pledge?"

"Yes, my pledge to make you suffer as far as possible as he suffered."

She put her hand to her side as if she had received a wound, and after a moment said wearily and coldly:

"Well, tell him that you succeeded, and be content;" and she turned to leave him.

"Stay," he cried impetuously. "It is now your turn. Take your revenge."

"My revenge?" she repeated in unfeigned astonishment.

"Yes, your revenge. I have loved you from the moment I hoped you had a woman's heart, yes, and before—when I feared I might not be able to save your life. I know it now, though the very thought of it enraged me then. I have watched and waited more to be sure that you had a woman's heart than for aught else, though a false sense of honor kept me true to my pledge. After I met you on the beach I determined at once to break my odious bond and place myself at your mercy. You may refuse me in view of my course—you probably will; but every one in that house there shall know that you refused me, and your triumph shall be more complete than mine."

She looked into his face with an expression of amazement and doubt; but instead of coldness, there was now a devotion and pleading that she had never seen before.

She was too confused and astounded, however, to comprehend his words immediately, nor could the impression of his hostility pass away readily.

"You are mocking me," she faltered, scarcely knowing what she said.

"I cannot blame you that you think me capable of mocking the noble candor which has cost you so dear, as I can now understand. I cannot ask you to believe that I appreciate your heroic impulse of self-sacrifice—your purpose to atone for wrong by inflicting irreparable wrong on yourself. It is natural that you should think of me only as an instrument of revenge with no more feeling than some keen-edged weapon would have. This also is the inevitable penalty of my course. When I speak of my love I cannot complain if you smile in bitter incredulity. But I have at least proved that I have a resolute will and that I keep my word; and I again assure you that it shall be known this very night that you have refused me, that I offered you my hand, that you already had my heart, where your image is enshrined with that of my mother, and that I entreated you to be my wife. My cousin alone guessed my miserable triumph; all shall know of yours."

As he spoke with impassioned earnestness, the confusion passed from her mind. She felt the truth of his words; she knew that her ambitious dream had been fulfilled, and that she had achieved the conquest of a man upon whom all others had smiled in vain. But how immeasurably different were her emotions from those which she had once anticipated! Not her beauty, not her consummate skill in fascination had wrought this miracle, but her woman's heart, awakened at last; and it thrilled with such unspeakable joy that she turned away to hide its reflex in her face. He was misled by the act into believing that she could not forgive him, and yet was perplexed when she murmured with a return of her old piquant humor:

"You are mistaken, Mr. Ackland; it shall never be known that I refused you."

"How can you prevent it?"

"If your words are sincere, you will submit to such terms as I choose to make."

"I am sincere, and my actions shall prove it; but I shall permit no mistaken self-sacrifice on your part, nor any attempt to shield me from the punishment I well deserve."

She suddenly turned upon him a radiant face in which he read his happiness, and faltered:

"Jack, I do believe you, although the change seems wrought by some heavenly magic. But it will take a long time to pay you up. I hope to be your dear torment for a lifetime."

He caught her in such a strong, impetuous embrace that she gasped:

"I thought you were—cold to our sex."

"It's not your sex that I am clasping, but you—YOU, my Eve. Like the first man, I have won my bride under the green trees and beneath the open sky."

"Yes, Jack; and I give you my whole heart as truly as did the first woman when there was but one man in all the world. That is MY REVENGE."

This is what Will Munson wrote some weeks later:

"Well, Jack, I've had the yellow fever, and it was the most fortunate event of my life. I was staying with a charming family, and they would not permit my removal to a hospital. One of my bravest and most devoted nurses has consented to become my wife. I hope you punished that little wretch Eva Van Tyne as she deserved."

"Confound your fickle soul!" muttered Ackland. "I punished her as she did not deserve; and I risked more than life in doing so. If her heart had not been as good as gold and as kind as Heaven she never would have looked at me again."

Ackland is quite as indifferent to the sex as ever, but Eva has never complained that he was cold to her.

A CHRISTMAS-EVE SUIT

The Christmas holidays had come, and with them a welcome vacation for Hedley Marstern. Although as yet a briefless young lawyer, he had a case in hand which absorbed many of his thoughts—the conflicting claims of two young women in his native village on the Hudson. It must not be imagined that the young women were pressing their claims except as they did so unconsciously, by virtue of their sex and various charms. Nevertheless, Marstern was not the first lawyer who had clients over whom midnight oil was burned, they remaining unaware of the fact.

If not yet a constitutional attorney, he was at least constitutionally one. Falling helplessly in love with one girl simplifies matters. There are no distracting pros and cons—nothing required but a concentration of faculties to win the enslaver, and so achieve mastery. Marstern did not appear amenable to the subtle influences which blind the eyes and dethrone reason, inspiring in its place an overwhelming impulse to capture a fortuitous girl because (to a heated imagination) she surpasses all her sex. Indeed, he was level-headed enough to believe that he would never capture any such girl; but he hoped to secure one who promised to make as good a wife as he would try to be a husband, and with a fair amount of self-esteem, he was conscious of imperfections. Therefore, instead of fancying that any of his fair acquaintances were angels, he had deliberately and, as some may think, in a very cold-blooded fashion, endeavored to discover what they actually were. He had observed that a good deal of prose followed the poetry of wooing and the lunacy of the honeymoon; and he thought it might be well to criticise a little before marriage as well as after it.

There were a number of charming girls in the social circle of his native town; and he had, during later years, made himself quite impartially agreeable to them. Indeed, without much effort on his part he had become what is known as a general favorite. He had been too diligent a student to become a society man, but was ready enough in vacation periods to make the most of every country frolic, and even on great occasions to rush up from the city and return at some unearthly hour in the morning when his partners in the dance were not half through their dreams. While on these occasions he had shared in the prevailing hilarity, he nevertheless had the presentiment that some one of the laughing, light-footed girls would one day pour his coffee and send him to his office in either a good or a bad mood to grapple with the problems awaiting him there. He had in a measure decided that when he married it should be to a girl whom he had played with in childhood and whom he knew a good deal about, and not to a chance acquaintance of the world at large. So, beneath all his diversified gallantries he had maintained a quiet little policy of observation, until his thoughts had gradually gathered around two of his young associates who, unconsciously to themselves, as we have said, put in stronger and stronger claims every time he saw them. They asserted these claims in the only way in which he would have recognized them—by being more charming, agreeable, and, as he fancied, by being better than the others. He had not made them aware, even by manner, of the distinction accorded to them; and as yet he was merely a friend.

But the time had come, he believed, for definite action. While he weighed and considered, some prompter fellows might take the case out of his hands entirely; therefore he welcomed this vacation and the opportunities it afforded.

The festivities began with what is termed in the country a "large party"; and Carrie Mitchell and Lottie Waldo were both there, resplendent in new gowns made for the occasion. Marstern thought them both charming. They danced equally well and talked nonsense with much the same ease and vivacity. He could not decide which was the prettier, nor did the eyes and attentions of others afford him any aid. They were general favorites, as well as himself, although it was evident that to some they might become more, should they give encouragement. But they were apparently in the heyday of their girlhood, and thus far had preferred miscellaneous admiration to individual devotion. By the time the evening was over Marstern felt that if life consisted of large parties he might as well settle the question by the toss of a copper.

It must not be supposed that he was such a conceited prig as to imagine that such a fortuitous proceeding, or his best efforts afterward, could settle the question as it related to the girls. It would only decide his own procedure. He was like an old marauding baron, in honest doubt from which town he can carry off the richest booty—that is, in case he can capture any one of them. His overtures for capitulation might be met with the "slings and arrows of outrageous fortune" and he be sent limping off the field. Nevertheless, no man regrets that he must take the initiative, and he would be less than a man who would fear to do so. When it came to this point in the affair, Marstern shrugged his shoulders and thought, "I must take my chances like the rest." But he wished to be sure that he had attained this point, and not lay siege to one girl only to wish afterward it had been the other.

His course that evening proved that he not only had a legal cast of mind but also a judicial one. He invited both Miss Mitchell and Miss Waldo to take a sleigh-ride with him the following evening, fancying that when sandwiched between them in the cutter he could impartially note his impressions. His unsuspecting clients laughingly accepted, utterly unaware of the momentous character of the trial scene before them.

As Marstern smoked a cigar before retiring that night, he admitted to himself that it was rather a remarkable court that was about to be held. He was the only advocate for the claims of each, and finally he proposed to take a seat on the bench and judge between them. Indeed, before he slept he decided to take that august position at once, and maintain a judicial impartiality while noting his impressions.

Christmas Eve happened to be a cold, clear, star-lit night; and when Marstern drove to Miss Waldo's door, he asked himself, "Could a fellow ask for anything daintier and finer" than the red-lipped, dark-eyed girl revealed by the hall-lamp as she tripped lightly out, her anxious mamma following her with words of unheeded caution about not taking cold, and coming home early. He had not traversed the mile which intervened between the residences of the two girls before he almost wished he could continue the drive under the present auspices, and that, as in the old times, he could take toll at every bridge, and encircle his companion with his arm as they bounced over the "thank-'ee mams." The frosty air appeared to give keenness and piquancy to Miss Lottie's wit, and the chime of the bells was not merrier or more musical than her voice. But when a little later he saw blue-eyed Carrie Mitchell in her furs and hood silhouetted in the window, his old dilemma became as perplexing as ever. Nevertheless, it was the most delightful uncertainty that he had ever experienced; and he had a presentiment that he had better make the most of it, since it could not last much longer. Meanwhile, he was hedged about with blessings clearly not in disguise, and he gave utterance to this truth as they drove away.

"Surely there never was so lucky a fellow. Here I am kept warm and happy by the two finest girls in town."

"Yes," said Lottie; "and it's a shame you can't sit on both sides of us."

"I assure you I wish it were possible. It would double my pleasure."

"I'm very well content," remarked Carrie, quietly, "as long as I can keep on the right side of people—"

"Well, you are not on the right side to-night," interrupted Lottie.

"Good gracious!" thought Marstern, "she's next to my heart. I wonder if that will give her unfair advantage;" but Carrie explained:

"Of course I was speaking metaphorically."

"In that aspect of the case it would be a shame to me if any side I have is not right toward those who have so honored me," he hastened to say.

"Oh, Carrie has all the advantage—she is next to your heart."

"Would you like to exchange places?" was the query flashed back by Carrie.
"Oh, no, I'm quite as content as you are."

"Why, then, since I am more than content—exultant, indeed—it appears that we all start from excellent premises to reach a happy conclusion of our Christmas Eve," cried Marstern.

"Now you are talking shop, Mr. Lawyer—Premises and Conclusions, indeed!" said Lottie; "since you are such a happy sandwich, you must be a tongue sandwich, and be very entertaining."

He did his best, the two girls seconding his efforts so genially that he found himself, after driving five miles, psychologically just where he was physically—between them, as near to one in his thoughts and preferences as to the other.

"Let us take the river road home," suggested Lottie.

"As long as you agree," he answered, "you both are sovereign potentates. If you should express conflicting wishes, I should have to stop here in the road till one abdicated in favor of the other, or we all froze."

"But you, sitting so snugly between us, would not freeze," said Lottie. "If we were obstinate we should have to assume our pleasantest expressions, and then you could eventually take us home as bits of sculpture. In fact, I'm getting cold already."

"Are you also, Miss Carrie?"

"Oh, I'll thaw out before summer. Don't mind me."

"Well, then, mind me," resumed Lottie. "See how white and smooth the river looks. Why can't we drive home on the ice? It will save miles—I mean it looks so inviting."

"Oh, dear!" cried Carrie, "I feel like protesting now. The longest way round may be both the shortest and safest way home."

"You ladies shall decide. This morning I drove over the route we would take to-night, and I should not fear to take a ton of coal over it."

"A comparison suggesting warmth and a grate-fire. I vote for the river," said Lottie, promptly.

"Oh, well, Mr. Marstern, if you've been over the ice so recently—I only wish to feel reasonably safe."

"I declare!" thought Marstern, "Lottie is the braver and more brilliant girl; and the fact that she is not inclined to forego the comfort of the home-fire for the pleasure of my company, reveals the difficulty of, and therefore incentive to, the suit I may decide to enter upon before New Year's."

Meanwhile, his heart on Carrie's side began to grow warm and alert, as if recognizing an affinity to some object not far off. Granting that she had not been so brilliant as Lottie, she had been eminently companionable in a more quiet way. If there had not been such bursts of enthusiasm at the beginning of the drive, her enjoyment appeared to have more staying powers. He liked her none the less that her eyes were often turned toward the stars or the dark silhouettes of the leafless trees against the snow. She did not keep saying, "Ah, how lovely! What a fine bit that is!" but he had only to follow her eyes to see something worth looking at.

"A proof that Miss Carrie also is not so preoccupied with the pleasure of my company that she has no thoughts for other things," cogitated Marstern. "It's rather in her favor that she prefers Nature to a grate fire. They're about even yet."

Meanwhile the horse was speeding along on the white, hard expanse of the river, skirting the west shore. They now had only about a mile to drive before striking land again; and the scene was so beautiful with the great dim outlines of the mountains before them that both the girls suggested that they should go leisurely for a time.

"We shouldn't hastily and carelessly pass such a picture as that, any more than one would if a fine copy of it were hung in a gallery," said Carrie. "The stars are so brilliant along the brow of that highland yonder that they form a dia—oh, oh! what IS the matter?" and she clung to Marstern's arm.

The horse was breaking through the ice.

"Whoa!" said Marstern, firmly. Even as he spoke, Lottie was out of the sleigh and running back on the ice, crying and wringing her hands.

"We shall be drowned," she almost screamed hysterically.

"Mr. Marstern, what SHALL we do? Can't we turn around and go back the way we came?"

"Miss Carrie, will you do what I ask? Will you believe me when I say that I do not think you are in any danger?"

"Yes, I'll do my best," she replied, catching her breath. She grew calm rapidly as he tried to reassure Lottie, telling her that water from the rising of the tide had overflowed the main ice and that thin ice had formed over it, also that the river at the most was only two or three feet deep at that point. But all was of no avail; Lottie stood out upon the ice in a panic, declaring that he never should have brought them into such danger, and that he must turn around at once and go back as they came.

"But, Miss Waldo, the tide is rising, and we may find wet places returning. Besides, it would bring us home very late. Now, Miss Carrie and I will drive slowly across this place and then return for you. After we have been across it twice you surely won't fear."

"I won't be left alone; suppose you two should break through and disappear, what would become of ME?"

"You would be better off than we," he replied, laughing.

"I think it's horrid of you to laugh. Oh, I'm so cold and frightened! I feel as if the ice were giving way under my feet."

"Why, Miss Lottie, we just drove over that spot where you stand. Here,
Miss Carrie shall stay with you while I drive back and forth alone."
"Then if you were drowned we'd both be left alone to freeze to death."

"I pledge you my word you shall be by that grate-fire within less than an hour if you will trust me five minutes."

"Oh, well, if you will risk your life and ours too; but Carrie must stay with me."

"Will YOU trust me, Miss Carrie, and help me out of this scrape?"

Carrie was recovering from her panic, and replied, "I have given you my promise."

He was out of the sleigh instantly, and the thin ice broke with him also. "I must carry you a short distance," he said. "I cannot allow you to get your feet wet. Put one arm around my neck, so; now please obey as you promised."

She did so without a word, and he bore her beyond the water, inwardly exulting and blessing that thin ice. His decision was coming with the passing seconds; indeed, it had come. Returning to the sleigh he drove slowly forward, his horse making a terrible crunching and splashing, Lottie meanwhile keeping up a staccato accompaniment of little shrieks.

"Ah, my charming creature," he thought, "with you it was only, 'What will become of ME?' I might not have found out until it was too late the relative importance of 'me' in the universe had we not struck this bad crossing; and one comes to plenty of bad places to cross in a lifetime."

The area of thin ice was not very narrow, and he was becoming but a dim and shadowy outline to the girls. Lottie was now screaming for his return. Having crossed the overflowed space and absolutely assured himself that there was no danger, he returned more rapidly and found Carrie trying to calm her companion.

"Oh," sobbed Lottie, "my feet are wet and almost frozen. The ice underneath may have borne you, but it won't bear all three of us. Oh, dear, I wish I hadn't—I wish I was home; and I feel as if I'd never get there."

"Miss Lottie, I assure you that the ice will hold a ton, but I'll tell you what I'll do. I shall put you in the sleigh, and Miss Carrie will drive you over. You two together do not weigh much more than I do. I'll walk just behind you with my hands on the back of the sleigh, and if I see the slightest danger I'll lift you out of the sleigh first and carry you to safety."

This proposition promised so well that she hesitated, and he lifted her in instantly before she could change her mind, then helped Carrie in with a quiet pressure of the hand, as much as to say, "I shall depend on you."

"But, Mr. Marstern, you'll get your feet wet," protested Carrie.

"That doesn't matter," he replied good-naturedly. "I shall be no worse off than Miss Lottie, and I'm determined to convince her of safety. Now go straight ahead as I direct."

Once the horse stumbled, and Lottie thought he was going down head first. "Oh, lift me out, quick, quick!" she cried.

"Yes, indeed I will, Miss Lottie, as soon as we are opposite that grate fire of yours."

They were soon safely over, and within a half-hour reached Lottie's home. It was evident she was a little ashamed of her behavior, and she made some effort to retrieve herself. But she was cold and miserable, vexed with herself and still more vexed with Marstern. That a latent sense of justice forbade the latter feeling only irritated her the more. Individuals as well as communities must have scapegoats; and it is not an unusual impulse on the part of some to blame and dislike those before whom they have humiliated themselves.

She gave her companions a rather formal invitation to come in and get warm before proceeding further; but Marstern said very politely that he thought it was too late, unless Miss Carrie was cold. Carrie protested that she was not so cold but that she could easily wait till she reached her own fireside.

"Well, good-night, then," and the door was shut a trifle emphatically.

"Mr. Marstern," said Carrie, sympathetically, "your feet must be very cold and wet after splashing through all that ice-water."

"They are," he replied; "but I don't mind it. Well, if I had tried for years I could not have found such a test of character as we had to-night."

"What do you mean?"

"Oh, well, you two girls did not behave exactly alike. I liked the way you behaved. You helped me out of a confounded scrape."

"Would you have tried for years to find a test?" she asked, concealing the keenness of her query under a laugh.

"I should have been well rewarded if I had, by such a fine contrast," he replied.

Carrie's faculties had not so congealed but that his words set her thinking. She had entertained at times the impression that she and Lottie were his favorites. Had he taken them out that night together in the hope of contrasts, of finding tests that would help his halting decision? He had ventured where the intuitions of a girl like Carrie Mitchell were almost equal to second-sight; and she was alert for what would come next.

He accepted her invitation to come in and warm his feet at the glowing fire in the grate, which Carrie's father had made before retiring. Mrs. Mitchell, feeling that her daughter was with an old friend and playmate, did not think the presence of a chaperon essential, and left the young people alone. Carrie bustled about, brought cake, and made hot lemonade, while Marstern stretched his feet to the grate with a luxurious sense of comfort and complacency, thinking how homelike it all was and how paradisiacal life would become if such a charming little Hebe presided over his home. His lemonade became nectar offered by such hands.

She saw the different expression in his eyes. It was now homage, decided preference for one and not mere gallantry to two. Outwardly she was demurely oblivious and maintained simply her wonted friendliness. Marstern, however, was thawing in more senses than one, and he was possessed by a strong impulse to begin an open siege at once.

"I haven't had a single suit of any kind yet, Carrie," he said, dropping the prefix of "Miss," which had gradually been adopted as they had grown up.

"Oh, well, that was the position of all the great lawyers once," she replied, laughing. Marstern's father was wealthy, and all knew that he could afford to be briefless for a time.

"I may never be great; but I shall work as hard as any of them," he continued. "To tell you the honest truth, however, this would be the happiest Christmas Eve of my life if I had a downright suit on my hands. Why can't I be frank with you and say I'd like to begin the chief suit of my life now and here—a suit for this little hand? I'd plead for it as no lawyer ever pleaded before. I settled that much down on the ice."

"And if I hadn't happened to behave on the ice in a manner agreeable to your lordship, you would have pleaded with the other girl?" she remarked, withdrawing her hand and looking him directly in the eyes.

"What makes you think so?" he asked somewhat confusedly.

"You do."

He sprang up and paced the room a few moments, then confronted her with the words, "You shall have the whole truth. Any woman that I would ask to be my wife is entitled to that," and he told her just what the attitude of his mind had been from the first.

She laughed outright, then gave him her hand as she said, "Your honesty insures that we can be very good friends; but I don't wish to hear anything more about suits which are close of kin to lawsuits."

He looked very dejected, feeling that he had blundered fatally in his precipitation.

"Come now, Hedley, be sensible," she resumed, half laughing, half serious. "As you say, we can be frank with each other. Why, only the other day we were boy and girl together coasting downhill on the same sled. You are applying your legal jargon to a deep experience, to something sacred—the result, to my mind, of a divine instinct. Neither you nor I have ever felt for each other this instinctive preference, this subtle gravitation of the heart. Don't you see? Your head has been concerned about me, and only your head. By a kindred process you would select one bale of merchandise in preference to another. Good gracious! I've faults enough. You'll meet some other girl that will stand some other test far better than I. I want a little of what you call silly romance in my courtship. See; I can talk about this suit as coolly and fluently as you can. We'd make a nice pair of lovers, about as frigid as the ice-water you waded through so good-naturedly;" and the girl's laugh rang out merrily, awakening echoes in the old house. Mr. and Mrs. Mitchell might rest securely when their daughter could laugh like that. It was the mirth of a genuine American girl whose self-protection was better than the care of a thousand duennas.

He looked at her with honest admiration in his eyes, then rose quietly and said, "That's fine, Carrie. Your head's worth two of mine, and you'd make the better lawyer. You see through a case from top to bottom. You were right—I wasn't in love with you; I don't know whether I'm in love with you now, and you haven't an infinitesimal spark for me. Nevertheless, I begin my suit here and now, and I shall never withdraw it till you are engaged to another fellow. So there!"

Carrie looked rather blank at this result of her reductio ad absurdum process; and he did not help her by adding, "A fellow isn't always in love. There must be a beginning; and when I arrive at this beginning under the guidance of reason, judgment, and observation, I don't see as I'm any more absurd than the fellow who tumbles helplessly in love, he doesn't know why. What becomes of all these people who have divine gravitations? You and I both know of some who had satanic repulsions afterward. They used their eyes and critical faculties after marriage instead of before. The romance exhaled like a morning mist; and the facts came out distinctly. They learned what kind of man and woman they actually were, and two idealized creatures were sent to limbo. Because I don't blunder upon the woman I wish to marry, but pick her out, that's no reason I can't and won't love her. Your analysis and judgment were correct only up to date. You have now to meet a suit honestly, openly announced. This may be bad policy on my part; yet I have so much faith in you and respect for you that I don't believe you will let my precipitation create a prejudice. Give me a fair hearing; that's all I ask."

"Well, well, I'll promise not to frown, even though some finer paragon should throw me completely in the shade."

"You don't believe in my yet," he resumed, after a moment of thought. "I felt that I had blundered awfully a while ago; but I doubt it. A girl of your perceptions would soon have seen it all. I've not lost anything by being frank from the start. Be just to me, however. It wasn't policy that led me to speak, but this homelike scene, and you appearing like the good genius of a home."

He pulled out his watch, and gave a low whistle as he held it toward her. Then his manner suddenly became grave and gentle. "Carrie," he said, "I wish you, not a merry Christmas, but a happy one, and many of them. It seems to me it would be a great privilege for a man to make a woman like you happy."

"Is this the beginning of the suit?" she asked with a laugh that was a little forced.

"I don't know. Perhaps it is; but I spoke just as I felt. Good-night."

She would not admit of a trace of sentiment on her part. "Good-night," she said. "Merry Christmas! Go home and hang up your stocking."

"Bless me!" she thought, as she went slowly up the stairs, "I thought I was going to be through with him for good and all, except as a friend; but if he goes on this way—"

The next morning a basket of superb roses was left at her home. There was no card, and mamma queried and surmised; but the girl knew. They were not displeasing to her, and somehow, before the day was over, they found their way to her room; but she shook her head decidedly as she said, "He must be careful not to send me other gifts, for I will return them instantly. Flowers, in moderation, never commit a girl."

But then came another gift—a book with pencillings here and there, not against sentimental passages, but words that made her think. It was his manner in society, however, that at once annoyed, perplexed, and pleased her. On the first occasion they met in company with others, he made it clear to every one that he was her suitor; yet he was not a burr which she could not shake off. He rather seconded all her efforts to have a good time with any and every one she chose. Nor did he, wallflower fashion, mope in the meanwhile and look unutterable things. He added to the pleasure of a score of others, and even conciliated Lottie, yet at the same time surrounded the girl of his choice with an atmosphere of unobtrusive devotion. She was congratulated on her conquest—rather maliciously so by Lottie. Her air of courteous indifference was well maintained; yet she was a woman, and could not help being flattered. Certain generous traits in her nature were touched also by a homage which yielded everything and exacted nothing.

The holidays soon passed, and he returned to his work. She learned incidentally that he toiled faithfully, instead of mooning around. At every coigne of vantage she found him, or some token of his ceaseless effort. She was compelled to think of him, and to think well of him. Though mamma and papa judiciously said little, it was evident that they liked the style of lover into which he was developing.

Once during the summer she said: "I don't think it's right to let you go on in this way any longer."

"Are my attentions so very annoying?"

"No, indeed. A girl never had a more agreeable or useful friend."

"Are you engaged to some other fellow?"

"Of course not. You know better."

"There is no 'of course not' about it. I couldn't and wouldn't lay a straw in the way. You are not bound, but I."

"You bound?"

"Certainly. You remember what I said."

"Then I must accept the first man that asks me—"

"I ask you."

"No; some one else, so as to unloose your conscience and give you a happy deliverance."

"You would leave me still bound and hopeless in that case. I love you now, Carrie Mitchell."

"Oh, dear! you are incorrigible. It's just a lawyer's persistence in winning a suit."

"You can still swear on the dictionary that you don't love me at all?"

"I might—on the dictionary. There, I won't talk about such things any more," and she resolutely changed the subject.

But she couldn't swear, even on the dictionary. She didn't know where she stood or how it would all end; but with increasing frequency the words, "I love you now," haunted her waking and dreaming hours.

The holidays were near again, and then came a letter from Marstern, asking her to take another sleigh-ride with him on Christmas Eve. His concluding words were: "There is no other woman in the world that I want on the other side of me." She kissed these words, then looked around in a startled, shamefaced manner, blushing even in the solitude of her room.

Christmas Eve came, but with it a wild storm of wind and sleet. She was surprised at the depth of her disappointment. Would he even come to call through such a tempest?

He did come, and come early; and she said demurely: "I did not expect you on such a night as this."

He looked at her for a moment, half humorously, half seriously, and her eyes drooped before his. "You will know better what to expect next time," was his comment.

"When is next time?"

"Any and every time which gives me a chance to see you. Who should know that better than you?"

"Are you never going to give up?" she asked with averted face.

"Not till you become engaged."

"Hush! They are all in the parlor."

"Well, they ought to know as much, by this time, also."

She thought it was astonishing how he made himself at home in the family circle. In half an hour there was scarcely any restraint left because a visitor was present. Yet, as if impelled by some mysterious influence, one after another slipped out; and Carrie saw with strange little thrills of dismay that she would soon be alone with that indomitable lawyer. She signalled to her mother, but the old lady's eyes were glued to her knitting.

At last they were alone, and she expected a prompt and powerful appeal from the plaintiff; but Marstern drew his chair to the opposite side of the hearth and chatted so easily, naturally, and kindly that her trepidation passed utterly. It began to grow late, and a heavier gust than usual shook the house. It appeared to waken him to the dire necessity of breasting the gale, and he rose and said:

"I feel as if I could sit here forever, Carrie. It's just the impression I had a year ago to-night. You, sitting there by the fire, gave then, and give now to this place the irresistible charm of home. I think I had then the decided beginning of the divine gravitation— wasn't that what you called it?—which has been growing so strong ever since. You thought then that the ice-water I waded was in my veins. Do you think so now? If you do I shall have to take another year to prove the contrary. Neither am I convinced of the absurdity of my course, as you put it then. I studied you coolly and deliberately before I began to love you, and reason and judgment have had no chance to jeer at my love."

"But, Hedley," she began with a slight tremor in her tones, "you are idealizing me as certainly as the blindest. I've plenty of faults."

"I haven't denied that; so have I plenty of faults. What right have I to demand a perfection I can't offer? I have known people to marry who imagined each other perfect, and then come to court for a separation on the ground of incompatibility of temperament. They learned the meaning of that long word too late, and were scarcely longer about it than the word itself. Now, I'm satisfied that I could cordially agree with you on some points and lovingly disagree with you on others. Chief of all it's your instinct to make a home. You appear better at your own fireside than when in full dress at a reception. You—"

"See here, Hedley, you've got to give up this suit at last. I'm engaged," and she looked away as if she could not meet his eyes.

"Engaged?" he said slowly, looking at her with startled eyes.

"Well, about the same as engaged. My heart has certainly gone from me beyond recall." He drew a long breath. "I was foolish enough to begin to hope," he faltered.

"You must dismiss hope to-night, then," she said, her face still averted.

He was silent and she slowly turned toward him. He had sunk into a chair and buried his face in his hands, the picture of dejected defeat.

There was a sudden flash of mirth through tear-gemmed eyes, a glance at the clock, then noiseless steps, and she was on her knees beside him, her arm about his neck, her blushing face near his wondering eyes as she breathed:

"Happy Christmas, Hedley! How do you like your first gift; and what room is there now for hope?"

THREE THANKSGIVING KISSES

It was the day before Thanksgiving. The brief cloudy November afternoon was fast merging into early twilight. The trees, now gaunt and bare, creaked and groaned in the passing gale, clashing their icy branches together with sounds sadly unlike the slumberous rustle of their foliage in June. And that same foliage was now flying before the wind, swept hither and thither, like exiles driven by disaster from the moorings of home, at times finding a brief abiding-place, and then carried forward to parts unknown by circumstances beyond control. The street leading into the village was almost deserted; and the few who came and went hastened on with fluttering garments, head bent down, and a shivering sense of discomfort. The fields were bare and brown; and the landscape on the uplands rising in the distance would have been utterly sombre had not green fields of grain, like childlike faith in wintry age, relieved the gloomy outlook and prophesied of the sunshine and golden harvest of a new year and life.

But bleak November found no admittance in Mrs. Alford's cosey parlor. Though, as usual, it was kept as the room for state occasions, it was not a stately room. It was furnished with elegance and good taste; but what was better, the genial home atmosphere from the rest of the house had invaded it, and one did not feel, on entering it from the free-and-easy sitting-room, as if passing from a sunny climate to the icebergs of the Pole. Therefore I am sure my reader will follow me gladly out of the biting, boisterous wind into the homelike apartment, and as we stand in fancy before the glowing grate, we will make the acquaintance of the May-day creature who is its sole occupant.

Elsie Alford, just turning seventeen, appeared younger than her years warranted. Some girls carry the child far into their teens, and Head the mirthful innocence of infancy with the richer, fuller life of budding womanhood. This was true of Elsie. Hers was not the forced exotic bloom of fashionable life; but rather one of the native blossoms of her New England home, having all the delicacy and at the same time hardiness of the windflower. She was also as shy and easily agitated, and yet, like the flower she resembled, well rooted among the rocks of principle and truth. She was the youngest and the pet of the household, and yet the "petting" was not of that kind that develops selfishness and wilfulness, but rather a genial sunlight of love falling upon her as a focus from the entire family. They always spoke of her as "little Sis," or the "child." And a child it seemed she would ever be, with her kittenish ways, quick impulses, and swiftly alternating moods. As she developed into womanly proportions, her grave, businesslike father began to have misgivings. After one of her wild sallies at the table, where she kept every one on the qui vive by her unrestrained chatter, Mr. Alford said:

"Elsie, will you ever learn to be a woman?"

Looking mischievously at him through her curls, she replied, "Yes; I might if I became as old as Mrs. Methuselah."

They finally concluded to leave Elsie's cure to care and trouble—two certain elements of earthly life; and yet her experience of either would be slight indeed, could their love shield her.

But it would not be exactly care or trouble that would sober Elsie into a thoughtful woman, as our story will show.

Some of the November wind seemed in her curling hair upon this fateful day; but her fresh young April face was a pleasant contrast to the scene presented from the window, to which she kept flitting with increasing frequency. It certainly was not the dismal and darkening landscape that so intensely interested her. The light of a great and coming pleasure was in her face, and her manner was one of restless, eager expectancy. Little wonder. Her pet brother, the one next older than herself, a promising young theologue, was coming home to spend Thanksgiving. It was time he appeared. The shriek of the locomotive had announced the arrival of the train; and her ardent little spirit could scarcely endure the moments intervening before she would almost concentrate herself into a rapturous kiss and embrace of welcome, for the favorite brother had been absent several long months.

Her mother called her away for a few moments, for the good old lady was busy indeed, knowing well that merely full hearts would not answer for a New England Thanksgiving. But the moment Elsie was free she darted back to the window, just in time to catch a glimpse, as she supposed, of her brother's well-remembered dark-gray overcoat, as he was ascending the front steps.

A tall, grave-looking young man, an utter stranger to the place and family, had his hand upon the doorbell; but before he could ring it, the door flew open, and a lovely young creature precipitated herself on his neck, like a missile fired from heavenly battlements, and a kiss was pressed upon his lips that he afterward admitted to have felt even to the "toes of his boots."

But his startled manner caused her to lift her face from under his side-whiskers; and though the dusk was deepening, she could see that her arms were around an utter stranger. She recoiled from him with a bound, and trembling like a windflower indeed, her large blue eyes dilating at the intruder with a dismay beyond words. How the awkward scene would have ended it were hard to tell had not the hearty voice of one coming up the path called out:

"Hi, there, you witch! who is that you are kissing, and then standing off to see the effect?"

There was no mistake this time; so, impelled by love, shame, and fear of "that horrid man," she fled, half sobbing, to his arms.

"No, he isn't a 'horrid man,' either," whispered her brother, laughing. "He is a classmate of mine. Why, Stanhope, how are you? I did not know that you and my sister were so well acquainted," he added, half banteringly and half curiously, for as yet he did not fully understand the scene.

The hall-lamp, shining through the open door, had revealed the features of the young man (whom we must now call Mr. Stanhope), so that his classmate had recognized him. His first impulse had been to slip away in the darkness, and so escape from his awkward predicament; but George Alford's prompt address prevented this and brought him to bay. He was painfully embarrassed, but managed to stammer: "I was taken for you, I think. I never had the pleasure—honor of meeting your sister."

"Oh, ho! I see now. My wild little sister kissed before she looked. Well, that was your good-fortune. I could keep two Thanksgiving days on the strength of such a kiss as that," cried the light-hearted student, shaking the diffident, shrinking Mr. Stanhope warmly by the hand. "You will hardly need a formal introduction now. But, bless me, where is she? Has the November wind blown her away?"

"I think your sist—the lady passed around to the side entrance. I fear
I have annoyed her sadly."
"Nonsense! A good joke—something to tease the little witch about. But come in. I'm forgetting the sacred rites."

And before the bewildered Mr. Stanhope could help himself, he was half dragged into the lighted hall, and the door shut between him and escape.

In the meantime, Elsie, like a whirlwind, had burst into the kitchen, where Mrs. Alford was superintending some savory dishes.

"Oh, mother, George has come and has a horrid man with him, who nearly devoured me."

And, with this rather feminine mode of stating the case, she darted into the dusky, fire-lighted parlor, from whence, unseen, she could reconnoitre the hall. Mr. Stanhope was just saying:

"Please let me go. I have stood between you and your welcome long enough. I shall only be an intruder; and besides, as an utter stranger, I have no right to stay." To all of which Elsie devoutly whispered to herself, "Amen."

But Mrs. Alford now appeared, and after a warm, motherly greeting to her son, turned in genial courtesy to welcome his friend, as she supposed.

George was so happy that he wished every one else to be the same. The comical episode attending Mr. Stanhope's unexpected appearance just hit his frolicsome mood, and promised to be a source of endless merriment if he could only keep his classmate over the coming holiday. Moreover, he long had wished to become better acquainted with this young man, whose manner at the seminary had deeply interested him. So he said:

"Mother, this is Mr. Stanhope, a classmate of mine. I wish you would help me persuade him to stay."

"Why, certainly, I supposed you expected to stay with us, of course," said Mrs. Alford, heartily.

Mr. Stanhope looked ready to sink through the floor, his face crimson with vexation.

"I do assure you, madam," he urged, "it is all a mistake. I am not an invited guest. I was merely calling on a little matter of business, when—" and there he stopped. George exploded into a hearty, uncontrollable laugh; while Elsie, in the darkness, shook her little fist at the stranger, who hastened to add, "Please let me bid you good-evening, I have not the slightest claim on your hospitality."

"Where are you staying?" asked Mrs. Alford, a little mystified. "We would like you to spend at least part of the time with us."

"I do not expect to be here very long. I have a room at the hotel."

"Now, look here, Stanhope," cried George, barring all egress by planting his back against the door, "do you take me, a half-fledged theologue, for a heathen? Do you suppose that I could be such a churl as to let a classmate stay at our dingy, forlorn little tavern and eat hash on Thanksgiving Day? I could never look you in the face at recitation again. Have some consideration for my peace of mind, and I am sure you will find our home quite as endurable as anything Mr. Starks can provide."

"Oh! as to that, from even the slight glimpse that I have had, this seems more like a home than anything I have known for many years; but I cannot feel it right that I, an unexpected stranger—"

"Come, come! No more of that! You know what is written about 'entertaining strangers;' so that is your strongest claim. Moreover, that text works both ways sometimes, and the stranger angel finds himself among angels. My old mother here, if she does weigh well on toward two hundred, is more like one than anything I have yet seen, and Elsie, if not an angel, is at least part witch and part fairy. But you need not fear ghostly entertainment from mother's larder. As you are a Christian, and not a Pagan, no more of this reluctance. Indeed, nolens volens, I shall not permit you to go out into this November storm to-night;" and Elsie, to her dismay, saw the new-comer led up to the "spare room" with a sort of hospitable violence.

With flaming cheeks and eyes half full of indignant tears, she now made onslaught on her mother, who had returned to the kitchen, where she was making preparations for a supper that might almost answer for the dinner the next day.

"Mother, mother," she exclaimed, "how could you keep that disagreeable stranger! He will spoil our Thanksgiving."

"Why, child, what is the matter?" said Mrs. Alford, raising her eyes in surprise to her daughter's face, that looked like a red moon through the mist of savory vapors rising from the ample cooking-stove. "I don't understand you. Why should not your brother's classmate add to the pleasure of our Thanksgiving?"

"Well, perhaps if we had expected him, if he had come in some other way, and we knew more about him—"

"Bless you, child, what a formalist you have become. You stand on a fine point of etiquette, as if it were the broad foundation of hospitality; while only last week you wanted a ragged tramp, who had every appearance of being a thief, to stay all night.

Your brother thinks it a special providence that his friend should have turned up so unexpectedly."

"Oh, dear!" sighed Elsie. "If that is what the doctrine of special providence means, I shall need a new confession of faith." Then, a sudden thought occurring to her, she vanished, while her mother smiled, saying:

"What a queer child she is, to be sure!"

A moment later Elsie gave a sharp knock at the spare room door, and in a second was in the further end of the dark hall. George put his head out.

"Come here," she whispered. "Are you sure it's you?" she added, holding him off at arm's-length.

His response was such a tempest of kisses and embraces that in her nervous state she was quite panic-stricken.

"George," she gasped, "have mercy on me!"

"I only wished to show you how he felt, so you would have some sympathy for him."

"If you don't stop," said the almost desperate girl, "I will shut myself up and not appear till he is gone. I will any way, if you don't make me a solemn promise."

"Leave out the 'solemn.'"

"No, I won't. Upon your word and honor, promise never to tell what has happened—my mistake, I mean."

"Oh, Elsie, it's too good to keep," laughed George.

"Now, George, if you tell," sobbed Elsie, "you'll spoil my holiday, your visit, and everything."

"If you feel that way, you foolish child, of course I won't tell. Indeed, I suppose I should not, for Stanhope seems half frightened out of his wits also."

"Serves him right, though I doubt whether he has many to lose," said Elsie, spitefully.

"Well, I will do my best to keep in," said George, soothingly, and stroking her curls. "But you will let it all out; you see. The idea of your keeping anything with your April face!"

Elsie acted upon the hint, and went to her room in order to remove all traces of agitation before the supper-bell should summon her to meet the dreaded stranger.

In the meantime, Mr. Alford and James, the second son, had come up from the village, where they had a thriving business. They greeted George's friend so cordially that it went some way toward putting the diffident youth at his ease; but he dreaded meeting Elsie again quite as much as she dreaded meeting him.

"Who is this Mr. Stanhope?" his parents asked, as they drew George aside for a little private talk after his long absence.

"Well, he is a classmate with whom I have long wished to get better acquainted; but he is so shy and retiring that I have made little progress. He came from another seminary, and entered our class in this the middle year. No one seems to know much about him; and indeed he has shunned all intimacies and devotes himself wholly to his books. The recitation-room is the one place where he appears well—for there he speaks out, as if forgetting himself, or rather, losing himself in some truth under contemplation. Sometimes he will ask a question that wakes up both class and professor; but at other times it seems difficult to pierce the shell of his reserve or diffidence. And yet, from little things I have seen, I know that he has a good warm heart; and the working of his mind in the recitation-room fascinates me. Further than this I know little about him, but have just learned, from his explanation as to his unexpected appearance at our door, that he is very poor, and purposed to spend his holiday vacation as agent for a new magazine that is offering liberal premiums. I think his poverty is one of the reasons why he has so shrunk from companionship with the other students. He thinks he ought to go out and continue his efforts tonight."

"This stormy night!" ejaculated kind Mrs. Alford. "It would be barbarous."

"Certainly it would, mother. We must not let him. But you must all be considerate, for he seems excessively diffident and sensitive; and besides—but no matter."

"No fear but that we will soon make him at home. And it's a pleasure to entertain people who are not surfeited with attention. I don't understand Elsie, however, for she seems to have formed a violent prejudice against him. From the nature of her announcement of his presence I gathered that he was a rather forward young man."

There was a twinkle in George's eye; but he merely said:

"Elsie is full of moods and tenses; but her kind little heart is always the same, and that will bring her around all right."

They were soon after marshalled to the supper-room. Elsie slipped in among the others, but was so stately and demure, and with her curls brushed down so straight that you would scarcely have known her. Her father caught his pet around the waist, and was about to introduce her, when George hastened to say with the solemnity of an undertaker that Elsie and Mr. Stanhope had met before.

Elsie repented the promise she had wrung from her brother, for any amount of badinage would be better than this depressing formality. She took her seat, not daring to look at the obnoxious guest; and the family noticed with surprise that they had never seen the little maiden so quenched and abashed before. But George good-naturedly tried to make the conversation general, so as to give them time to recover themselves.

Elsie soon ventured to steal shy looks at Mr. Stanhope, and with her usual quickness discovered that he was more in terror of her than she of him, and she exulted in the fact.

"I'll punish him well, if I get a chance," she thought with a certain phase of the feminine sense of justice. But the sadness of his face quite disarmed her when her mother, in well-meant kindness, asked:

"Where is your home located, Mr. Stanhope?"

"In the seminary," he answered in rather a low tone.

"You don't mean to say that you have no better one than a forlorn cell in Dogma Hall?" exclaimed George, earnestly.

Mr. Stanhope crimsoned, and then grew pale, but tried to say lightly,
"An orphan of my size and years is not a very moving object of
sympathy; but one might well find it difficult not to break the Tenth
Commandment while seeing how you are surrounded."
Elsie was vexed at her disposition to relent toward him; she so hardened her face,
however, that James rallied her:

"Why, Puss, what is the matter? Yours is the most unpromising
Thanksgiving phiz I have seen today. 'Count your marcies.'"
Elsie blushed so violently, and Mr. Stanhope looked so distressed that James finished
his supper in puzzled silence, thinking, however, "What has come over the little witch?

For a wonder, she seems to have met a man that she is afraid of: but the joke is, he seems even more afraid of her."

In the social parlor some of the stiffness wore off; but Elsie and Mr. Stanhope kept on opposite sides of the room and had very little to say to each other. Motherly Mrs. Alford drew the young man out sufficiently, however, to become deeply interested in him.

By the next morning time for thought had led him to feel that he must trespass on their hospitality no longer. Moreover, he plainly recognized that his presence was an oppression and restraint upon Elsie; and he was very sorry that he had stayed at all. But when he made known his purpose the family would not listen to it.

"I should feel dreadfully hurt if you left us now," said Mrs. Alford, so decidedly that he was in a dilemma, and stole a timid look toward Elsie, who at once guessed his motive in going away. Her kind heart got the better of her; and her face relented in a sudden reassuring smile. Then she turned hastily away. Only George saw and understood the little side scene and the reason Mr. Stanhope was induced to remain. Then Elsie, in her quickly varying moods, was vexed at herself, and became more cold and distant than ever. "He will regard me as only a pert, forward miss, but I will teach him better," she thought; and she astonished the family more and more by a stateliness utterly unlike herself. Mr. Stanhope sincerely regretted that he had not broken away, in spite of the others; but in order not to seem vacillating he resolved to stay till the following morning, even though he departed burdened with the thought that he had spoiled the day for one of the family. Things had now gone so far that leaving might only lead to explanations and more general annoyances, for George had intimated that the little mistake of the previous evening should remain a secret.

And yet he sincerely wished she would relent toward him, for she could not make her sweet little face repellent. The kiss she had given him still seemed to tingle in his very soul, while her last smile was like a ray of warmest sunshine. But her face, never designed to be severe, was averted.

After having heard the affairs of the nation discussed in a sound, scriptural manner, they all sat down to a dinner such as had never blessed poor Mr. Stanhope's vision before. A married son and daughter returned after church, and half a dozen grandchildren enlivened the gathering. There was need of them, for Elsie, usually in a state of wild effervescence upon such occasions, was now demure and comparatively silent. The children, with whom she was accustomed to romp like one of them, were perplexed indeed; and only the intense excitement of a Thanksgiving dinner diverted their minds from Aunt Elsie, so sadly changed. She was conscious that all were noting her absent manner, and this embarrassed and vexed her more; and yet she seemed under a miserable paralysis that she could neither explain nor escape.

"If we had only laughed it off at first," she groaned to herself; "but now the whole thing grows more absurd and disagreeable every moment."

"Why, Elsie," said her father, banteringly, "you doubted the other day whether Mrs. Methuselah's age would ever sober you; and yet I think that good old lady would have looked more genial on Thanksgiving Day. What is the matter?"

"I was thinking of the sermon," she said.

Amid the comic elevation of eyebrows, George said slyly:

"Tell us the text."

Overwhelmed with confusion, she darted a reproachful glance at him and muttered:

"I did not say anything about the text."

"Well, tell us about the sermon then," laughed James.

"No," said Elsie, sharply. "I'll quote you a text: 'Eat, drink, and be merry,' and let me alone."

They saw that for some reason she could not bear teasing, and that such badinage troubled Mr. Stanhope also. George came gallantly to the rescue, and the dinner-party grew so merry that Elsie thawed perceptibly and Stanhope was beguiled into several witty speeches. At each one Elsie opened her eyes in wider and growing appreciation. At last, when they rose from their coffee, she come to the surprising conclusion—

"Why, he is not stupid and bad-looking after all."

George was bent on breaking the ice between them, and so proposed that the younger members of the family party should go up a swollen stream and see the fall. But Elsie flanked herself with a sister-in-law on one side and a niece on the other, while Stanhope was so diffident that nothing but downright encouragement would bring him to her side. So George was almost in despair. Elsie's eyes had been conveying favorable impressions to her reluctant mind throughout the walk. She sincerely regretted that such an absurd barrier had grown up between her and Stanhope, but could not for the life of her, especially before others, do anything to break the awkward spell.

At last they were on their return, and were all grouped together on a little bluff, watching the water pour foamingly through a narrow gorge.

"Oh, see," cried Elsie, suddenly pointing to the opposite bank, "what beautiful moss that is over there! It is just the kind I have been wanting. Oh, dear! there isn't a bridge within half a mile."

Stanhope glanced around a moment, and then said gallantly, "I will get you the moss, Miss Alford." They saw that in some inconceivable way he intended crossing where they stood. The gorge was much too wide for the most vigorous leap, so Elsie exclaimed eagerly:

"Oh, please don't take any risk! What is a little moss?"

"I say, Stanhope," remonstrated George, seriously, "it would be no laughing matter if you should fall in there."

But Stanhope only smiled, threw off his overcoat, and buttoned his undercoat closely around him. George groaned to himself, "This will be worse than the kissing scrape," and was about to lay a restraining grasp upon his friend. But he slipped away, and lightly went up hand-over-hand a tall, slender sapling on the edge of the bank, the whole party gathering round in breathless expectation. Having reached its slender, swaying top, he threw himself out on the land side. The tree bent at once to the ground with his weight, but without snapping, showing that it was tough and fibrous. Holding firmly to the top, he gave a strong spring, which, with the spring of the bent sapling, sent him well over the gorge on the firm ground beyond.

There was a round of applause from the little group he had just left, in which Elsie joined heartily. Her eyes were glowing with admiration, for when was not power and daring captivating to a woman? Then, in sudden alarm and forgetfulness of her former coolness, she exclaimed:

"But how will you get back?"

"This is my bridge," he replied, smiling brightly across to her, and holding on to the slender young tree. "You perceive that I was brought up in the country."

So saying, he tied the sapling down to a root with a handkerchief, and then proceeded to fill another with moss.

As George saw Elsie's face while she watched Stanhope gather the coveted trifle, he chuckled to himself—

"The ice is broken between them now."

But Stanhope had insecurely fastened the sapling down. The strain upon the knot was too severe, and suddenly the young tree flew up and stood erect but quivering, with his handkerchief fluttering in its top as a symbol of defeat. There was an exclamation of dismay and Elsie again asked with real anxiety in her tone:

"How will you get back now?"

Stanhope shrugged his shoulders.

"I confess I am defeated, for there is no like sapling on this side; but I have the moss, and can join you at the bridge below, if nothing better offers."

"George," said Elsie, indignantly, "don't go away and leave Mr.
Stanhope's handkerchief in that tree."
"Bless you, child," cried George, mischievously, and leading the way down the path, "I can't climb anymore than a pumpkin. You will have to go back with him after it, or let it wave as a memento of his gallantry on your behalf."

"If I can only manage to throw them together without any embarrassing third parties present, the ridiculous restraint they are under will soon vanish," he thought; and so he hastened his steps. The rest trooped after him, while Stanhope made his way with difficulty on the opposite bank, where there was no path. His progress therefore was slow; and Elsie saw that if she did not linger he would be left behind. Common politeness forbade this, and so she soon found herself alone, carrying his overcoat on one bank, and he keeping pace with her on the other. She comforted herself at first with the thought that with the brawling, deafening stream between them, there would be no chance for embarrassing conversation. But soon her sympathies became aroused, as she saw him toilsomely making his way over the rocks and through the tangled thickets: and as she could not speak to him, she smiled her encouragement so often that she felt it would be impossible to go back to her old reserve.

Stanhope now came to a little opening in the brush. The cleared ground sloped evenly down to the stream, and its current was divided by a large rock. He hailed the opportunity here offered with delight, for he was very anxious to speak to her before they should join the others. So he startled Elsie by walking out into the clearing, away from the stream.

"Well, I declare; that's cool, to go and leave me alone without a word," she thought.

But she was almost terror-stricken to see him turn and dart to the torrent like an arrow. With a long flying leap, he landed on the rock in the midst of the stream, and then, without a second's hesitation, with the impetus already acquired, sprang for the solid ground where she stood, struck it, wavered, and would have fallen backward into the water had not she, quick as thought, stepped forward and given him her hand.

"You have saved me from a ducking, if not worse," he said, giving the little rescuing hand a warm pressure.

"Oh!" exclaimed she, panting, "please don't do any more dreadful things. I shall be careful how I make any wishes in your hearing again."

"I am sorry to hear you say that," he replied. And then there was an awkward silence.

Elsie could think of nothing better than to refer to the handkerchief they had left behind.

"Will you wait for me till I run and get it?" he asked.

"I will go back with you, if you will permit me," she said timidly.

"Indeed, I could not ask so much of you as that."

"And yet you could about the same as risk your neck to gratify a whim of mine," she said more gratefully than she intended.

"Please do not think," he replied earnestly, "that I have been practicing cheap heroics. As I said, I was a country boy, and in my early home thought nothing of doing such things." But even the brief reference to that vanished home caused him to sigh deeply, and Elsie gave him a wistful look of sympathy.

For a few moments they walked on in silence. Then Mr. Stanhope turned, and with some hesitation said:

"Miss Alford, I did very wrong to stay after—after last evening. But my better judgment was borne down by invitations so cordial that I hardly knew how to resist them. At the same time I now realize that I should have done so. Indeed, I would go away at once, would not such a course only make matters worse. And yet, after receiving so much kindness from your family, more than has blessed me for many long years—for since my dear mother died I have been quite alone in the world—I feel I cannot go away without some assurance or proof that you will forgive me for being such a kill-joy in your holiday."

Elsie's vexation with herself now knew no bounds. She stopped in the path, determining that she would clear up matters, cost what it might.

"Mr. Stanhope," she said, "will you grant a request that will contain such assurance, or rather, will show you that I am heartily ashamed of my foolish course? Will you not spend next Thanksgiving with us, and give me a chance to retrieve myself from first to last?"

His face brightened wonderfully as he replied, "I will only be too glad to do so, if you truly wish it."

"I do wish it," she said earnestly. "What must you think of me?" (His eyes then expressed much admiration; but hers were fixed on the ground and half filled with tears of vexation.) Then, with a pretty humility that was exquisite in its simplicity and artlessness, she added:

"You have noticed at home that they call me 'child'—and indeed, I am little more than one—and now see that I have behaved like a very silly and naughty one toward you. I have trampled on every principle of hospitality, kindness, and good-breeding. I have no patience with myself, and I wish another chance to show that I can do better. I—"

"Oh, Miss Alford, please do not judge yourself so harshly and unjustly," interrupted Stanhope.

"Oh, dear!" sighed Elsie, "I'm so sorry for what happened last night.
We all might have had such a good time."
"Well, then," said Stanhope, demurely, "I suppose I ought to be also."

"And do you mean to say that you are not?" she asked, turning suddenly upon him.

"Oh, well, certainly, for your sake," he said with rising color.

"But not for your own?" she asked with almost the naivete of a child.

He turned away with a perplexed laugh and replied: "Really, Miss
Alford, you are worse than the Catechism."

She looked at him with a half-amused, half-surprised expression, the thought occurring to her for the first time that it might not have been so disagreeable to him after all; and somehow this thought was quite a relief to her. But she said: "I thought you would regard me as a hoyden of the worst species."

"Because you kissed your brother? I have never for a moment forgotten that it was only your misfortune that I was not he."

"I should have remembered that it was not your fault. But here is your handkerchief, flying like a flag of truce; so let bygones be bygones. My terms are that you come again another year, and give me a chance to entertain my brother's friend as a sister ought."

"I am only too glad to submit to them," he eagerly replied, and then added, so ardently as to deepen the roses already in her cheeks, "If such are your punishments, Miss Alford, how delicious must be your favors!"

By common consent the subject was dropped; and with tongues released from awkward restraint, they chatted freely together, till in the early twilight they reached her home. The moment they entered George exultingly saw that the skies were serene.

But Elsie would never be the frolicsome child of the past again. As she surprised the family at dinner, so now at supper they could scarcely believe that the elegant, graceful young lady was the witch of yesterday. She had resolved with all her soul to try to win some place in Mr. Stanhope's respect before he departed, and never did a little maiden succeed better.

In the evening they had music; and Mr. Stanhope pleased them all with his fine tenor, while Elsie delighted him by her clear, birdlike voice. So the hours fled away.

"You think better of the 'horrid man,' little Sis," said George, as he kissed her good-night.

"I was the horrid one," said Elsie, penitently. "I can never forgive myself my absurd conduct. But he has promised to come again next Thanksgiving, and give me a chance to do better; so don't you fail to bring him."

George gave a long, low whistle, and then said: "Oh! ah! Seems to me you are coming on, for an innocent. Are we to get mixed up again in the twilight?"

"Nonsense!" said Elsie, with a peony face, and she slammed her door upon him.

The next morning the young man took his leave, and Elsie's last words were:

"Mr. Stanhope, remember your promise."

And he did remember more than that, for this brief visit had enshrined a sweet, girlish face within his heart of hearts, and he no longer felt lonely and orphaned. He and George became the closest friends, and messages from the New England home came to him with increasing frequency, which he returned with prodigal interest. It also transpired that he occasionally wrote for the papers, and Elsie insisted that these should be sent to her; while he of course wrote much better with the certainty that she would be his critic. Thus, though separated, they daily became better acquainted, and during the year George found it not very difficult to induce his friend to make several visits.

But it was with joy that seemed almost too rich for earthly experience that he found himself walking up the village street with George the ensuing Thanksgiving Eve. Elsie was at the door; and he pretended to be disconsolate that his reception was not the same as on the previous year. Indeed she had to endure not a little chaffing, for her mistake was a family joke now.

It was a peerless Thanksgiving eve and day—one of the sun-lighted heights of human happiness.

After dinner they all again took a walk up the brawling stream, and Stanhope and Elsie became separated from the rest, though not so innocently as on the former occasion.

"See!" cried Elsie, pointing to the well-remembered sapling, which she had often visited. "There fluttered our flag of truce last year."

Stanhope seized her hand and said eagerly: "And here I again break the truce, and renew the theme we dropped at this place. Oh, Elsie, I have felt that kiss in the depths of my heart every hour since; and in that it led to my knowing and loving you, it has made every day from that time one of thanksgiving. If you could return my love, as I have dared to hope, it would be a happiness beyond words. If I could venture to take one more kiss, as a token that it is returned, I could keep Thanksgiving forever."

Her hand trembled in his, but was not withdrawn. Her blushing face was turned away toward the brawling stream; but she saw not its foam, she heard not its hoarse murmurs. A sweeter music was in her ears. She seemed under a delicious spell, but soon became conscious that a pair of dark eyes were looking down eagerly, anxiously for her answer. Shyly raising hers, that now were like dewy violets, she said, with a little of her old witchery:

"I suppose you will have to kiss me this Thanksgiving, to make things even."

Stanhope needed no broader hint.

"I owe you a heavy grudge," said Mr. Alford, in the evening. "A year ago you robbed me of my child, for little, kittenish Elsie became a thoughtful woman from the day you were here; and now you are going to take away the daughter of my old age."

"Yes, indeed, husband. Now you know how my father felt," said Mrs. Alford, at the same time wiping something from the corner of her eye.
"Bless me, are you here?" said the old gentleman, wheeling round to his wife. "Mr. Stanhope, I have nothing more to say."

"I declare," exulted George, "that 'horrid man' will devour Elsie yet."

"Haw! haw! haw!" laughed big-voiced, big-hearted James. "The idea of our little witch of an Elsie being a minister's wife!"

* * * * * * *

It is again Thanksgiving Eve. The trees are gaunt, the fields bare and brown, with dead leaves whirling across them; but a sweeter than June sunshine seems filling the cosey parlor where Elsie, a radiant bride, is receiving her husband's first kiss almost on the moment that she with her lips so unexpectedly kindled the sacred fire, three years before.

SUSIE ROLLIFFE'S CHRISTMAS

Picnicking in December would be a dreary experience even if one could command all the appliances of comfort which outdoor life permitted. This would be especially true in the latitude of Boston and on the bleak hills overlooking that city and its environing waters. Dreary business indeed Ezekiel Watkins regarded it as he shivered over the smoky camp-fire which he maintained with difficulty. The sun was sinking into the southwest so early in the day that he remarked irritably: "Durned if it was worth while for it to rise at all."

Ezekiel Watkins, or Zeke, as he was generally known among his comrades, had ceased to be a resident on that rocky hillside from pleasure. His heart was in a Connecticut valley in more senses than one; and there was not a more homesick soldier in the army. It will be readily guessed that the events of our story occurred more than a century ago. The shots fired at Bunker Hill had echoed in every nook and corner of the New England colonies, and the heart of Zeke Watkins, among thousands of others, had been fired with military ardor. With companions in like frame of mind he had trudged to Boston, breathing slaughter and extermination against the red-coated instruments of English tyranny. To Zeke the expedition had many of the elements of an extended bear-hunt, much exalted. There was a spice of danger and a rich promise of novelty and excitement. The march to the lines about Boston had been a continuous ovation; grandsires came out from the wayside dwellings and blessed the rustic soldiers; they were dined profusely by the housewives, and if not wined, there had been slight stint in New England rum and cider; the apple-cheeked daughters of the land gave them the meed of heroes in advance, and abated somewhat of their ruddy hues at the thought of the dangers to be incurred. Zeke was visibly dilated by all this attention, incense, and military glory; and he stepped forth from each village and hamlet as if the world were scarcely large enough for the prowess of himself and companions. Even on parade he was as stiff as his long-barrelled flintlock, looking as if England could hope for no quarter at his hands; yet he permitted no admiring glances from bright eyes to escape him. He had not traversed half the distance between his native hamlet and Boston before he was abundantly satisfied that pretty Susie Rolliffe had made no mistake in honoring him among the recruits by marks of especial favor. He wore in his squirrel-skin cap the bit of blue ribbon she had given him, and with the mien of a Homeric hero had intimated darkly that it might be crimson before she saw it again. She had clasped her hands, stifled a little sob, and looked at him admiringly. He needed no stronger assurance than her eyes conveyed at that moment. She had been shy and rather unapproachable before, sought by others than himself, yet very chary of her smiles and favors to all. Her ancestors had fought the Indians, and had bequeathed to the demure little maiden much of their own indomitable spirit. She had never worn her heart on her sleeve, and was shy of her rustic admirers chiefly because none of them had realized her ideals of manhood created by fireside stories of the past.

Zeke's chief competitor for Susie's favor had been Zebulon Jarvis; and while he had received little encouragement, he laid his unostentatious devotion at her feet unstintedly, and she knew it. Indeed, she was much inclined to laugh at him, for he was singularly bashful, and a frown from her overwhelmed him. Unsophisticated Susie reasoned that any one who could be so afraid of HER could not be much of a man. She had never heard of his doing anything bold and spirited. It might be said, indeed, that the attempt to wring a livelihood for his widowed mother and for his younger brothers and sisters from the stumpy, rocky farm required courage of the highest order; but it was not of a kind that appealed to the fancy of a romantic young girl. Nothing finer or grander had Zebulon attempted before the recruiting officer came to Opinquake, and when he came, poor Zeb appeared to hang back so timorously that he lost what little place he had in Susie's thoughts. She was ignorant of the struggle taking place in his loyal heart. More intense even than his love for her was the patriotic fire which smouldered in his breast; yet when other young men were giving in their names and drilling on the village green, he was absent. To the war appeals of those who sought him, he replied briefly. "Can't leave till fall."

"But the fighting will be over long before that," it was urged.

"So much the better for others, then, if not for me."

Zeke Watkins made it his business that Susie should hear this reply in the abbreviated form of, "So much the better, then."

She had smiled scornfully, and it must be added, a little bitterly. In his devotion Zeb had been so helpless, so diffidently unable to take his own part and make advances that she, from odd little spasms of sympathy, had taken his part for him, and laughingly repeated to herself in solitude all the fine speeches which she perceived he would be glad to make. But, as has been intimated, it seemed to her droll indeed that such a great stalwart fellow should appear panic-stricken in her diminutive presence. In brief, he had been timidity embodied under her demurely mischievous blue eyes; and now that the recruiting officer had come and marched away with his squad without him, she felt incensed that such a chicken-hearted fellow had dared to lift his eyes to her.

"It would go hard with the Widow Jarvis and all those children if Zeb 'listed," Susie's mother had ventured in half-hearted defence, for did she not look upon him as a promising suitor.

"The people of Opinquake wouldn't let the widow or the children starve," replied Susie, indignantly. "If I was a big fellow like him, my country would not call me twice. Think how grandfather left grandma and all the children!"

"Well, I guess Zeb thinks he has his hands full wrastling with that stony farm."

"He needn't come to see me any more, or steal glances at me 'tween meetings on Sunday," said the girl, decisively. "He cuts a sorry figure beside Zeke Watkins, who was the first to give in his name, and who began to march like a soldier even before he left us."

"Yes," said Mrs. Rolliffe; "Zeke was very forward. If he holds out as he began—Well, well, Zeke allus was a little forward, and able to speak for himself. You are young yet, Susan, and may learn before you reach my years that the race isn't allus to the swift. Don't be in haste to promise yourself to any of the young men."

"Little danger of my promising myself to a man who is afraid even of me! I want a husband like grandfather. He wasn't afraid to face anything, and he honored his wife by acting as if she wasn't afraid either."

Zeb gave Susie no chance to bestow the rebuffs she had premeditated. He had been down to witness the departure of the Opinquake quota, and had seen Susie's farewell to Zeke Watkins. How much it had meant he was not sure—enough to leave no hope or chance for him, he had believed; but he had already fought his first battle, and it had been a harder one than Zeke Watkins or any of his comrades would ever engage in. He had returned and worked on the stony farm until dark. From dawn until dark he continued to work every secular day till September.

His bronzed face grew as stern as it was thin; and since he would no longer look at her, Susie Rolliffe began to steal an occasional and wondering glance at him "'tween meetings."

No one understood the young man or knew his plans except his patient, sad-eyed mother, and she learned more by her intuitions than from his spoken words. She idolized him, and he loved and revered her: but the terrible Puritan restraint paralyzed manifestations of affection. She was not taken by surprise when one evening he said quietly, "Mother, I guess I'll start in a day or two."

She could not repress a sort of gasping sob however, but after a few moments was able to say steadily, "I supposed you were preparing to leave us."

"Yes, mother, I've been a-preparing. I've done my best to gather in everything that would help keep you and the children and the stock through the winter. The corn is all shocked, and the older children can help you husk it, and gather in the pumpkins, the beans, and the rest. As soon as I finish digging the potatoes I think I'll feel better to be in the lines around Boston. I'd have liked to have gone at first, but in order to fight as I ought I'd want to remember there was plenty to keep you and the children."

"I'm afraid, Zebulon, you've been fighting as well as working so hard all summer long. For my sake and the children's, you've been letting Susan Rolliffe think meanly of you."

"I can't help what she thinks, mother; I've tried not to act meanly."

"Perhaps the God of the widow and the fatherless will shield and bless you, my son. Be that as it may," she added with a heavy sigh, "conscience and His will must guide in everything. If He says go forth to battle, what am I that I should stay you?" Although she did not dream of the truth, the Widow Jarvis was a disciplined soldier herself. To her, faith meant unquestioning submission and obedience; she had been taught to revere a jealous and an exacting God rather than a loving one. The heroism with which she pursued her toilsome, narrow, shadowed pathway was as sublime as it was unrecognized on her part. After she had retired she wept sorely, not only because her eldest child was going to danger, and perhaps death, but also for the reason that her heart clung to him so weakly and selfishly, as she believed. With a tenderness of which she was half-ashamed she filled his wallet with provisions which would add to his comfort, then, both to his surprise and her own, kissed him good-by. He left her and the younger brood with an aching heart of which there was little outward sign, and with no loftier ambition than to do his duty; she followed him with deep, wistful eyes till he, and next the long barrel of his rifle, disappeared in an angle of the road, and then her interrupted work was resumed.

Susie Rolliffe was returning from an errand to a neighbor's when she heard the sound of long rapid steps.

A hasty glance revealed Zeb in something like pursuit. Her heart fluttered slightly, for he had looked so stern and sad of late that she had felt a little sorry for him in spite of herself. But since he could "wrastle" with nothing more formidable than a stony farm, she did not wish to have anything to say to him, or meet the embarrassment of explaining a tacit estrangement. She was glad, therefore, that her gate was so near, and passed in as if she had not recognized him. She heard his steps become slower and pause at the gate, and then almost in shame in being guilty of too marked discourtesy, she turned to speak, but hesitated in surprise, for now she recognized his equipment as a soldier.

"Why, Mr. Jarvis, where are you going?" she exclaimed.

A dull red flamed through the bronze of his thin cheeks as he replied awkwardly, "I thought I'd take a turn in the lines around Boston."

"Oh, yes," she replied, mischievously, "take a turn in the lines. Then we may expect you back by corn-husking?"

He was deeply wounded, and in his embarrassment could think of no other reply than the familiar words, "'Let not him that girdeth on his harness boast himself as he that putteth it off.'"

"I can't help hoping, Mr. Jarvis, that neither you nor others will put it off too soon—not, at least, while King George claims to be our master. When we're free I can stand any amount of boasting."

"You'll never hear boasting from me, Miss Susie;" and then an awkward silence fell between them.

Shyly and swiftly she raised her eyes. He looked so humble, deprecatory, and unsoldier-like that she could not repress a laugh. "I'm not a British cannon," she began, "that you should be so fearful."

His manhood was now too deeply wounded for further endurance even from her, for he suddenly straightened himself, and throwing his rifle over his shoulder, said sternly, "I'm not a coward. I never hung back from fear, but to keep mother from charity, so I could fight or die as God wills. You may laugh at the man who never gave you anything but love, if you will, but you shall never laugh at my deeds. Call that boasting or not as you please," and he turned on his heel to depart.

His words and manner almost took away the girl's breath, so unexpected were they, and unlike her idea of the man. In that brief moment a fearless soldier had flashed himself upon her consciousness, revealing a spirit that would flinch at nothing—that had not even quailed at the necessity of forfeiting her esteem, that his mother might not want. Humiliated and conscience-stricken that she had done him so much injustice, she rushed forward, crying, "Stop, Zebulon; please do not go away angry with me! I do not forget that we have been old friends and playmates. I'm willing to own that I've been wrong about you, and that's a good deal for a girl to do. I only wish I were a man, and I'd go with you."

Her kindness restored him to his awkward self again, and he stammered, "I wish you were—no, I don't—I merely stopped, thinking you might have a message; but I'd rather not take any to Zeke Watkins—will, though, if you wish. It cut me all up to have you think I was afraid," and then he became speechless.

"But you acted as if you were afraid of me, and that seemed so ridiculous."

He looked at her a moment so earnestly with his dark, deep-set eyes that hers dropped. "Miss Susie," he said slowly, and speaking with difficulty, "I AM afraid of you, next to God. I don't suppose I've any right to talk to you so, and I will say good-by. I was reckless when I spoke before. Perhaps—you'll go and see mother. My going is hard on her."

His eyes lingered on her a moment longer, as if he were taking his last look, then he turned slowly away.

"Good-by, Zeb," she called softly. "I didn't—I don't understand. Yes, I will go to see your mother."

Susie also watched him as he strode away. He thought he could continue on steadfastly without looking back, but when the road turned he also turned, fairly tugged right about by his loyal heart. She stood where he had left her, and promptly waved her hand. He doffed his cap, and remained a moment in an attitude that appeared to her reverential, then passed out of view.

The moments lapsed, and still she stood in the gateway, looking down the vacant road as if dazed. Was it in truth awkward, bashful Zeb Jarvis who had just left her? He seemed a new and distinct being in contrast to the youth whom she had smiled at and in a measure scoffed at. The little Puritan maiden was not a reasoner, but a creature of impressions and swift intuitions. Zeb had not set his teeth, faced his hard duty, and toiled that long summer in vain. He had developed a manhood and a force which in one brief moment had enabled him to compel her recognition.

"He will face anything," she murmured. "He's afraid of only God and me; what a strange thing to say—afraid of me next to God! Sounds kind of wicked. What can he mean? Zeke Watkins wasn't a bit afraid of me. As mother said, he was a little forward, and I was fool enough to take him at his own valuation. Afraid of me! How he stood with his cap off. Do men ever love so? Is there a kind of reverence in some men's love? How absurd that a great strong, brave man, ready to face cannons, can bow down to such a little—" Her fragmentary exclamations ended in a peal of laughter, but tears dimmed her blue eyes.

Susie did visit Mrs. Jarvis, and although the reticent woman said little about her son, what she did say meant volumes to the girl who now had the right clew in interpreting his action and character. She too was reticent. New England girls rarely gushed in those days, so no one knew she was beginning to understand. Her eyes, experienced in country work, were quick, and her mind active. "It looks as if a giant had been wrestling with this stony farm," she muttered.

Zeb received no ovations on his lonely tramp to the lines, and the vision of Susie Rolliffe waving her hand from the gateway would have blinded him to all the bright and admiring eyes in the world. He was hospitably entertained, however, when there was occasion; but the advent of men bound for the army had become an old story. Having at last inquired his way to the position occupied by the Connecticut troops, he was assigned to duty in the same company with Zeke Watkins, who gave him but a cool reception, and sought to overawe him by veteran-like airs. At first poor Zeb was awkward enough in his unaccustomed duties, and no laugh was so scornful as that of his rival. Young Jarvis, however, had not been many days in camp before he guessed that Zeke's star was not in the ascendant. There was but little fighting required, but much digging of intrenchments, drill, and monotonous picket duty. Zeke did not take kindly to such tasks, and shirked them when possible. He was becoming known as the champion grumbler in the mess, and no one escaped his criticism, not even "Old Put"—as General Putnam, who commanded the Connecticut quota, was called. Jarvis, on the other hand, performed his military duties as he had worked the farm, and rapidly acquired the bearing of a soldier. Indomitable Putnam gave his men little rest, and was ever seeking to draw his lines nearer to Boston and the enemy's ships. He virtually fought with pick and shovel, and his working parties were often exposed to fire while engaged in fortifying the positions successively occupied. The Opinquake boys regarded themselves as well seasoned to such rude compliments, and were not a little curious to see how Zeb would handle a shovel with cannon-balls whizzing uncomfortably near. The opportunity soon came. Old Put himself could not have been more coolly oblivious than the raw recruit. At last a ball smashed his shovel to smithereens; he quietly procured another and went on with his work. Then his former neighbors gave him a cheer, while his captain clapped him on the shoulder and said, "Promote you to be a veteran on the spot!"

The days had grown shorter, colder, and drearier, and the discomforts of camp-life harder to endure. There were few tents even for the officers, and the men were compelled to improvise such shelter as circumstances permitted. Huts of stone, wood, and brush, and barricades against the wind, lined the hillside, and the region already was denuded of almost everything that would burn. Therefore, when December came, Zeke Watkins found that even a fire was a luxury not to be had without trouble. He had become thoroughly disgusted with a soldier's life, and the military glory which had at first so dazzled him now wore the aspect of the wintry sky. He had recently sought and attained the only promotion for which his captain now deemed him fitted—that of cook for about a dozen of his comrades; and the close of the December day found him preparing the meagre supper which the limited rations permitted. By virtue of his office, Zeke was one of the best-fed men in the army, for if there were any choice morsels he could usually manage to secure them; still, he was not happy. King George and Congress were both pursuing policies inconsistent with his comfort, and he sighed more and more frequently for the wide kitchen-hearth of his home, which was within easy visiting distance of the Rolliffe farmhouse. His term of enlistment expired soon, and he was already counting the days. He was not alone in his discontent, for there was much homesickness and disaffection among the Connecticut troops. Many had already departed, unwilling to stay an hour after the expiration of their terms; and not a few had anticipated the periods which legally released them from duty. The organization of the army was so loose that neither appeals nor threats had much influence, and Washington, in deep solicitude, saw his troops melting away.

It was dark by the time the heavy tramp of the working party was heard returning from the fortifications. The great mess-pot, partly filled with pork and beans, was bubbling over the fire; Zeke, shifting his position from time to time to avoid the smoke which the wind, as if it had a spite against him, blew in his face, was sourly contemplating his charge and his lot, bent on grumbling to the others with even greater gusto than he had complained to himself. His comrades carefully put away their intrenching tools, for they were held responsible for them, and then gathered about the fire, clamoring for supper.

"Zeke, you lazy loon," cried Nat Atkinson, "how many pipes have you smoked to-day? If you'd smoke less and forage and dun the commissary more, we'd have a little fresh meat once in a hundred years."

"Yes, just about once in a hundred years!" snarled Zeke.

"YOU find something to keep fat on, anyhow. We'll broil you some cold night. Trot out your beans if there's nothing else."

"Growl away," retorted Zeke. "'Twon't be long before I'll be eating chickens and pumpkin-pie in Opinquake, instead of cooking beans and rusty pork for a lot of hungry wolves."

"You'd be the hungriest wolf of the lot if you'd 'a' been picking and shovelling frozen ground all day."

"I didn't 'list to be a ditch-digger!" said Zeke. "I thought I was going to be a soldier."

"And you turned out a cook!" quietly remarked Zeb Jarvis.

"Well, my hero of the smashed shovel, what do you expect to be—Old Put's successor? You know, fellows, it's settled that you're to dig your way into Boston, tunnel under the water when you come to it. Of course Put will die of old age before you get half there. Zeb'll be the chap of all others to command a division of shovellers. I see you with a pickaxe strapped on your side instead of a sword."

"Lucky I'm not in command now," replied Zeb, "or you'd shovel dirt under fire to the last hour of your enlistment. I'd give grumblers like you something to grumble about. See here, fellows, I'm sick of this seditious talk in our mess. The Connecticut men are getting to be the talk of the army. You heard a squad of New Hampshire boys jeer at us to-day, and ask, 'When are ye going home to mother?' You ask, Zeke Watkins, what I expect to be. I expect to be a soldier, and obey orders as long as Old Put and General Washington want a man. All I ask is to be home summers long enough to keep mother and the children off the town. Now what do you expect to be after you give up your cook's ladle?"

"None o' your business."

"He's going home to court Susie Rolliffe," cried Nat Atkinson. "They'll be married in the spring, and go into the chicken business. That'd just suit Zeke."

"It would not suit Susie Rolliffe," said Zeb, hotly. "A braver, better girl doesn't breathe in the colonies, and the man that says a slurring word against her's got to fight me."

"What! Has she given Zeke the mitten for your sake, Zeb?" piped little
Hiram Woodbridge.
"She hasn't given me anything, and I've got no claim; but she is the kind of girl that every fellow from Opinquake should stand up for. We all know that there is nothing chicken-hearted about her."

"Eight, by George—George W., I mean, and not the king," responded Hiram Woodbridge. "Here's to her health, Zeb, and your success! I believe she'd rather marry a soldier than a cook."

"Thank you," said Zeb. "You stand as good a chance as I do; but don't let's bandy her name about in camp any more'n we would our mother's. The thing for us to do now is to show that the men from Connecticut have as much backbone as any other fellows in the army, North or South. Zeke may laugh at Old Put's digging, but you'll soon find that he'll pick his way to a point where he can give the Britishers a dig under the fifth rib. We've got the best general in the army. Washington, with all his Southern style, believes in him and relies on him. Whether their time's up or not, it's a burning shame that so many of his troops are sneaking off home."

"It's all very well for you to talk, Zeb Jarvis," growled Zeke. "You haven't been here very long yet; and you stayed at home when others started out to fight. Now that you've found that digging and not fighting is the order of the day, you're just suited. It's the line of soldiering you are cut out for. When fighting men and not ditch-diggers are wanted, you'll find me—-"

"All right, Watkins," said the voice of Captain Dean from without the circle of light. "According to your own story you are just the kind of man needed to-night—no ditch-digging on hand, but dangerous service. I detail you, for you've had rest compared with the other men. I ask for volunteers from those who've been at work all day."

Zeb Jarvis was on his feet instantly, and old Ezra Stokes also began to rise with difficulty. "No, Stokes," resumed the officer, "you can't go. I know you've suffered with the rheumatism all day, and have worked well in spite of it. For to-night's work I want young fellows with good legs and your spirit. How is it you're here anyhow Stokes? Your time's up."

"We ain't into Boston yet," was the quiet reply.

"So you want to stay?"

"Yes, sir."

"Then you shall cook for the men till you're better. I won't keep so good a soldier, though, at such work any longer than I can help. Your good example and that of the gallant Watkins has brought out the whole squad. I think I'll put Jarvis in command, though; Zeke might be rash, and attempt the capture of Boston before morning;" and the facetious captain, who had once been a neighbor, concluded, "Jarvis, see that every man's piece is primed and ready for use. Be at my hut in fifteen minutes." Then he passed on to the other camp-fires.

In a few minutes Ezra Stokes was alone by the fire, almost roasting his lame leg, and grumbling from pain and the necessity of enforced inaction. He was a taciturn, middle-age man, and had been the only bachelor of mature years in Opinquake. Although he rarely said much, he had been a great listener, and no one had been better versed in neighborhood affairs. In brief, he had been the village cobbler, and had not only taken the measure of Susie Rolliffe's little foot, but also of her spirit. Like herself he had been misled at first by the forwardness of Zeke Watkins and the apparent backwardness of Jarvis. Actual service had changed his views very decidedly. When Zeb appeared he had watched the course of this bashful suitor with interest which had rapidly ripened into warm but undemonstrative goodwill. The young fellow had taken pains to relieve the older man, had carried his tools for him, and more than once with his strong hands had almost rubbed the rheumatism out of the indomitable cobbler's leg. He had received but slight thanks, and had acted as if he didn't care for any. Stokes was not a man to return favors in words; he brooded over his gratitude as if it were a grudge. "I'll get even with that young Jarvis yet," he muttered, as he nursed his leg over the fire. "I know he worships the ground that little Rolliffe girl treads on, though she don't tread on much at a time. She never trod on me nuther, though I've had her foot in my hand more'n once. She looked at the man that made her shoes as if she would like to make him happier.

When a little tot, she used to say I could come and live with her when I got too old to take care of myself. Lame as I be, I'd walk to Opinquake to give her a hint in her choosin'. Guess Hi Woodbridge is right, and she wouldn't be long in making up her mind betwixt a soger and a cook—a mighty poor one at that. Somehow or nuther I must let her know before Zeke Watkins sneaks home and parades around as a soldier 'bove ditch-digging. I've taken his measure.

"He'll be putting on veteran airs, telling big stories of what he's going to do when soldiers are wanted, and drilling such fools as believe in him. Young gals are often taken by such strutters, and think that men like Jarvis, who darsn't speak for themselves, are of no account. But I'll put a spoke in Zeke's wheel, if I have to get the captain to write."

It thus may be gathered that the cobbler had much to say to himself when alone, though so taciturn to others.

The clouds along the eastern horizon were stained with red before the reconnoitring party returned. Stokes had managed, by hobbling about, to keep up the fire and to fill the mess-kettle with the inevitable pork and beans. The hungry, weary men therefore gave their new cook a cheer when they saw the good fire and provision awaiting them. A moment later, however, Jarvis observed how lame Stokes had become; he took the cobbler by the shoulder and sat him down in the warmest nook, saying, "I'll be assistant cook until you are better. As Zeke says, I'm a wolf sure enough; but as soon's the beast's hunger is satisfied, I'll rub that leg of yours till you'll want to dance a jig;" and with the ladle wrung from Stokes's reluctant hand, he began stirring the seething contents of the kettle.

Then little Hi Woodbridge piped in his shrill voice, "Another cheer for our assistant cook and ditch-digger! I say, Zeke, wouldn't you like to tell Ezra that Zeb has showed himself fit for something more than digging? You expressed your opinion very plain last night, and may have a different one now."

Zeke growld something inaudible, and stalked to his hut in order to put away his equipments.

"I'm cook-in-chief yet," Stokes declared; "and not a bean will any one of you get till you report all that happened."

"Well," piped Hi, "you may stick a feather in your old cap, Ezra, for our Opinquake lad captured a British officer last night, and Old Put is pumping him this blessed minute."

"Well, well, that is news. It must have been Zeke who did that neat job," exclaimed Stokes, ironically; "he's been a-pining for the soldier business."

"No, no; Zeke's above such night scrimmages. He wants to swim the bay and walk right into Boston in broad daylight, so everybody can see him. Come, Zeb, tell how it happened. It was so confounded dark, no one can tell but you."

"There isn't much to tell that you fellows don't know," was Zeb's laconic answer. "We had sneaked down on the neck so close to the enemy's lines—-"

"Yes, yes, Zeb Jarvis," interrupted Stokes, "that's the kind of sneaking you're up to—close to the enemy's lines. Go on."

"Well, I crawled up so close that I saw a Britisher going the round of the sentinels, and I pounced on him and brought him out on the run, that's all."

"Oho! you both ran away, then? That wasn't good soldiering either, was it, Zeke?" commented Stokes, in his dry way.

"It's pretty good soldiering to stand fire within an inch of your nose," resumed Hi, who had become a loyal friend and adherent of his tall comrade. "Zeb was so close on the Britisher when he fired his pistol that we saw the faces of both in the flash; and a lot of bullets sung after us, I can sell you, as we dusted out of those diggin's."

"Compliments of General Putnam to Sergeant Zebulon Jarvis," said an orderly, riding out of the dim twilight of the morning. "The general requests your presence at headquarters."

"Sergeant! promoted! Another cheer for Zeb!" and the Opinquake boys gave it with hearty goodwill.

"Jerusalem, fellows! I'd like to have a chance at those beans before I go!" but Zeb promptly tramped off with the orderly.

When he returned he was subjected to a fire of questions by the two or three men still awake, but all they could get out of him was that he had been given a good breakfast. From Captain Dean, who was with the general at the time of the examination, it leaked out that Zeb was in the line of promotion to a rank higher than that of sergeant.

The next few days passed uneventfully; and Zeke was compelled to resume the pick and shovel again. Stokes did his best to fulfil his duties, but it had become evident to all that the exposure of camp would soon disable him utterly. Jarvis and Captain Dean persuaded him to go home for the winter, and the little squad raised a sum which enabled him to make the journey in a stage. Zeke, sullen toward his jeering comrades, but immensely elated in secret, had shaken the dust—snow and slush rather—of camp-life from his feet the day before. He had the grace to wait till the time of his enlistment expired, and that was more than could be said of many.

It spoke well for the little Opinquake quota that only two others besides Zeke availed themselves of their liberty. Poor Stokes was almost forced away, consoled by the hope of returning in the spring. Zeb was sore-hearted on the day of Zeke's departure. His heart was in the Connecticut Valley also. No message had come to him from Susie Rolliffe. Those were not the days of swift and frequent communication. Even Mrs. Jarvis had written but seldom, and her missives were brief. Mother-love glowed through the few quaint and scriptural phrases like heat in anthracite coals. All that poor Zeb could learn from them was that Susie Rolliffe had kept her word and had been to the farm more than once; but the girl had been as reticent as the mother. Zeke was now on his way home to prosecute his suit in person, and Zeb well knew how forward and plausible he could be. There was no deed of daring that he would not promise to perform after spring opened, and Zeb reasoned gloomily that a present lover, impassioned and importunate, would stand a better chance than an absent one who had never been able to speak for himself.

When it was settled that Stokes should return to Opinquake, Zeb determined that he would not give up the prize to Zeke without one decisive effort; and as he was rubbing the cobbler's leg, he stammered, "I say Ezra, will you do me a turn? 'Twon't be so much, what I ask, except that I'll like you to keep mum about it, and you're a good hand at keeping mum."

"I know what yer driving at, Zeb. Write yer letter and I'll deliver it with my own hands."

"Well, now, I'm satisfied, I can stay on and fight it out with a clear mind. When Zeke marched away last summer, I thought it was all up with me; and I can tell you that any fighting that's to do about Boston will be fun compared with the fighting I did while hoeing corn and mowing grass. But I don't believe that Susie Rolliffe is promised to Zeke Watkins, or any one else yet, and I'm going to give her a chance to refuse me plump."

"That's the way to do it, Zeb," said the bachelor cobbler, with an emphasis that would indicate much successful experience. "Asking a girl plump is like standing up in a fair fight. It gives the girl a chance to bowl you over, if that's her mind, so there can't be any mistake about it; and it seems to me the women-folks ought to have all the chances that in any way belong to them. They have got few enough anyhow."

"And you think it'll end in my being bowled over?"

"How should I know, or you either, unless you make a square trial? You're such a strapping, fighting feller that nothing but a cannon-ball or a woman ever will knock you off your pins."

"See here, Ezra Stokes, the girl of my heart may refuse me just as plump as I offer myself; and if that's her mind she has a right to do it. But I don't want either you or her to think I won't stand on my feet. I won't even fight any more recklessly than my duty requires. I have a mother to take care of, even if I never have a wife."

"I'll put in a few pegs right along to keep in mind what you say; and I'll give you a fair show by seeing to it that the girl gets your letter before Zeke can steal a march on you."

"That's all I ask," said Zeb, with compressed lips. "She shall choose between us. It's hard enough to write, but it will be a sight easier than facing her. Not a word of this to another soul, Ezra; but I'm not going to use you like a mail-carrier, but a friend. After all, there are few in Opinquake, I suppose, but know I'd give my eyes for her, so there isn't much use of my putting on secret airs."

"I'm not a talker, and you might have sent your letter by a worse messenger'n me," was the laconic reply.

Zeb had never written a love-letter, and was at a loss how to begin or end it. But time pressed, and he had to say what was uppermost in his mind. It ran as follows:

"I don't know how to write so as to give my words weight. I cannot come home; I will not come as long as mother and the children can get on without me. And men are needed here; men are needed. The general fairly pleads with the soldiers to stay. Stokes would stay if he could. We're almost driving him home. I know you will be kind to him, and remember he has few to care for him. I cannot speak for myself in person very soon, if ever. Perhaps I could not if I stood before you. You laugh at me; but if you knew how I love you and remember you, how I honor and almost worship you in my heart, you might understand me better. Why is it strange I should be afraid of you? Only God has more power over me than you. Will you be my wife? I will do anything to win you that YOU can ask. Others will plead with you in person. Will you let this letter plead for the absent?"

Zeb went to the captain's quarters and got some wax with which to seal this appeal, then saw Stokes depart with the feeling that his destiny was now at stake.

Meanwhile Zeke Watkins, with a squad of homeward-bound soldiers, was trudging toward Opinquake. They soon began to look into one another's faces in something like dismay. But little provision was in their wallets when they had started, for there was little to draw upon, and that furnished grudgingly, as may well be supposed. Zeke had not cared. He remembered the continuous feasting that had attended his journey to camp, and supposed that he would only have to present himself to the roadside farmhouses in order to enjoy the fat of the land. This hospitality he proposed to repay abundantly by camp reminiscences in which it would not be difficult to insinuate that the hero of the scene was present.

In contrast to these rose-hued expectations, doors were slammed in their faces, and they were treated little better than tramps. "I suppose the people near Boston have been called on too often and imposed on, too," Zeke reasoned rather ruefully. "When we once get over the Connecticut border we'll begin to find ourselves at home;" and spurred by hunger and cold, as well as hope, they pushed on desperately, subsisting on such coarse provisions as they could obtain, sleeping in barns when it stormed, and not infrequently by a fire in the woods. At last they passed the Connecticut border, and led by Zeke they urged their way to a large farmhouse, at which, but a few months before, the table had groaned under rustic dainties, and feather-beds had luxuriously received the weary recruits bound to the front. They approached the opulent farm in the dreary dark of the evening, and pursued by a biting east wind laden with snow. Not only the weather, but the very dogs seemed to have a spite against them; and the family had to rush out to call them off.

"Weary soldiers ask for shelter," began Zeke.

"Of course you're bound for the lines," said the matronly housewife.
"Come in."
Zeke thought they would better enter at once before explaining; and truly the large kitchen, with a great fire blazing on the hearth, seemed like heaven. The door leading into the family sitting-room was open, and there was another fire, with the red-cheeked girls and the white-haired grandsire before it, their eyes turned expectantly toward the new-comers. Instead of hearty welcome, there was a questioning look on every face, even on that of the kitchen-maid. Zeke's four companions had a sort of hang-dog look—for they had been cowed by the treatment received along the road; but he tried to bear himself confidently, and began with an insinuating smile, "Perhaps I should hardly expect you to remember me. I passed this way last summer—-"

"Passed this way last summer?" repeated the matron, her face growing stern. "We who cannot fight are ready and glad to share all we have with those who fight for us. Since you carry arms we might very justly think you are hastening forward to use them."

"These are our own arms; we furnished them ourselves," Zeke hastened to say.

"Oh, indeed," replied the matron, coldly; "I supposed that not only the weapons, but the ones who carry them, belonged to the country. I hope you are not deserting from the army."

"I assure you we are not. Our terms of enlistment have expired."

"And your country's need was over at the same moment? Are you hastening home at this season to plow and sow and reap?"

"Well, madam, after being away so long we felt like having a little comfort and seeing the folks. We stayed a long as we agreed. When spring opens, or before, if need be—-"

"Pardon me, sir; the need is now. The country is not to be saved by men who make bargains like day-laborers, and who quit when the hour is up, but by soldiers who give themselves to their country as they would to their wives and sweethearts. My husband and sons are in the army you have deserted. General Washington has written to our governor asking whether an example should not be made of the men who have deserted the cause of their country at this critical time when the enemy are receiving re-enforcements. We are told that Connecticut men have brought disgrace on our colony and have imperilled the whole army. You feel like taking comfort and seeing the folks. The folks do not feel like seeing you. My husband and the brave men in the lines are in all the more danger because of your desertion, for a soldier's time never expires when the enemy is growing stronger and threatening every home in the land. If all followed your example, the British would soon be upon your heels, taking from us our honor and our all. We are not ignorant of the critical condition of our army; and I can tell you, sir, that if many more of our men come home, the women will take their places."

Zeke's companions succumbed to the stern arraignment, and after a brief whispered consultation one spoke for the rest. "Madam," he said, "you put it in a way that we hadn't realized before. We'll right-about-face and march back in the morning, for we feel that we'd rather face all the British in Boston than any more Connecticut women."

"Then, sirs, you shall have supper and shelter and welcome," was the prompt reply.

Zeke assumed an air of importance as he said: "There are reasons why I must be at home for a time, but I not only expect to return, but also to take many back with me."

"I trust your deeds may prove as large as your words," was the chilly reply; and then he was made to feel that he was barely tolerated. Some hints from his old associates added to the disfavor which the family took but little pains to conceal. There was a large vein of selfish calculation in Zeke's nature, and he was not to be swept away by any impulses. He believed he could have a prolonged visit home, yet manage so admirably that when he returned he would be followed by a squad of recruits, and chief of all he would be the triumphant suitor of Susie Rolliffe. Her manner in parting had satisfied him that he had made go deep an impression that it would be folly not to follow it up. He trudged the remainder of the journey alone, and secured tolerable treatment by assuring the people that he was returning for recruits for the army. He reached home in the afternoon of Christmas; and although the day was almost completely ignored in the Puritan household, yet Mrs. Watkins forgot country, Popery, and all, in her mother love, and Zeke supped on the finest turkey of the flock. Old Mr. Watkins, it is true, looked rather grim, but the reception had been reassuring in the main; and Zeke had resolved on a line of tactics which would make him, as he believed, the military hero of the town. After he had satisfied an appetite which had been growing ever since he left camp, he started to call on Susie in all the bravery of his best attire, filled with sanguine expectations inspired by memories of the past and recent potations of cider.

Meanwhile Susie had received a guest earlier in the day. The stage had stopped at the gate where she had stood in the September sunshine and waved her bewildered farewell to Zeb. There was no bewilderment or surprise now at her strange and unwonted sensations. She had learned why she had stood looking after him dazed and spellbound. Under the magic of her own light irony she had seen her drooping rustic lover transformed into the ideal man who could face anything except her unkindness. She had guessed the deep secret of his timidity. It was a kind of fear of which she had not dreamed, and which touched her innermost soul.

When the stage stopped at the gate, and she saw the driver helping out Ezra Stokes, a swift presentiment made her sure that she would hear from one soldier who was more to her than all the generals. She was soon down the walk, the wind sporting in her light-gold hair, supporting the cobbler on the other side.

"Ah, Miss Susie!" he said, "I am about worn out, sole and upper. It breaks my heart, when men are so sorely needed, to be thrown aside like an old shoe."

The girl soothed and comforted him, ensconced him by the fireside, banishing the chill from his heart, while Mrs. Rolliffe warmed his blood by a strong, hot drink. Then the mother hastened away to get dinner, while Susie sat down near, nervously twisting and untwisting her fingers, with questions on her lips which she dared not utter, but which brought blushes to her cheeks. Stokes looked at her and sighed over his lost youth, yet smiled as he thought: "Guess I'll get even with that Zeb Jarvis to-day." Then he asked, "Isn't there any one you would like to hear about in camp?"

She blushed deeper still, and named every one who had gone from Opinquake except Zeb. At last she said a little ironically: "I suppose Ezekiel Watkins is almost thinking about being a general about this time?"

"Hasn't he been here telling you what he is thinking about?"

"Been here! Do you mean to say he has come home?"

"He surely started for home. All the generals and a yoke of oxen couldn't 'a' kept him in camp, he was so homesick—lovesick too, I guess. Powerful compliment to you, Miss Susie," added the politic cobbler, feeling his way, "that you could draw a man straight from his duty like one of these 'ere stump-extractors."

"No compliment to me at all!" cried the girl, indignantly. "He little understands me who seeks my favor by coming home at a time like this. The Connecticut women are up in arms at the way our men are coming home. No offence to you, Mr. Stokes. You're sick, and should come; but I'd like to go myself to show some of the strong young fellows what we think of them."

"Coming home was worse than rheumatism to me, and I'm going back soon's I kin walk without a cane. Wouldn't 'a' come as 'tis, if that Zeb Jarvis hadn't jes' packed me off. By Jocks! I thought you and he was acquainted, but you don't seem to ask arter him."
"I felt sure he would try—I heard he was doing his duty," she replied with averted face.

"Zeke Watkins says he's no soldier at all—nothing but a dirt-digger."

For a moment, as the cobbler had hoped, Susie forgot her blushes and secret in her indignation. "Zeke Watkins indeed!" she exclaimed. "He'd better not tell ME any such story. I don't believe there's a braver, truer man in the—Well," she added in sudden confusion, "he hasn't run away and left others to dig their way into Boston, if that's the best way of getting there."

"Ah, I'm going to get even with him yet," chuckled Stokes to himself. "Digging is only the first step, Miss Susie. When Old Put gets good and ready, you'll hear the thunder of the guns a'most in Opinquake."

"Well, Mr. Stokes," stammered Susie, resolving desperately on a short cut to the knowledge she craved, "you've seen Mr. Jarvis a-soldiering. What do you think about it?"

"Well, now, that Zeb Jarvis is the sneakin'ist fellow—-"

"What?" cried the girl, her face aflame.

"Wait till I get in a few more pegs," continued Stokes, coolly. "The other night he sneaked right into the enemy's lines and carried off a British officer as a hawk takes a chicken. The Britisher fired his pistol right under Zeb's nose; but, law! he didn't mind that any more'n a 'sketer-bite. I call that soldiering, don't you? Anyhow, Old Put thought it was, and sent for him 'fore daylight, and made a sergeant of him. If I had as good a chance of gettin' rid of the rheumatiz as he has of bein' captain in six months, I'd thank the Lord."

Susie sat up very straight, and tried to look severely judicial; but her lip was quivering and her whole plump little form trembling with excitement and emotion. Suddenly she dropped her face in her hands and cried in a gust of tears and laughter: "He's just like grandfather; he'd face anything!"

"Anything in the 'tarnal universe, I guess, 'cept you, Miss Susie. I seed a cannon-ball smash a shovel in his hands, and he got another, and went on with his work cool as a cucumber. Then I seed him writin' a letter to you, and his hand trembled—-"

"A letter to me!" cried the girl, springing up.

"Yes; 'ere it is. I was kind of pegging around till I got to that; and you know—-"

But Susie was reading, her hands trembling so she could scarcely hold the paper. "It's about you," she faltered, making one more desperate effort at self-preservation. "He says you'd stay if you could; that they almost drove you home. And he asks that I be kind to you, because there are not many to care for you—and—and—-"

"Oh, Lord! never can get even with that Zeb Jarvis," groaned Ezra. "But you needn't tell me that's all the letter's about."

Her eyes were full of tears, yet not so full but that she saw the plain, closing words in all their significance. Swiftly the letter went to her lips, then was thrust into her bosom, and she seized the cobbler's hand, exclaiming: "Yes, I will! I will! You shall stay with us, and be one of us!" and in her excitement she put her left hand caressingly on his shoulder.

"SUSAN!" exclaimed Mr. Rolliffe, who entered at that moment, and looked aghast at the scene.

"Yes, I WILL!" exclaimed Susie, too wrought up now for restraint.

"Will what?" gasped the mother.

"Be Zebulon Jarvis's wife. He's asked me plump and square like a soldier; and I'll answer as grandma did, and like grandma I'll face anything for his sake."

"WELL, this IS suddent!" exclaimed Mrs. Rolliffe, dropping into a chair. "Susan, do you think it is becoming and seemly for a young woman—-"

"Oh, mother dear, there's no use of your trying to make a prim Puritan maiden of me. Zeb doesn't fight like a deacon, and I can't love like one. Ha! ha! ha! to think that great soldier is afraid of little me, and nothing else! It's too funny and heavenly—-"

"Susan, I am dumfounded at your behavior!"

At this moment Mr. Rolliffe came in from the wood-lot, and he was dazed by the wonderful news also. In his eagerness to get even with Zeb, the cobbler enlarged and expatiated till he was hoarse. When he saw that the parents were almost as proud as the daughter over their prospective son-in-law, he relapsed into his old taciturnity, declaring he had talked enough for a month.

Susie, the only child, who apparently had inherited all the fire and spirit of her fighting ancestors, darted out, and soon returned with her rosebud of a face enveloped in a great calyx of a woollen hood.

"Where are you going?" exclaimed her parents.

"You've had the news. I guess Mother Jarvis has the next right." And she was off over the hills with almost the lightness and swiftness of a snowbird.

In due time Zeke appeared, and smiled encouragingly on Mrs. Rolliffe, who sat knitting by the kitchen fire. The matron did not rise, and gave him but a cool salutation. He discussed the coldness of the weather awkwardly for a few moments, and then ventured: "Is Miss Susan at home?"

"No, sir," replied Mrs. Rolliffe; "she's gone to make a visit to her mother-in-law that is to be, the Widow Jarvis. Ezra Stokes is sittin' in the next room, sent home sick. Perhaps you'd like to talk over camp-life with him."

Not even the cider now sustained Zeke. He looked as if a cannon-ball had wrecked all his hopes and plans instead of a shovel. "Good-evening, Mrs. Rolliffe," he stammered; "I guess I'll—I'll—go home."

Poor Mrs. Jarvis had a spiritual conflict that day which she never forgot. Susie's face had flashed at the window near which she had sat spinning, and sighing perhaps that Nature had not provided feathers or fur for a brood like hers; then the girl's arms were about her neck, the news was stammered out—for the letter could never be shown to any one—in a way that tore primness to tatters. The widow tried to act as if it were a dispensation of Providence which should be received in solemn gratitude; but before she knew it she was laughing and crying, kissing her sweet-faced daughter, or telling how good and brave Zeb had been when his heart was almost breaking.

Compunction had already seized upon the widow. "Susan," she began, "I fear we are not mortifyin' the flesh as we ought—-"

"No mortifying just yet, if you please," cried Susie. "The most important thing of all is yet to be done. Zeb hasn't heard the news; just think of it! You must write and tell him that I'll help you spin the children's clothes and work the farm; that we'll face everything in Opinquake as long as Old Put needs men. Where is the ink-horn? I'll sharpen a pen for you and one for me, and SUCH news as he'll get! Wish I could tell him, though, and see the great fellow tremble once more. Afraid of me! Ha! ha! ha! that's the funniest thing—Why, Mother Jarvis, this is Christmas Day!"

"So it is," said the widow, in an awed tone. "Susie, my heart misgives me that all this should have happened on a day of which Popery has made so much."

"No, no," cried the girl. "Thank God it IS Christmas! and hereafter I shall keep Christmas as long as love is love and God is good."